A 'COP FOR CRIMINALS'

FIND — THE — LADY

NEW YORK TIMES #1 BESTSELLER **TONY LEE** WRITING AS

JACK GATLAND

Hooded Man
MEDIA
INSPIRATION • PRODUCTION • PUBLICATION

———————

Published by Hooded Man Media.
Cover photo by Paul Thomas Gooney

First Edition: November 2023

PRAISE FOR JACK GATLAND

'This is one of those books that will keep you up past your bedtime, as each chapter lures you into reading just one more.'

'This book was excellent! A great plot which kept you guessing until the end.'

'Couldn't put it down, fast paced with twists and turns.'

'The story was captivating, good plot, twists you never saw and really likeable characters. Can't wait for the next one!'

'I got sucked into this book from the very first page, thoroughly enjoyed it, can't wait for the next one.'

'Totally addictive. Thoroughly recommend.'

'Moves at a fast pace and carries you along with it.'

'Just couldn't put this book down, from the first page to the last one it kept you wondering what would happen next.'

There's a new Detective Inspector in town...

Before Ellie Reckless, there was DI Declan Walsh!

LIQUIDATE
THE PROFITS

COUNTER ATTACK

STEALTH STRIKE

DAMIAN LUCAS BOOKS

THE LIONHEART CURSE

STANDALONE BOOKS

THE BOARDROOM

AS TONY LEE

DODGE & TWIST

For Mum, who inspired me to write.

For Tracy, who inspires me to write.

CONTENTS

1

LIGHT MY FIRE

THE MOMENT THE FLAMES STARTED MOVING UP HER LEGS ZOEY Park knew the audience could sense she was in trouble.

If she was being honest, however, the flames were the last part of the problem. The first part was that she was upside down. The second was that she was currently strapped into a straitjacket. The third was that she was secured, while in the straitjacket, to the length of thick metal chain that attached her to the ceiling, and the fourth was that she was in front of five hundred paying people, watching horrified at the flaming vision, currently in the auditorium of the West End's Piccadilly Theatre on a six-week, limited run of her touring show.

This wasn't the first time Zoey had been in this predicament, however. In fact, she did this trick once a night, five days a week, sometimes with a matinee. She had performed this trick all over the world. It had been performed in front of kings, heads of state, celebrities; she'd even performed a cutdown version of this trick at the Edinburgh Festival as a street performer a few years earlier.

The problem was that *this* time she didn't have the key.

It was a very simple trick once you knew how to do the various things needed to make it work correctly. For a start, she would be secured by a large, almost oval, linked chain – which basically meant a one foot wide hoop with two straight, longer sides with rounded ends, with two additional chains on either side. These, padlocked around each ankle earlier on by a member of the audience, were now visibly locked together, to give her some kind of inability to move her legs while trapped. She would then have a straitjacket strapped around her and then two winding lengths of chain over her shoulders, which also went around her waist, connecting her to the chain that her ankle chain was also attached to.

Obviously, there was a little street theatre here; there was no way two such connections could hold her upside down, there was a third secure for that; the strap of the straitjacket was also a fully connectible climbing belt, keeping her secure while upside down. Only an idiot risked slamming their head into the stage from twenty feet up, following a slip.

After this, she would have the chain connected to a winch, which would pull her upwards, using the anchor-point chains to hold her steady upside down. Finally, the straitjacket itself would be set on fire as she was raised upwards, the accelerant on her trousers creating a rapid burst of fire, where the flames would go upwards, keeping away from her head, only concentrating on her legs and shoes – which, unknown to the audience, were also flame retardant.

She had no fear of the flames – she'd grown up on the streets of Covent Garden with jugglers and fire breathers, swinging her first fire poi at twelve, so the white spirit flames were like an old friend. In over ten years of doing the trick, she'd only been burnt twice, and both were because of her own stupidity.

As she rose, a curtain was set to fall down in front of her, to hide the audience from the last few seconds of the trick.

This was where the real fun began.

The flames were the most dynamic part of the entire show and, as the curtain fell during a usual performance of this trick, the flames, stronger than usual would catch the edges of it, as the curtain itself caught fire.

As far as the audience was concerned, the trick had gone wrong.

The flames were too strong and the fact that the curtain itself was now ablaze – with terrified crew running around the edges of the stage, screaming into radios and headsets – filled the audience with horror. Even more so when black-clad stage crew came running onto the stage to extinguish the flames, holding up their arms to hide their faces from the flames intensity as they sprayed fire extinguishers up, turning the entire stage area into some dry-ice-style scene, as the fire finally stopped, and an eerie silence now came over the theatre.

The curtain was destroyed.

Zoey was still not visible.

As the audience stared stunned, one of the crew, in a fire-retardant balaclava and who'd been there from the start of the fire extinguishing part of the show would step forward, telling everyone in the audience to stay calm, and that every-thing is fine – before pulling off the balaclava to show it was Zoey Park all along – to rapturous applause.

It was a stupidly simple trick.

When the key was there.

Usually, under an external flap on the right-hand sleeve,

missed by the member of the audience who examined it, and with a magnet holding it secure, would be a metal key within reach, attached to a thin length of cotton to keep it from falling to the floor and giving everything away. As she hung upside down, she would be able to manipulate her body around to shimmy out of the straitjacket sleeve, pulling one hand over her head to free both arms, but still in the jacket. However, as the jacket was just material, she could now grab the key through the sleeve with her other hand, using it to unlock the padlock that kept it secured. This was all performed once the curtain fell down and a loose hoop of flame retardant cloth also fell, thanks to a second item under the flap, a remote control that dropped it around her bottom half. Although, while upside down this was her top half and by some judicious swinging, she'd quickly pat out the flames on her legs. The surrounding chains weren't an issue, being there purely for theatrical value, so she would then use the major chain as a rope, pulling herself upward quickly.

The bulk of the escape was the straitjacket escape, and most of the movements to get herself into position had been arranged during preparation for the trick – as she was secured, connected to the chain and then winched up, all while talking to the audience, building up the suspense – while secretly making sure she was ready for this. It was a trick she'd learned from a street performer friend years earlier, who'd be placed into a sack with the same manacles on his hands and feet as she had now around her own, with his connected by two feet of chain, with the bag's open end tightened around his throat and then padlocked. He would then attempt to escape from the bag within a ten second countdown. When doing so, jumping out of the top of the sack on the final number, not only would he be free, but he would be in a completely different set of clothing.

The way he could do this was because of a two-minute soliloquy he gave once the trick was ready – and while the padlock was against his neck – where he explained to the audience how street performing worked, and, how if they enjoyed the show, they should give him some money. There was always a lot of banter that went into this, and it took the period up to the buildup, by which time he'd already got out of the manacles and changed his clothes. This done, he just had to wait out the countdown, and struggle around and pretend to be escaping. When he was ready, all he had to do was jump up, the padlock on the bag only there, like her waist locks, for theatrical value.

He could have jumped out at any point of the ten counts, but he needed to build the tension.

This, years later, was what Zoey had added to her trick. She could have clambered out of this within fifteen seconds on a good day. She could have been out before the flames had even licked up to her shoes. But she waited, so as her legs caught alight and she became effectively a human candle, the curtain now fell from above, blocking her from the horrified audience, flames still licking up and appearing over the top, as the curtain itself now set alight.

The moment the curtain came down, she pressed the button which released the fire-retardant cloth down, smothering the flames. By this point, she was already free, apart from her feet, which could be removed from the shackles quickly because the manacles were trick ones, known as *electronic release handcuffs*, using the simple fact that the two smaller, padlocked chains holding the ankles together would slide down the large middle parts, away from the ankles, allowing her to pull her foot out without any problems. By this point, there'd be somebody waiting above, usually her partner in crime, Jacob, who would help pull her up.

So, as the audience stared in horror at the flames licking up the curtain's side, now hidden and free she would run down the stairs, pulling off the straitjacket, leaving her black sweatshirt underneath, putting on a pair of baggy black joggers and a balaclava, and running out to join the others.

It was an impressive trick when it went right.

Currently, it wasn't.

The flames were already flickering up her legs, and even though at this point she'd press the button to drop the flame retardant cloth, the key being gone now a minor problem compared to the first-degree burns she was about to receive, as nothing was happening there either. She could feel the heat on her feet now, and looked up, seeing Jacob staring down in utter horror. He was a couple of years younger, slim built with spiked-up peroxide hair making him look even younger. But right now, his face aged him past his actual age as he gaped at her.

She'd gained one arm free – even without the key she could still escape, in time, But even escaping now, she didn't have time to get down to the stage. The trick was ruined, as Jacob waved the crew to run out already, so he could mask his own fire extinguisher with theirs.

She could see from his expression that he knew who had done this as well. That was the worst part; this wasn't even an accident, or a mistake by a careless member of the crew.

This has been Flanagan. It had her fingers all over. That and the audience volunteer who'd checked the straitjacket. The one she recognised, realising that if *she* was there, then Flanagan was there too.

The volunteer who'd spoken to her; a single phrase that had thrown Zoey's life into paranoia and disarray before returning to the audience, her job done.

She didn't know who to trust anymore.

Jacob, giving up on any kind of subtlety started visibly pulling the chain up, trying to bring her to the gantry as the curtain was gassed with extinguishers, filling the entire stage with smoke, more than ever before, as usually it'd been purely for show, while this time it was to save a life.

The audience outside were horrified as the flames licked up the outside cloth and the crew came running out to extinguish the flames. However, this time there was no last line from Zoey, no miraculous appearance as, on the galley above, coughing and waving away the smoke, Jacob stared in shock at the chains and straitjacket in front of him.

Of Zoey Park, there was no sign. It was as if she'd performed the ultimate magic trick ... and disappeared.

JOSEPH KERRIGAN WAS EXHAUSTED.

He'd spent the night at *Brasserie Zédel* in Piccadilly Circus, performing sleight-of-hand tricks for diners, wandering from table to table, pulling coins out of people's ears, and playing a version of three-card monte that was quick, to the point, and allowed them to keep on eating while being entertained by his tricks. It was simple fare, but it was a break from his usual job in the city, where he worked as an associate for a legal firm. He only did shows three times a week, and he'd only really started getting back into it after Zoey came into his life.

They had dated for six months before they moved in together, although Joseph wasn't too sure if one could call it "moving in". Half the time, she was on tour across the country, or even to other countries and continents, but he knew this was a fact of the matter when he signed up for the relationship.

Joseph, or "Joe" as he liked to use in his stage name "Joe Kerr," had been a street performer in Covent Garden many years ago while working his way through university, and had met Zoey when she was first starting out. They both had gone their different ways, though; Joseph becoming a member of the bar and working as a lawyer in the city, and Zoey into the cabaret scene. Meeting again seemingly randomly a decade or so later at a Christmas party, he'd explained to Zoey he was at a low part of his life, wondering if he'd made the right career choice, whether his family commitments were contrary to his own needs, and whether he was in a rut he couldn't get free of. After a month together, he told her she'd inspired him to start his sleight-of-hand tricks again.

He'd been working on a YouTube channel with her to do that as well, one that taught people how to do the simple tricks he did in a show. They were quite popular, it seemed, and it was probably quite easy money if you could get it going as a side hustle.

Joseph was all about the side hustles.

It was close to midnight when he arrived at the apartment at the Liverpool Street end of Shoreditch, and although the evening itself hadn't been that taxing, it was a busy time at work. He had been effectively working eighteen-hour days, especially with the added side-hustle dates, and he was considering dropping the shows until he could get things more under control in the office.

Zoey was already in bed as he walked in, and he was careful to keep the light turned off so as not to wake her. The adrenaline crash after one of her shows always had her sleeping heavily, and the last thing he ever wanted to do was wake her up after one, just to go back to sleep again.

He glanced up at the red light of the motion-sensitive camera in the bedroom's corner; he'd found Zoey suffered from sleep terrors when she first moved in, and had been sleepwalking. As she couldn't remember any of this, they'd decided together – well, more *he'd* decided – that a record should be made, and the camera had been placed there. The fact it could also catch their more *intimate* moments was a surprise addition, but also a bit of a logistical nightmare, especially if anyone hacked the feed.

But, with Joseph walking in, the camera had started recording. Quietly, and ignoring it, he tiptoed into the bedroom, took off his clothes, placed his iPhone onto the wireless stand beside the bed, and snuggled in beside her as he turned away and shut his eyes.

A moment later, the iPhone flashed a message.

He cursed himself for leaving the phone off "Do Not Disturb," but he was still awake enough to glance across at the phone facing him from his nightstand and see the message.

FROM: JACOB MORRISON

> Have you seen Zoey? She's gone missing.
> Call me.

He was looking at the phone at a sideways angle and couldn't quite work out if he'd read it correctly. So he sat up, staring at the message before it blinked out of existence. Glancing back at Zoey, he realised she wasn't breathing. Turning on the side lamp, he could see the figure beside him, snuggled into the duvet as much as he had been a minute earlier, but there was no sound, no breathing ...

Nothing.

Slowly, and with great trepidation, making sure not to stare at the camera recording this moment of horror, Joseph pulled aside the duvet to stare at the lifeless face of Zoey Park.

He jumped, but only for a moment, as he realised what it was. A full-sized stunt double of Zoey, which she had had made for a trick on "Britain's Got Talent," two years earlier. From a distance, the face looked exactly like her, created in the same way they'd make wax models for *Madame Tussauds*. She'd kept it in the back of the wardrobe when not using it, and it had been the basis of a few practical jokes she'd played on him since moving in.

But this didn't feel like a joke.

As Joseph pulled at the shoulder of the fake Zoey, letting it roll onto its back, he jumped back from the bed as he saw the knife jutting from the silicone chest. On it was a note pinned to the model.

Do what I say you bitch or the next knife goes through you.

Joseph staggered back from the bed, picking up the iPhone and dialling Jacob's number.

'It's me,' he said. 'I got your message. What the hell is going on? Where's Zoey? I've got her bloody dummy here with a note stabbed into it.'

There was a moment where he paused, listening to the voice down the line.

'What the hell do you mean, "she's gone missing?"' he snapped. 'She's—'

He stopped, listened some more, and as Jacob promised to contact him the moment he had any news, Joseph disconnected the call, staring down at the fake Zoey.

He then looked back down at his phone; the logical idea would be to call the police, but he knew they'd be slow; was a "magician who disappeared" really a priority? They'd claim that there was nothing about this yet, that it was probably some PR stunt and they wanted nothing to do with it. No, he needed someone who was good at this and there was only one person he could think of, someone who had made a name for themselves finding things that couldn't be found, someone who had been in the news recently. Not in terms of using magic, that was, but after all, they owed him a favour.

Dialling another number, he stared at the knife in the chest, almost tempted to pull it out, to touch it, until the call answered.

'Robbie, it's me,' he said. 'Do you still work for that company that finds things?'

His heart pounded in his chest as he listened to the response, the surreal and terrifying circumstances swirling in chaos around him. The room seemed to close in, the reality of Zoey's disappearance hitting him all at once, mingled with the bizarre and morbid joke that lay in his bed.

'Great,' he finally said. 'In that case, I've got a job for you.'

2

TELEVISION DREAMS

THE TELEVISION SHOW "PETER MORRIS IN THE AFTERNOON," known to most people as "PM in the PM," was a show that Ellie Reckless barely ever watched.

It was a daytime talk show on one of the terrestrial TV channels, where the titular Peter Morris, a smarmy wannabe GB News anchor waited out his contract, talking to various people in the news. That was a "loose" terminology of "in the news" as many of the guests weren't anything to do with it whatsoever, keeping abreast of topical situations and events.

Often, it was politicians or diplomats, usually people who needed to boost their "branding," that prevailed themselves of his services. He'd even interviewed Charles Baker during the Victoria Davies case, before Baker was even a suspect, and had a very good research team – quite expert actually – who found him snippets of information, usually from deep forums and blind items on Reddit he could adapt to his own needs, sprinkle them into the conversations and then, when these broke as news stories months later, he'd personally claim to be involved in the breaking of them – even though all he'd done is hint at things that were mostly false. He also took credit for solving several crimes thanks to his show, none of which could be confirmed by his producers.

Either way, whether you liked or disliked the man and his practises, it was a place where reputations could be salvaged.

And Ellie Reckless could do with a little salvaging right now.

She sat in a chair at a forty-five-degree angle from Peter, positioned so both faces could be picked up by the cameras on his overly bright daytime set. Peter himself was dressed colourfully while Ellie had opted for a more muted look than she usually had. He was in one of his usual shiny blue suits, his greying hair obviously doctored, and combed in a stylish side parting that was decades too young for him. The only thing she wore outside of her quite surprising business attire was her usual pair of Converse sneakers, Ox style, which she always wore and now seemed to be her lucky talisman.

'So, Ellie,' Peter said, having already discussed her past with the audience, 'am I right to say that with the arrest of Paddy Simpson, you feel vindicated now?'

Ellie thought about the question.

'No,' she replied. 'I mean, yes, to an extent. I feel like there's a vindication in that I always said I was innocent, and now I've proven that I wasn't guilty of the crime.'

'Did it change you?'

'Yes, I think I've changed as a person since the trial,' Ellie nodded warily. So far, these had been straightforward questions, and it concerned her.

'How does it feel to have the weight of Bryan Noyce's death, placed on your shoulders by the police and public opinion, taken away from you?'

'I lost my job because of it,' Ellie said carefully, still

expecting a "gotcha" moment. 'The trial claimed there was no evidence to state that I *had* killed him. However, I couldn't also claim that I hadn't, and therefore, I was never claimed innocent.'

She shifted in the chair.

'We hope now, with this new information, that I will finally be cleared of all charges and allowed to move on with my life.'

'We certainly hope so too,' Peter smiled to the audience before leaning closer. 'What does that entail? Moving on with your life? Are you going to rejoin the force, for example?'

Ellie went to laugh a response, but then stopped. The whole reason she had joined *Finders*, created a team and worked for favours for years was to clear her name so she could become a police officer once more, to be readmitted into the police ranks, and to return to duty. But, in the time she'd been working with Robert Lewis and Finders, she'd found a new camaraderie, one she'd never expected.

She'd also found that the freedom Finders gave her allowed her to take her own cases and solve them, often to the police's chagrin.

Now with her reasoning for doing such things gone, she wasn't too sure what she wanted to do next.

'No,' she said, realising as she spoke this was the first time she'd actually admitted it, even to herself. 'I don't want to return to the police. I think it's a different unit to the one I left anyway, what with Mark Whitehouse now gone, and Kate Delgado now promoted to his old role—'

'And how are you with Detective Inspector Delgado?' Peter pressed, and Ellie knew he was looking for an angle. 'Is there a long-term rivalry still?'

'She believed I killed somebody, and that I was a corrupt

cop,' Ellie replied diplomatically. 'I understand why she'd think that, even if her methods were off, in my opinion. However, I've proven I wasn't.'

She looked into the camera. She'd been told by Ramsey Allen this was a way to gain empathy from the audience, but was now realising she didn't have a clue how a retired ex-thief would know such a thing.

'There's no love there, but at the same time, I think her mission to have me taken down has been put on hold.'

'What of your partners at Finders?' Peter asked, steepling his fingers as he considered the questions he was asking. 'Your boss, for example, Robert Lewis, has recently come out of hospital where he'd been treated for severe head injuries while beaten to within an inch of his life, allegedly by then-DI Mark Whitehouse.'

'Allegedly?' Ellie half rose in anger, but paused herself. The trial was still a month or two away, and Mark had been giving up everyone he knew for some kind of new life. She needed to back down and settled back into the chair, nodding for Peter to continue. 'Sorry. Sore point.'

'I can sympathise,' Peter cooed, and Ellie forced herself not to punch the annoying scroat, wondering if she still had any favours owed to her that could get him taken off air. 'He suffered major brain injuries, didn't he? We hear he's only now becoming the man he used to be.'

'No, they weren't as extensive as you're claiming, and it's only been a few weeks. We're—'

'Then, there's Ramsey Allen, your "retrieval specialist," who was attacked by the Lumetta family, almost losing his life and his ability to use his fingers.'

'Ah, no, I see—'

'Plus there are the others in your "family" at Finders,'

Peter carried on, talking over her. 'Casey Noyce, the teenage son of Bryan Noyce who, while you both secretly worked to find proof Bryan was killed by YouTube influencer and health club extraordinaire Nicky Simpson, was placed in mortal danger frequently, learning in the process you'd had an illicit relationship with his father. And then there's Nicky Simpson, who, after months of an ongoing hate campaign by you against him, turned out not to be the man who had done this, with you yourself proving—'

'No, wait,' Ellie interrupted, waving her hand now. 'Sure, Nicky wasn't the man we thought he was, but he was still connected. His bodyguard killed Bryan. You can't say he ...'

'Well, let's check into that,' Peter leant even closer now, his voice dropping to a breathy whisper. 'Let's speak to a few people who claim to know you and who want to talk to you. Let's bring out Nicky Simpson!'

The audience applauded, but no one entered through the door.

'My mistake,' Peter said, listening to his earpiece. 'It's not Nicky who's coming out today, as apparently he doesn't think you're worth helping. In fact, many of the guests we asked didn't want to help you out, and we really had to dig deep for today's surprise character witness. So, please welcome Bryan Noyce!'

Ellie stared in horror as the door at the side of the set opened, and her onetime lover entered.

He was dead.

His eyes were pale, his body mottled green. He looked like a zombie from a movie.

But he walked and spoke like the Bryan she knew.

'Wait,' she said. 'This can't be—'

'You should leave my son alone,' the body of Bryan said.

'You can't have me, so what, you decided to groom him to *be* me, in your image of what I was to you?'

'It's not like that,' Ellie rose now, looking around imploringly. 'He came to me, we wanted to solve your murder.'

'You've solved my murder. It's time to step back. Forget about me, and move on.'

Ellie went to reply, but then shook her head, staring around the studio in realisation.

'This is a dream,' she said calmly now.

As the thought crossed her mind, she relaxed, looking back at the long-dead man in front of her.

'You're not real,' she said, her voice calm and measured. 'You're my past. You made me what I am now, and I appreciate that. But you're not here. Goodbye—'

———

'Ellie.'

The voice was panicked, and Ellie opened her eyes, finding herself sprawled forward on her desk, Ramsey Allen shaking her urgently.

'Are you okay?' he asked, the concern obvious on his face.

'Why wouldn't I be?' she asked, feeling that momentary confusion of which world you were in when waking quickly from a dream.

'You were screaming for a start,' he said. 'That's usually a good sign of someone not being okay.'

Today, Ramsey was in a vintage tweed suit, a burgundy cravat around his neck. His almost white, short hair was a little wind-bedraggled, and he held his silver-tipped cane in his hand as he placed the other hand on her. He could have been here to work, go to a film premiere or solve a 1920s crime. Ellie genuinely didn't know.

'How long have I been out?'

'I was talking to you fifteen minutes ago, so ten at best.'

Ellie cracked her neck, stretching. It felt far longer, but then that was the style of dreams.

'Was it the TV studio again?'

Ellie nodded.

'Peter sodding Morris,' she said. 'It's like I'm reliving the interview, but adding a ton of extra bits.'

'The interview was good,' Ramsey replied. 'Short, simple, to the point. You didn't give him anything.'

'He didn't want anything,' Ellie muttered. 'It was like I was filler, not wanted.'

'Don't take offence at this, but you were filler,' Ramsey smiled softly. 'Look, they asked, you went on, it was a couple of weeks ago now. We got work from it, so give up, move onwards.'

Ellie nodded, staring at the wall. She still felt the interview had been a mistake, an impatient urge to clear her name before the police did, but it had been and gone. Ramsey was right; it was time to move on.

'Sorry,' she said. 'I haven't slept much recently.'

'I know,' Ramsey smiled, passing a hot mug of coffee across. 'You've been trying to run everything while Robert's been recovering. Which means you're doing your job *and* his as well, picking easy jobs from the partners.'

As she continued to stretch, hearing her back crack, probably from lying in a bad position, he continued.

'But now, you can take a break,' he smiled.

Ellie, however, shook her head.

'He's back soon, though he's not one hundred percent yet, but—'

'Actually, I think he's back closer than your diagnosis, Eleanor,' Ramsey said, nodding out of the room. In a glass windowed boardroom across the corridor, they could see Robert Lewis sitting, checking his phone's messages. 'It seems he's back today, and he has a job for us.'

Ellie rose, sipping the coffee, allowing the caffeine to kick-start her metabolism and spark her neurons as she walked out of the office and across the corridor, entering the boardroom.

'You're not supposed to be here till Monday,' she grumbled.

Robert nodded. His dirty-blond hair had almost grown back from where they had shaved it for the operation, and because of this, the scar, given during his attack, was no longer visible. He'd lost a little weight, and his slightly gaunter face had aged him about five years in the process. His weight loss also meant the suits he usually wore impeccably fitted now hung off him a little more than usual. However, in the previous weeks, he had put weight back on, and Ellie knew it'd be a matter of time before he looked just like he did before.

It wasn't just the look, though; he wasn't *acting* the same way he did before, either. Now he was more cautious, slower in speech, as if considering every word that he spoke.

Ellie understood this; the doctors had said he'd be worried about what he was saying. The attack several weeks earlier had given him the brain equivalent of a stroke. He had developed a slight tic in his hands that he hadn't had before. But when he looked up at her, his eyes were as intelligent as ever, and he gave a slight half-smile.

'I've got us a job,' he said. 'A missing person.'

'We don't do missing persons,' Ramsey interjected. 'And we've got a list of jobs—'

'We're called Finders,' Robert interrupted. 'We find.'

'Yes, but people ...' Ellie trailed off. 'Is there a reason we're doing this?'

'I owe someone a favour,' Robert nodded. 'I'm sure you can understand the irony of that. Someone I used to know back in Uni when I was training to be a lawyer. It's been hanging over my head a long time, but he never called it in, and if I'm being honest, I'd almost forgotten.'

He sighed, leaning back in the chair.

'He phoned me last night and called it in. He was in a bit of a state, too, to be honest. His partner's disappeared.'

'Okay,' Ramsey said. 'People disappear all the time. Sometimes they just go for a walk, sometimes they—'

'This is the problem,' Robert interrupted. 'His partner disappeared live on stage in front of five hundred people, and he believes that someone is trying to kill her.'

'So, we're investigating a missing person with a potential criminal background—'

'Why do you say that?'

'Because his first call was to you, rather than the police,' Ellie shrugged. 'That's usually a red flag.'

She stopped, looking around.

'Where's Millie?'

'Davey's taking her for a walk,' Ramsey said.

'It's your day today.'

'I was told I feed her too much on walks,' Ramsey, obviously miffed at this, replied. 'Not my fault she's a good girl who deserves treats.'

'Okay, so for the moment, let's say we're hunting a missing

person with a potentially threatening background, while racing against a deranged killer who wants her dead?' Ellie summarised, looking back at Robert before smiling widely. 'Added to that, we're doing all of this for a favour. Sounds like old times.'

Robert nodded.

'I've already called the team,' he said. 'I think this one's going to be a quick one, and then we can return to the other jobs.'

'You do? Why?' Ramsey frowned.

At the question, Robert's face fell.

'Because I think the longer we take, the more chance there is that Zoey Park will be dead.'

JOANNE DAVEY HADN'T EXPECTED TO, BUT SHE REALLY ENJOYED the walks with Millie. She would have preferred more off-the-lead strolls across countryside vistas, but a walk around the block was good for the soul, especially when seen through the eyes of a Spaniel.

She'd heard once that dogs eyes were only sixty percent as good as human ones, but their sense of smell was a million times that of humans. It sounded like made up numbers, but Davey knew there was a little truth to the rumours, if only by watching Millie inhale every smell she could, leaving little wees, like Facebook replies, every few yards.

In fact, she was so engrossed with the microcosm of dog behaviour, she hadn't noticed the car pull up beside her, and the old man emerge from the side. A wizened old Chinese gentleman, he was dressed immaculately in a three-piece pinstripe suit, his long, thinning white hair pulled back over his liver-spotted skull and a pair of thick-rimmed varifocal glasses peering myopically at her.

'You're the one they call Davey, yes?' he asked.

Davey paused, looking at the man, his driver, and his two bodyguards in a slow panning glance.

'Jimmy Tsang,' she said. 'Has Ellie called in your family's favour?'

Jimmy's mouth twitched slightly, and Davey knew she'd caught a nerve. Instead, he walked over to Millie, crouching down and stroking her.

'Lovely dog,' he said. 'She's a Show Cocker? Is she yours?'

'You know she isn't,' Davey was feeling that moment of unease when things were going off kilter. 'So tell me your message and let me continue with my walk.'

'What if this lovely Spaniel – Millie, isn't it – what if this dog *is* the message?' Jimmy kept stroking with his left hand while the right hand pulled out a butterfly knife, flicking it open.

Davey instinctively moved forward.

'Touch her and die,' she said. 'You know me? Then you know my rep. I trained under Rosanna Marcos, who knew your cousin well. Too well. You think I couldn't make one call and destroy you?'

It was bravado, but it wasn't needed. Tsang was just playing, as he pulled out a bag of dog treats, using the blade to slice open the top. He placed some down, allowing Millie, overjoyed at this, to start eating.

'She's too thin,' he explained. 'She needs fattening up.'

He rose now to face Davey.

'Pass a message to your boss,' he said. 'She made herself clear, told me to keep my nose clean and as a favour, I've done that for the last few weeks.'

'I thought it was because you lost a chess game to her?'

There was a flicker of annoyance in Jimmy Tsang's eye, but it was momentary, replaced by his fixed smile.

'I understand she's no longer in the market for favours,' he continued, ignoring the comment. 'But she needs to use the ones she has soon, yes?'

'I didn't realise there was a time limit on them.'

'Neither did I,' Jimmy replied, and this time his voice was tired, reluctant. 'But someone's making a play at us, taking out our infrastructure, and ...'

He looked uncomfortable.

'... bad things are being said about me,' he finished.

'I didn't peg you as the sort of guy that listens to rumours,' Davey picked the bag up, pulling it away from Millie, furious her bag of joy had been removed.

'I don't mean insults,' Jimmy shook his head. 'I mean bad things in the way of curses.'

'Wait, you're here because someone's put a *curse* on you?'

Jimmy didn't reply, but eventually and reluctantly nodded.

'Someone has placed a curse on me and my family by default,' he explained, as if this was the most natural thing in the world. 'If Ellie Reckless can find out who, how, why, and also remove it, I'll owe her whatever she wants. My man Chow will send more details.'

With this, Jimmy Tsang nodded to himself, turned and walked back to his car, leaving Davey and Millie alone together on the street.

Before he could get into his car, however, Davey looked back over.

'Mister Tsang,' she said, loud enough for Jimmy to be forced to look back at her. 'Why us?'

Jimmy frowned. 'What do you mean?

'You've been cursed,' Davey explained. 'You're convinced of this. You know it needs to be stopped, and you want to find who did it, but why come to us? Surely there are people out there better placed to discover curses and break them? I don't know much, but I know a good Chinese curse needs a good Chinese curse breaker.'

'You weren't my first choice,' Jimmy nodded at the question. 'Let's just say a mutual acquaintance suggested you, and you were suggested as an opportunity to use.'

'Who suggested us?'

Jimmy shrugged, already climbing back into the car.

'I have a lot of contacts,' he said. 'You can't expect me to know them all. Or even remember them. Suffice to say, I have a curse; it needs to be removed and I was told on good authority that you are the people to do it.'

And with that, the car drove off.

'Well damn,' Davey said with a smile. 'I should speak to someone about this.'

She looked down at Millie.

'Right after we walk off these new treats,' she said. 'Come on, or they'll rate me lower than Ramsey, and we're not having that.'

3

THE CLIENT

IT HAD TAKEN ANOTHER HOUR TO GATHER THE TEAM IN. FIRST was Davey, her curly red hair pulled back in a bun, a waggy and slightly fuller Cocker Spaniel at her feet. Then Tinker Jones arrived, in her usual olive-green army coat, her hair bunched under a baseball cap. Sitting next to Ramsey in his cravat and suit, she couldn't have looked more like a style counterpoint if she'd tried.

'No Casey?' she asked, looking around. 'It's been a while since he's been here.'

'Only when needed on this one,' Ellie replied, sitting back down, Millie the Spaniel climbing up happily on her lap.

'You still having problems with Pauline?'

Ellie winced and shrugged at the name of Bryan's widow. She'd been quite clear when she told Ellie she could use Casey's skills when needed, but mainly on holidays and weekends. That had been a few weeks earlier, and Ellie had tried to keep to her wishes.

'I'd rather wait until we knew what the case was before bringing him in.'

'You're scared of calling her, aren't you?' Ramsey smiled. 'I don't blame you. She scares the piss out of me.'

'Is Millie getting fat again?' Tinker leant forward, peering. 'She looks a little chunky.'

'She is,' Davey admitted. 'She was over-treated by Jimmy Tsang in a drive-by feeding.'

She quickly explained the strange conversation she'd had downstairs, and Ramsey nodded sagely at this.

'Can't muck about with a curse,' he said. 'It's like the yips. You need to nip it in the bud.'

'The yips?'

Ramsey nodded again at this.

'A sudden and unexplained loss of ability to execute certain skills,' he explained. 'If you're an athlete, it could spell the end of your career. It gets dumped in with superstition, and you have to do something to offset the yip. I had it about twenty years ago. Couldn't pick a pocket to save my life. Had to give fifty quid to a charity of my last mark's choice.'

'Because that's what your brain had decided it needed to do,' Tinker smiled. 'We had it on the range, but we just said it was losing nerve when shooting. But Jimmy says this is a curse, not the yips.'

'It's only a curse because he believes it is,' Ramsey sniffed, folding his arms. 'Same thing. We find who did this, magically the curse lifts because he has an explanation, and he gets closure.'

'Or because we remove the curse,' Davey smiled.

'Et tu, Brute?' Ramsey bemoaned as he stared across the table at her.

'Can we get started?' Ellie, tiring of the banter, shuffled around in her chair to face Robert. 'Want to give us the skinny?'

'Zoey Park,' Robert nodded, leaning forward on the desk as he looked around it at the team. 'Thirty-one years old, built herself up as one of the most well-known escapologists and magicians in the UK. Not famous, but one of those entertainers you see on TV and go "oh I know her." Over the last ten years, she's been a finalist on shows like *Britain's Got Talent,* did a piece of her show on *Jonathan Ross,* and she even had a small residence in Las Vegas two years back.'

'I don't understand exactly why we're looking at her,' Ellie said, confused. 'I mean, if she's gone missing, surely this is a matter for the police.'

'I agree, and that's what I told Joe,' Robert said.

'Joe is?' Tinker asked now.

'Joseph Kerrigan, her partner,' Robert explained. 'Yes, I get your concern. However, this is very much the remit of an Ellie Reckless case.'

'How do you see that?' Ellie raised an eyebrow.

'I owe him a favour,' Rober shrugged. 'I'll be frank – Joe and me, we were at law school together. I was struggling, I had a few problems. Joe sorted them out for me.'

'What sorts of problems?' Tinker asked.

'The sorts of problems that get someone kicked out of law school,' Robert replied coldly. 'That's all I'm saying, Tinker. So don't expect anything juicy to come out of this.'

'So, Joe helped you, you feel you owe him, and now he's called in his favour?' Ellie asked.

Robert gave a reluctant smile.

'Yeah,' he said. 'It really is an Ellie Reckless favour. Whatever he needs, time and place of his choosing, all of that.'

He sighed, leaning back on the chair, still tired.

'I know this isn't what we were going to do now things were over,' he said. 'I know we agreed we were moving away from favours. But this is different. There's something more going on here.'

'How so?'

Robert looked at the file in front of him.

'A lot of this is just from talking to Joe,' he said. 'We still need more information. But Zoey's been doing a series of shows in London, at the Piccadilly Theatre. They end with a show-stopping trick which involves her being suspended over the stage, upside down with a straitjacket on – whilst on fire.'

'So a normal Wednesday for Ramsey,' Tinker suggested.

'I could be out of it within thirty seconds,' Ramsey scoffed at the suggestion. 'Straitjackets are very simple once you know how to do it.'

'Either way, it's an exciting trick which ends with the curtain blocking her going up in flames, a load of her crew coming out and extinguishing them, and one of the crew turning to the audience and revealing herself to be Zoey,' Robert finished.

'Well, that's mildly more exciting, I suppose,' Ramsey grumbled. 'That might take a little longer. So what happened last night?'

'I'm not going to go into how the trick's done or anything like that,' Robert looked at the others. 'I'm sure Ramsey will tell you all exactly how it was done, with his intimate knowledge of getting out of straitjackets. Suffice to say, there was a secret compartment where items were supposed to be and those items weren't there.'

'Carelessness or deliberate?'

'Joe doesn't know. But Jacob, who's her partner in the show, thinks that somebody did it deliberately. They wanted

Zoey to be trapped on a chain, as flames spread up her legs, immolating her.'

'I get that,' Ellie stroked Millie as she spoke. 'Is there anything else that makes you think that somebody's after her?'

Robert nodded, passing across a printed screenshot.

'Joe sent me this,' he said.

'What the hell is that?' Tinker looked up. 'If this is sex toys ...'

'It's a stunt double doll,' Robert explained. 'Used in one of her tricks a while back, and it's been left in the apartment while she looked for a new lockup.'

'What's wrong with the old lockup?'

'Broken into. Unconnected though, apparently it was a teenage magician hoping to find a few cool tricks to duplicate. Either way, Joe was under the assumption that only he and Zoey knew the model was in a wardrobe in the bedroom.'

He looked around the table.

'It's a double, not like Tinker just suggested though, but as you can see, somebody else obviously did know where it was, and they decided to leave a message.'

Everyone took a moment to look at the photo, passing it around. Eventually, Ellie looked up.

'So, let me guess,' she said. 'Zoey's doing a trick, she finds that someone's tried to sabotage it. She obviously gets out because we didn't see any news of "tragic magician dies on stage" in the press. Then she disappears.'

'Almost,' Robert said. 'The end of the trick is quite chaotic. They spray fire extinguisher everywhere and create a lot of smoke, as a part of the effect, helping her get down from a gantry above without being seen, and sneaking onto the stage in the smoke and confusion. The problem was this time, Jacob was also using a fire extinguisher because, well, as the flames on the outside curtain were being sorted, the fire sheet that usually fell on her once hidden hadn't gone down.'

He leant back as he finished.

'In doing so, he managed to create a foggy scenario up there in which, by the time the smoke had cleared, Zoey had gone.'

'She wasn't on the gantry anymore?' Ramsey asked.

'She wasn't anywhere,' Robert shook his head. 'She wasn't on the gantry, she wasn't still attached to the chain, she hadn't left through the stage door, she wasn't in her dressing room. They checked everywhere, and she was gone. It was the ultimate disappearance act. Then, an hour or two later, Jacob contacts Joe, who had gone to bed not realising that the figure beside him wasn't Zoey, asleep.'

'So, we're talking about somebody who not only knew how the trick worked and could throw a spanner into it, but they also knew where she lived, they knew the human-sized doll was there, and they knew what time Joe would get in at night. Does he know anything else?' Ramsey asked.

Robert shook his head.

'It was one quick phone call, and I'm still not one hundred percent on whether I heard it all correctly,' he replied. 'Anyway, he was nervous and scared and it was late at night. You can ask him all the questions you want when you see him. He's meeting us in the diner in half an hour.'

As he said this, the others in the boardroom looked confused.

'Why the diner?'

'Come on, Ramsey, that's Ellie's unofficial office,' Robert

said with a smile. 'Surely this isn't a normal Finder's job. As I said, it fits the remit, so we go with the flow.'

'But—'

'I know that's what you're going to say,' Ellie now spoke, pausing Ramsey. 'Officially, we work with insurance fraud. We find items that have been lost. We don't really have a remit for people, so we can't take it on with an official capability. At the same time, as Robert said, he's doing this for a favour, which means it's effectively one of our usual jobs. So why not meet in the same place?'

She looked at Ramsey.

'We keep it as it's supposed to be,' she said. 'Don't want a case of the yips.'

Ramsey nodded slowly at this, as if an impressive statement had been made.

'I can see the logic in that,' Davey nodded. 'But I still have one question that hasn't been asked. Why *haven't* the police been involved in this? I know you said you owed a favour, and he probably thought you could do a better job ...'

Davey let the question trail off, and Robert nodded.

'I think there's something going on here that they don't want the police to look into,' he said. 'My first suggestion was for him to go to the police. But Joe said not to. He'll explain everything when we see him.'

'He'd bloody better,' Ramsey muttered. 'Because right now it's sounding like a right royal stitch-up.'

'That's what I love about you,' Tinker grinned. 'Your unwavering optimism.'

'What about Tsang?' Ellie asked the table. 'Do we help him or let the course of the curse take effect?'

'I'd say help,' Davey replied. 'He gave Millie treats. You

didn't see him, boss. He was thrown by this. Almost like it's the one thing he can't fix.'

'Curses can be specific,' Ramsey rubbed at his chin. 'Things like "only a woman can remove it" or "only by repaying a debt," things like that. Maybe he can't fix it? Maybe he has to use us?'

'I thought I might speak to Doctor Marcos at Temple Inn,' Davey suggested. 'She knows the Tsangs well.'

'As long as you don't start working for them again,' Ellie nodded. 'I don't need to hunt for a new forensics again, okay?'

'No chance of that,' Davey grinned. 'They couldn't have me, even if they wanted me. They don't have spaniels in the office for a start.'

4

DINER DATE

DOWNSTAIRS AND A SHORT WALK FROM THE FINDERS' OFFICES, Caesar's Diner was a strange addition to the chrome and glass city buildings that surrounded it, and to enter the inside of Caesar's was to enter a fifties diner, with the floor a checkerboard black and white design, with the walls tiled white. There were tables in the middle, and along the side were large, opulent red-leather booths, easily big enough for six or seven people to sit and eat in. In fact, the furthest along had been unofficially classed as Ellie's "other office" for a couple of years now.

On the wall were fifties' advertising posters for milk-shakes, burgers and soft drinks, and on each table was a small jukebox, where for a coin, you could change the fifties song to another fifties song. It was an atypical city diner, serving great, if simple food, and its clientele were often rich, hungry, and nostalgic. The only alteration was a small flat-screen television on the wall, set to subtitles and with the sound turned down, mainly for Ali the owner to watch as he worked at the hot plate.

Sandra, the long-suffering server of the diner, stormed over to them with a face of fury as they entered.

'I don't know what you're playing at this time, but you need to stop it,' she snapped, nodding her head over to their usual booth, where, sitting alone was a man in his thirties, tall and gangly with mid-length brown hair hanging around his shoulders, next to what looked like some kind of surfboard bag.

'He's got a body,' she said. 'I saw the face. It scared the living hell out of me.'

Robert patted her on the shoulder.

'It's a mannequin,' he said. 'I didn't realise you were so squeamish, Sandra. I mean, you serve Ramsey his dinner, and I've seen the man eat.'

Sandra glared at them all before storming off. As they continued walking over to the booth, the man that she had pointed out, obviously Joe Kerrigan, stood up, turning and shaking Robert's hand.

'Thank you so much,' he said. 'Thank you all so much.'

'I wouldn't start thanking us yet,' Tinker replied. 'We still don't know what the situation is.'

She looked at the bag.

'I'm guessing that's your sex toy,' she grinned, as both Robert and Joe gave her the same look, both of which gave the same message.

Deciding not to reply directly to Tinker, Joe nodded, unzipping the bag.

'I've left the knife in it,' he said. 'It's a stage knife from one of Zoey's acts. But they're still quite sharp, easily enough to puncture the silicone chest.'

Davey leant closer, having a peek at it.

'Do you mind?' she asked.

Joe stepped aside, looking at Robert quizzically.

'This is our forensics expert,' Robert explained. 'If there's anything there to be seen, she'll see it.'

Davey had already placed latex gloves on and was peering at it.

'I reckon we can get prints off the note and the blade,' she said. 'It's handwritten, which is helpful. We can get a graphologist onto it. I reckon I can even find out where the headed notepaper came from.'

She tapped at the top where it had been carefully torn, and where there had been some kind of line of text above it.

'How can you tell the notepaper is headed?' Joe frowned, looking back at it.

'There,' Davey pointed to the tear. 'Probably a hotel or some kind of restaurant. They've torn off the top to make sure we don't know where they wrote it, but they haven't done a great job. They should have used scissors. Give me time, I'll see what I can do.'

'Did you see anyone enter the house?' Ellie asked. 'Like a doorbell camera or anything?'

'No, and the CCTV in the bedroom was scrubbed,' Joe added. 'Zoey has night terrors. She's been documenting them. But the video was removed for three hours before I returned.'

'Can you send us what you have?'

Joe nodded.

Davey looked back at Ellie, who also nodded, but this was more a quiet agreement to get out with the evidence. Davey zipped up the body bag, picked it up, and lugged it out of the diner.

'Do you think one day she'll actually stay for a full lunch?' Ramsey asked.

'Davey just doesn't do people,' Ellie shrugged. 'She's fine. She'll have a look at it upstairs while we're chatting down here.'

She turned back to Joe.

'You know who I am and what I do, right?'

'Robert explained it,' Joe nodded. 'I get that I'm not paying you for this, but I'll cover any expenses. It's unfair of me to expect Robert would cover that as well.'

Robert held up a hand to stop him.

'I cover all expenses,' he said. 'This is on me. You did enough back at university.'

'Thank you,' Joe said gratefully.

'So why don't you tell me what exactly happened last night?'

'I'd been working at *Zédel*, the brasserie off Piccadilly Circus,' Joe sighed.

'I thought you were a lawyer?'

'Oh, I am. I'm an associate at *Oberman Davies* in Liverpool Street. But I used to be a street performer back when I was at university, earning a bit of scratch here and there and I'd picked up a few magic tricks – you know how it goes – and I'd perform them now and then.'

'Sure,' Ramsey replied with a straight face, and Ellie wasn't sure if he was mocking or not. 'We've all been there.'

'Anyway, I hadn't done it for years, and then, at the end of the year I bumped into Zoey again at a Christmas party. I was a guest, she was the show they'd booked.'

'You knew her how?'

'I'd known her from when I was a street performer,' Joe replied. 'She was incredible back then, and now she was successful. I think she was happy I was one of the few people there who wasn't asking about her shows, rather talking about her. She remembered me, we got chatting. Next thing I know, we ...'

'We don't need all the details,' Ramsey held his hand up.

Joe laughed.

'Six months later we're moving in together,' he said, editing out any salacious moments. 'I've got a large apartment in Shoreditch. She was having problems with the house she was staying in. Despite appearing in Vegas, she still rented a shared house. She told me once that she couldn't live alone. She said she'd grown up with a big family.'

'I thought she was an only child,' Robert interjected, opening the file, looking into it.

'She was, but when she was fostered as a kid, most of her time was spent in foster homes with a handful of various children,' Joe quickly added. 'She spent her teenage years trying to escape, but she was never alone, so to speak. When she was fifteen, she was performing street magic. By the time she was sixteen, she was working full time at Covent Garden.'

'How do you work full time as a street performer?' Ellie asked.

'You spend a lot more hours there than you expect,' Joe replied, and Ellie felt there was an element of professional pride in his voice. 'They have a list where they used to ... I mean, I don't know what they do now, but back when I was there, they had a list that you had to place your name on before ten in the morning. First person on the list by ten am got the pick of the show times, all half-hour slots throughout the day, then the second name, then the third, until all performances had been given out. Then, if there were any slots left, the first person got a second show.'

'So, what, you turn up at nine, write a name, wait until ten and pick a spot?'

'It's a little more complicated,' Joe shook his head. 'The problem was, "is first on our list by ten" didn't mean turning up at half-past nine. In the summer months, you had people turning up at four in the morning. Also, they had rules – once you signed your name, you had to stay near St Martin's Church, where the sheet was. So, you couldn't have a night out, write your name down on the way home, have a couple of hours' kip and come back.'

Joe smiled faintly, lost in a memory.

'I'd often turn up about six during the summer months, when I wasn't at university,' he said. 'You'd sign your name, and already there were seven or eight people ahead of you. Some might not turn up, though. Some just wrote their name and took a chance, some might have wandered off ... you'd spend hours just sitting around, doing nothing. There was a guy who practised the saxophone for hours there, in the empty square, while we played football. Then at ten, you'd pick the time you wanted, timing it, in case you had an inside spot on a second, smaller street performing area inside the palisade. Once you'd picked your time, you could then go off.'

He paused, considering his words.

'Of course, you might have picked a two in the afternoon slot, but if three people before you overstep their time, it might now be an hour later. Most of them were okay. But some of them were right pricks. There was this one guy who knew he only had half an hour. He'd spend that gathering an audience and then continue, not caring he was overrunning and screwing one of us over. He was called Pipé, was one of the kings of the Garden, and people let him do what he wanted. I hated that prick so much.'

He shrugged.

'What can you do?' he said. 'One thing it taught me,

though, was how to read people. Anyway, before I graduated, I'd met Zoey during an Edinburgh Festival and we had a bit of a fling, but nothing serious. We were from different worlds. I was a student; she was the street. Then I went off and became a lawyer.'

'So why were you performing street magic last night?'

'Getting back with Zoey reminded me of what I used to do,' Joe mouth-shrugged the answer. 'I remembered the tricks; as I said, I'd always done them as party tricks over the years and I thought maybe I should do something more with myself. Zoey had a friend who did small bookings for restaurants and places where they had close-up magicians, and I started doing it for fun.'

'But you don't need the money.'

'It's not about the money,' Joe smiled. 'Zoey was making plenty, almost as much as I was in the City, and I make a lot. It was an opportunity to not be myself, you know? I tired of being the corporate suit. When I found Zoey again, it gave me an opportunity to return to a more innocent time. A time when I was eager to see what the future held.'

'It sounds to me like you're having a midlife crisis,' Tinker said.

'Maybe, but that doesn't stop the fact she's missing,' Joe replied.

'You've been together a while, do you know anyone who might have a problem with her?' Ellie asked.

'Luana Flanagan,' Joe nodded. 'You should start with her. Right vicious bitch.'

Ellie noted down the name.

'You've met her?'

Joe shook his head.

'No, I only go on what I was told by Zoey,' he replied.

'Luana knew Zoey's mum, and was one of the reasons Zoey was dumped in a foster home.'

'Why was that?'

'Zoey's mum was circus folk,' Joe explained. 'Worked for Luana in Ireland. Left when she became pregnant with Zoey, but was convinced to go back by Luana about ten years later. Zoey was at primary school, Luana promised to have her looked after. She didn't.'

'Zoey's mum is ...'

'Dead. Died of a drug overdose in Bunratty about fifteen years ago,' Joe replied. 'She never talks about it. By then she was on the streets, performing.'

'So why do you think this Luana Flanagan is after Zoey?'

Joe paused, considered his words, and then sighed.

'Because Zoey's mum screwed her out of a hundred grand when thirty years ago she stole an item that's never been found, and now Zoey owes the debt,' he said. 'That's why we can't get the police involved.'

5

STAGE HANDS

IF SHE WAS BEING HONEST WITH HERSELF, DAVEY MISSED THIS side of her old life as a forensic officer and detective; crime scenes were always thrilling for her, the idea that any single item could break open a case, and you were the only person to see all angles was something you never moved away from. However, Davey had also expected some kind of police presence to be outside the theatre. It took a moment to realise that although Zoey Park was missing, there hadn't been any kind of crime – as Joe hadn't even mentioned her absence to the police, and the audience were under the belief this had been a slightly anti-climactic ending to a good evening's entertainment.

Ramsey, strolling along with Davey, currently grumbling beside her, looked up at the entrance.

'I used to come here as a kid,' he said. 'They used to do variety routines and Vaudeville shows. Do you remember the TV show "The Good Old Days?"'

'Jesus Christ,' Davey stared at him. 'How old do you think

I am? For that matter, how old are *you*? My granddad used to love that stuff and he's in his eighties.'

'I'm an old soul,' Ramsey shrugged. 'I wonder if it's haunted. Old theatres are always haunted. I bet the place is filled with ghosts.'

Arthur, the elderly, stick-thin man at the stage door hadn't been informed that they were turning up, but after a few minutes chatting to Ramsey allowed them straight through – now the firmest of friends. Davey was impressed with this; making friends was something she'd never been able to do before, apart from a few, close people. Though even they had been forgotten as Davey moved on. She made a mental note to check in with Rosanna Marcos soon, and not just because of the Tsang case. But then, as they entered the auditorium, all thoughts of friends went away, as the case beckoned.

The stage itself was dark.

Davey was surprised at this.

'They don't have a lead star here,' Ramsey said, noting the expression and recognising it. 'There's no point lighting it up.'

Davey nodded, and they made their way onto the stage with nobody stopping them.

'Maybe they're at lunch?' Ramsey suggested, checking his watch. 'You'd have thought some people would have been around. You know, in case Zoey was just having some kind of "diva strop," and returned for tonight's show.'

He stopped himself.

'No, they refunded tonight, so maybe they're having a day off,' he continued.

'Theatre folk don't have lunch at one o'clock,' Davey replied, checking her watch. 'They don't get up until around now. They work in a completely different time zone to us—'

'Unless there's a matinee.'

'Well, obviously, with a matinee, the rules change.'

A man appeared at the far edge of the stage, and started walking across it, towards them. He was young, mid-twenties at best, with short, spiked, peroxide hair, and a black band T-shirt on, the word "Suede" written in a white font the only text on it.

'Are you friends of Joe?' he asked.

'Not really,' Davey smiled. 'But if by "Joe" you mean "were we sent here to look at the magical act that saw a seasoned professional disappear," then yes.'

Ramsey stepped back into the shadows, allowing Davey to take over, but it was a second too late.

'Hold on,' the man said, noting the movement and looking over Davey's shoulder. 'Bloody hell. Ramsey Allen. Not dead after all, it seems.'

'Hello, Jacob,' Ramsey said softly, sighing as he reluctantly stepped forward, back into the lit area of the stage.

'Wait, hold on, you know this guy?'

Ramsey wasn't sure whether Davey was asking the question of him or Jacob, but both of them nodded in response.

'Ramsey here taught me how to pickpocket,' Jacob replied, but his expression gave no recollection of fond memories. 'I was what, ten? Maybe eleven?'

'You were teaching ten-year-old kids how to steal things?' Davey stared back at Ramsey. 'You're bloody lucky I'm not a copper anymore.'

'It was purely for educational reasons,' Ramsey said. 'I had just come out of a five-stretch in Wandsworth and was given community service looking after kids – you know, teaching them life skills.'

'Pick-pocketing counts as a life skill?'

Ramsey smiled, waving around the theatre.

'Look where Jacob has got to,' he said. 'I'd say that's a success.'

Jacob smiled, and then the smile of recognition turned to an expression of anger.

'You left us,' he snapped. 'Mum was bereft.'

'Wait, you dated his mum?' Davey didn't know whether to be delighted or horrified at these fresh revelations, and was wondering if she had Tinker on speed dial. However, her surprised tone was a complete opposite to Jacob's icy response.

'He did a damn sight more than date her,' Jacob replied. 'Then not a single bloody word after he disappeared.'

'I was in prison,' Ramsey said, voice brittle with regret.

'You could have written,' Jacob replied. 'At least we'd have known if you were dead or not.'

'I'm sorry, Jacob,' Ramsey nodded slowly, as if realising there wasn't really an answer he could give here that made everything all right. 'I was in a bad place, addicted to gambling and many other bad vices. I should have contacted you, especially when I got out. But by that point, you were older, and I assumed your lives had moved on.'

'You left us with nothing, Ramsey. Nothing to remember you with. Not even a cigarette holder.'

Jacob paused, then looked as if he was about to continue, but stopped, checked himself, and nodded curtly.

'So, you've been sent to check into Zoey's disappearance,' he said, changing the subject. 'I understand I was the last person to see her?'

'From what Joe tells us,' Davey nodded.

'She was doing an escapology trick,' Jacob continued, pointing up at the gantry. 'I was pulling her up. The far side of the fire curtain hadn't fallen on her to smother the flames—'

'Were you worried she would burn?'

'Not really,' Jacob added quickly. 'Zoey's always quick. She'd have worked out a way of getting out of it, but she didn't want the audience to see the smothering. Always keep the trick hidden, you know?'

He looked up, reliving the moment.

'There were a lot of flames. Downstairs they were setting off fire extinguishers, putting out the fake fire—'

'Fake fire?'

'We put accelerants on the outside of the curtain. It's fire-proof, too, so the flames only last while they have something to burn. We put it out before that happens, so the audience thinks we're fighting a real fire. So they were down here, fogging the place up, while up there, I was using one as well, just to make sure Zoey wasn't still alight. But, in the fog, she well ... disappeared.'

He pointed back the way they came.

'The corridor you came up, via the stage door was the only way she could have escaped, and she didn't go out that way. I spoke to Arthur, the man at the door. He said the only people who came in or out were at the end of the show.'

'Could she have hidden inside the theatre?' Davey asked.

'Possibly,' Jacob accepted the question with a shrug. 'But by that point, we were checking around, worried she'd been injured and passed out somewhere – not because of the flames, but if she'd inhaled too much fire extinguisher. You know, CO_2 and stuff like that ...'

He let the sentence trail off; they understood what he meant.

'So, hypothetically, she escaped out of her binds, got onto

the gantry, and ran while it was smoky. How else could she have gotten out?' Davey walked to the edge of the stage now, looking up at the gantry above her.

'The only other way would be to go through the audience,' Jacob pointed into the auditorium. 'Though, at that point, they weren't moving, they thought the trick was still going. Even when we stood at the front and said the show was being closed, they didn't move. We even had the promoter come out.'

'Promoter being ...'

'Claudette Storm. She's been running the show for the last six months,' Jacob added, and Davey nodded.

'We'll need to have a chat with her,' she said to Ramsey.

'Oh, you're in charge now, are you?'

'Do *you* have any police experience?'

Ramsey grinned.

'Oh, I have a lot of police experience,' he said. 'Just possibly not the type that you're thinking of.'

Davey turned her attention back to Jacob.

'Do you have the straitjacket around?'

Jacob nodded, pointing at the props table to the side of the stage.

'I'm afraid I can't really show it to you,' he said. 'It's a trick, you know, and the Magic Circle—'

'We know how the trick works,' Davey replied impatiently. 'We're not children, and we have brains.'

She smiled.

'Also, Joe Kerrigan told us what was going on.'

'Joe can't keep his sodding mouth shut,' Jacob groaned, frustrated. 'Honest to God, you tell him anything and within five minutes everybody and their dog knows.'

'We understand it's something to do with a flap and a key on a piece of string?'

Jacob sighed, nodding as he walked the pair of them over to the props table now, muttering under his breath about how *nobody could keep a secret these days.*

'Yeah, but as you can see, the key isn't there,' he said, indicating the sleeve of the jacket on the table. 'It usually hangs on a piece of cotton so it can't fall onto the stage, and there's a wire connected to the button you can see here, that's been cut. I think someone took a knife to both of them, made sure that neither could be used, then sealed the flap back over so no one would know.'

'Surely you check this before the trick?' Ramsey asked.

Jacob nodded, his face angering now.

'That's the point,' he said. 'I looked at this three or four minutes before we put it on her. The only way this could have been tampered with was during the trick itself.'

Ramsey considered this.

'How many people touched the straitjacket between the moment you checked it, and the moment Zoey put it on?'

'Barely anyone.'

'Barely anyone isn't a number,' Davey added.

Jacob glared at her for a moment and then started scratching his head as he cast his mind back to the previous day.

'The prop manager would have held it to make sure it was ready to go on,' he started, counting the mentions off on his fingers. 'One of the crew would have placed it onto the stand, another bringing it out onto the stage. Then there are the audience members.'

'What do you mean, audience members?'

Jacob frowned, looking confused at the question.

'It's a staple of every magician's trick,' he said, as if expecting both people to know this. 'You pull out an item, you show it to the audience. You let them look at it, touch it, move it, play with it. Then they give it back to you. They've seen that it's an item that's perfectly fine, perfectly legitimate in their eyes, and then you do something magical with it.'

He tapped the straitjacket.

'With the straitjacket, we gave it to audience members to examine,' he said. 'Zoey brings out three or four people from the audience onto the stage, and each one of them has a job. One checks the manacles around her feet; they're basic electronic release manacles – you can just slip your foot in and out, but they look really cool. The second examines the straitjacket, the third examines the lock that secures it, the fourth examines the chains and the fire torches that will light up the jacket when she's in it.'

He stared out into the auditorium, reliving the moment.

'Realistically, a single one of them could have looked at all four pieces, but it looks cooler when there's more than one person on stage. Your audience feels they're getting a more detailed examination of what's going on.'

'Like when you bring ringers in to sell a con,' Ramsey nodded, noting Davey's expression at this. 'More people saying something's legit makes you feel more secure in investing. So I've been told. I've never done anything like that.'

'How many of them were ringers?' Davey asked.

'What do you mean?' Jacob said.

'You know, part of the show.'

'Oh, you mean "stooge" or "shill."'

'Shill?'

'It's an abbreviation of "shillaber," a word originally

denoting a carnival worker who pretended to be a member of the audience, in an attempt to gain an interest in an attraction,' Jacob gave a small smile. 'Zoey doesn't use them. At this point, she didn't need it. It's just purely an escapology trick. There's no way they were going to find the flap. It's not really given to them when they look around.'

'How do you manage that?'

'When she holds the straitjacket, she makes a point of holding that arm,' Jacob replied. 'Most of the time, they'll just play around with the torso section, maybe look at the straps. No one really gives a damn about the sleeves, the wrists.'

'Do you know who the people were?' Davey asked as she was pulling on a pair of latex gloves.

'Differs every night,' Jacob said, watching the gloves. 'I don't consent to a cavity search.'

Davey looked over at Ramsey, ignoring Jacob's attempt at a joke.

'Somebody checks this straitjacket before giving it back to Zoey,' she said. 'In the time this was done, the cable to the button and the cord holding the keys were both slashed. If you were standing in front of five hundred people and you were given this to examine, how would you have done it?'

Ramsey took the straitjacket and examined it carefully.

'Razor blade,' he said. 'I'd have it hidden in my hand, keep it out of sight, slash the two cords, move on quickly. It'd take less than a second if done right. But I'd need to know the flap was there, especially if Zoey's holding the other side, trying to keep me away from it.'

'Can we borrow this?' Davey asked, picking the straitjacket up.

'I don't know how—' Jacob started, but stopped as Davey held up an authoritative hand.

'I'm forensics,' she said. 'Hence your oh-so-funny "cavity search" joke. There are fingerprints on this. Sure, we'll have a load of them, but the tips are leather. If someone held it to open the flap quickly, we should get a good mark. Once we remove you, the prop manager, Zoey, and a few other fingerprints, we'll narrow it down.'

'Sure,' Jacob nodded, looking off to the side of the stage, where a young stagehand was cleaning up. 'I'll get it sorted, but we need it back ASAP, in case Zoey turns up, ready to perform. Damian, can you have a chat with the forensics lady here?'

As Damian, one of the stage hands walked over to speak to Davey, Ramsey turned to face Jacob.

'How well did you know Zoey?' he asked. 'Joe's under the belief you guys are like thick as thieves.'

Jacob hesitated before responding.

'I've been working with her for five years now,' he said. 'I was on a talent show she was on. I didn't even pass the second round, and she went through to the finals. But in my routine, I did a trick that Zoey couldn't work out.'

'What trick?'

'Nobody's worked it out yet,' Jacob grinned. 'The last thing I'm going to do is tell you.'

There was a long, uncomfortable moment between the two men.

'I really am sorry, Jacob,' Ramsey nodded. 'If it makes you feel any better, your mum told me not to return. We'd had a fight. I went out, I got drunk, I was gambling in a casino. Next I was in a cell, the police finding me telling everybody, in great detail about a theft I performed.'

Jacob shook his head, actually chuckling now.

'Are you telling me that an argument with my mum is what put you in prison?'

'In a way, yes,' Ramsey smiled. 'I would never have walked away from the pair of you. You should know that.'

Jacob's expression softened slightly.

'Well, it's water under the bridge, isn't it?' he said. 'You've apologised and I'm willing to forgive.'

Ramsey grasped Jacob's hands, giving him a double-handed handshake.

'Thank you,' he said. 'We will find Zoey, don't worry.'

As Jacob nodded silently, removing his hands from Ramsey's and walking off, Davey, holding the straitjacket, walked over.

'We good to go?'

Ramsey nodded, looking around.

'Got what you need?' he asked.

However, Davey now stared at Ramsay, a curious expression on her face.

'Was that the truth?' she asked, frowning. 'You know, about how his mum dumped you and you got drunk?'

Ramsey stared sadly back at Jacob, now moving other items around the stage, packing things away until the next show.

'No,' he replied. 'To be honest, I was captured, went to prison, and I didn't give them a second thought.'

He stopped, looking back at Davey.

'Oh, I'm not a good man, Joanne. Never claimed to be, never was. I'm trying to be better these days, but when you spend most of your life being an absolute prick, it's very hard to move away from it.'

'I get that,' Davey nodded. 'So, what did you take from him?'

'What do you mean?' Ramsey asked, his tone a little too innocent for the conversation.

'You gave him a double-handed handshake,' Davey replied with the slightest hint of a smile. 'You've never done that in the time I've known you, which isn't that long in the grand scheme of things – but let's just say you don't strike me as the person who gives overly emotive responses.'

Ramsey smiled, pulling out a watch.

'I took his watch,' he said.

'Why?'

'Because it's *my* watch,' Ramsey replied. 'When I was arrested, I'd left it in the house. I hadn't intended to be arrested that night. It was one of my favourites.'

'What about his mum? How'd you know he won't just ask her if she really banned you from coming back?'

'She passed away five years ago,' Ramsey said, sadness dripping from his voice. 'I checked into it when I got out, not to catch up, I was ... I was just curious. You know, on how they were doing. Without me.'

'So, even if he disagrees with what you're saying, or disbelieves what you're saying, he can't prove it,' Davey nodded. 'Shitty, but clever.'

Ramsey looked down at the watch in his hand.

'It meant a lot to me,' he said. 'It was given to me by my uncle, when I was no older than he was when I left them.'

'Well I'm guessing it meant a lot to Jacob, for him to still wear it ...'

'Either that, or he found out how much it was worth.' Ramsey looked back as he scanned the auditorium. 'But it does make me wonder how much of a reliable narrator the man is. After all, he said he was left with nothing.'

'Maybe he didn't class the watch as anything?'

'It's been well cared for,' Ramsey retorted, examining it. 'This isn't nothing, Joanne. If he's going to lie about something like *this*, what does that mean about something important, like a friend?'

Davey went to reply, but noticed Ramsey had already moved on mentally, now staring off to the side of the stage, across from Jacob.

'Actually, you take the straitjacket back, I'll stay here,' he said. 'I want to see how our missing Miss Park got out of the theatre.'

Davey went to contest this, but stopped. She was still new to the team and wasn't sure how some things worked. This also seemed to be Ramsey Allen's modus operandi – to wander off until something connected to the case tried to kill him.

'See you back at the office,' she said. 'Try not to die.'

'Compassion, Joanne?'

'I just hate filling out forms,' Davey grinned as she walked away.

Ramsey chuckled to himself and then stared back at the side of the stage—

And the old woman watching him.

'Anna Lever,' he said to himself. 'I heard you were dead.'

Maybe the theatre had ghosts in it, after all.

6

CARNY GHOSTS

ALTHOUGH RAMSEY HAD BEEN IN THE THEATRE AS A YOUNGER man, he'd always been part of the audience, not backstage as such, apart from the brief stroll from the stage door up to the main auditorium.

Now, he was hurrying down the corridor towards the dressing rooms, hunting the mysterious woman he was absolutely certain was dead.

He found Anna Lever in one of the downstairs dressing rooms, sitting alone at a table, staring into the mirror, the lights on around it, watching the reflection of Ramsey as he entered through the door.

He hadn't realised that Anna was still alive. The woman had to be pushing eighty, maybe ninety by now. She was skeletally thin, her skin stretched across her bones, her hair, bright-white, pulled back into a harsh bun. She wore a long black skirt, and a thick cable-style jumper that hid what he knew would be a skinny, muscled frame. She may be old, but Anna Lever had always been exceptionally fit, blaming good genes rather than exercise regimes.

'Ramsey Allen,' she said with a smile. 'I thought you were in prison.'

'Well I thought you'd be in a box by now, Anna,' Ramsey smiled in response. 'But you didn't think I was there, did you?'

Anna smiled.

'You're not as quiet as you used to be,' she said. 'I hear your name everywhere these days. Like how you were courting Maureen Lumetta a couple of months back.'

'It was a party, and I was a chaperone,' Ramsey replied icily. 'Why are you here?'

'I'm a consultant,' Anna said, turning away from the mirror now to face him. 'I've been doing it for about thirty years now.'

'Since you retired, then?' Ramsey laughed as he walked over and sat down, facing her. 'It's good to see you.'

'Is it?' Anna asked. 'The circumstances aren't fortuitous, shall we say?'

Ramsey watched the old woman cautiously.

'Are you here with Zoey or Jacob?'

'Does it matter?' Anna folded her arms, almost defensively.

'You were friends with his mum.'

'I was also friends with his grandmother,' Anna smiled slightly. 'They never listened to me, though.'

'You sure about that?'

'Oh, absolutely. I told her not to date you, and look where that got her.'

She sighed.

'Jacob started working with Zoey, and I'd seen her around,' she explained. 'I'm here with both of them, in a way.'

Ramsey wasn't sure if he believed her, but he let it slide for the moment.

'What do you know about Zoey Park's disappearance?' he asked.

'Why would I know anything?'

Ramsey leant forward, resting his elbows on his knees and his head upon his hands.

'Anna, you were one of the greatest escape artists I have ever known,' he said. 'When the police turned up while you were street hustling, you'd be out of there in a second, and no one would know how you did it. Three times I saw you in buildings with no escape, only to find you gone when you needed to. Now, you happen to be in a West End theatre the day after Zoey Park does the same thing. What do *you* think I'm talking about?'

Anna chuckled, leaning back on her chair as she watched Ramsey for a long moment.

'Zoey has demons,' she said.

'What sorts of demons?'

'Carny demons.'

'Is this Flanagan?'

'Among others,' Anna reached to the side, pulling out an old battered "bicycle" deck of cards.

'Come, Ramsey,' she said. 'Play with me.'

'Oh no,' Ramsey shook his head. 'I remember playing three-card monte with you when I was younger and I remember losing a lot of money in the process. And even with your old fingers, you're still more dextrous than people half your age.'

'Not for money,' Anna said. 'For information.'

She pulled three cards from the top.

'Do you trust me?'

'Of course not,' Ramsey smiled.

She turned them over, showing him the cards: a Two of Clubs, a Two of Spades, and an Ace of Hearts.

'No longer "Find the Lady" then?' Ramsey smiled.

'We can do that if you want,' Anna grinned, revealing a line of mostly false, yellowing teeth.

'Go on, then. Surprise me with your magic,' Ramsey shrugged.

'It's not magic when we already know how it ends,' Anna smiled, picking up the three cards. 'Here you are, gentlemen, this Ace of Hearts is the winning card. Watch it closely.'

She flipped the three cards now, shuffling them from spot to spot, now and then revealing the Ace as she continued.

'Follow it with your eye as I shuffle. Here it is, and now here, now here, and now – where?' She held up a hand. 'If you point it out the first time, you win; but if you miss, you lose.'

She flipped one card over.

'Here it is, you see! Now watch it again. This Ace of Hearts, gentlemen, is the winning card.'

She carried on shuffling, now deep into the role of the three-card monte dealer, the patter coming easily as she spoke.

'I take no bets from paupers, cripples or orphan children. The Ace of Hearts. It's my regular trade, gentlemen, to move my hands quicker than your eyes. I always have two chances to your one. The Ace of Hearts. If your sight is quick enough, you beat me and I pay; if not, I beat you and take your money. The Ace of Hearts; who will go me twenty? It is very plain and simple, but you can't always tell. Here you are, gentlemen, the Ace, and the Ace. Who will go me twenty dollars?'

Ramsey sighed, tapping the card on the left and turning it over.

The Ace of Hearts stared up at them.

'Albert D. Richardson, *Beyond the Mississippi,* 1869,' he said, looking up at Anna. 'Taken from an account of a trip from Sacramento to Salt Lake that Richardson made at the invitation of Leland Stanford, to inspect the ongoing construction of the line.'

'Did you ever read the book?'

'God no,' Ramsey chuckled. 'I only remember it because you used the bloody thing word for word in Leicester Square in the early eighties.'

'Well done. You remember the training I gave you.'

'More likely, you let me see that one,' Ramsey shook his head. 'That's how the hustle works, isn't it? Let the mark think they've beaten the dealer, give them a few wins, and then take them for everything they've got.'

'Let's see,' Anna said, placing the cards down again. 'Follow it with your eye as I shuffle—'

'Do we need the patter every time?' Ramsey interrupted.

Anna glared at him.

'Do I tell you how to break into a house or steal a watch from a young man?' she asked.

Ramsey reddened as he realised she'd seen his double-handed handshake on Jacob.

'Ask your questions, Mister Allen,' Anna responded, a sparkle in her eye. 'I'll save you the Mississippi banter this time.'

Ramsey watched the three cards being shuffled on the table.

'How did Zoey get out?' he asked.

'How do you think she got out?' Anna replied, placing the three cards on the table in front of him.

Ramsey tapped the one on the left, and Anna nodded.

'She could have exited through the stage door,' she said, turning it over, revealing the Two of Spades. 'But we know that didn't happen. Arthur would have seen her. There were no other entrances or exits on the lower level.'

Ramsey tapped the second card, the one in the centre.

'She could have gone through the main entrance,' Anna continued, turning the card to show *another* Two of Spades, looking up at Ramsey with a knowing smile. 'All it would take is to change her clothes and exit with the crowd, but she had no idea how long they would still be there, waiting for the trick that was never going to end too well.'

'What other options are there?' Ramsey said. 'Or are you just showing me an entire deck of Twos of Spades now?'

Anna took the last card, not quite turning it over and revealing it yet.

'If you can't go out through the front or from down below, that only leaves you one direction,' she said.

Ramsey looked up at the ceiling.

'The roof?' he asked, confused.

Anna smiled, turning the card. It was a Queen of Hearts.

'The roof,' she said.

She took the cards, shuffling them into the deck, passing those to Ramsey for him to shuffle, and then taking them back, pulling off the top three cards, showing them once more to be the Ace of Hearts, the Two of Spades, and now the returned Two of Clubs.

Ramsey applauded slowly. It was a good trick. The one thing he knew about Anna, more than anything, was that three-card monte was her speciality.

'Next question,' she said.

'Who should we be looking into?' he asked.

Anna shuffled the three cards.

'Pick a card,' she said, placing them on the table, side by side.

Ramsey tapped the one on the left, turning it over.

It wasn't any of the cards she'd originally shown; now it was the Queen of Spades.

'Do you understand cartomancy?' Anna asked.

'The art of using playing cards as a focus, like tarot,' Ramsey nodded.

'Do you understand what the royal cards mean?'

'Yes,' Ramsey continued. 'The Queen of Spades is a dark-haired woman or widow, usually angry or bitter. But you knew that when you placed it into your hand. This isn't some kind of occult trick. I'm very aware of how these things work.'

Anna shrugged, tapping the Queen of Spades.

'It could be Claudette Storm,' she said. 'She's run Zoey's shows for a few months. But Zoey's not been working as much as she used to. The shows aren't making as much money. She's getting less TV time. Maybe there's an issue there? Perhaps Claudette has been asking her to change her act a little to fit with the changing times?'

'How so?' Ramsey asked.

'Maybe she has offers from other people, offers that give more profits?'

Ramsey nodded, tapping the second card. Anna turned over the card to reveal another woman, this time the Queen of Diamonds.

'An outgoing, flirtatious woman with light hair, a definite player,' Anna said. 'Maybe Luana Flanagan. Self-proclaimed Queen of Conjuring, the Duchess of the Gypsies. Ran circuses with her father across Ireland. Knew Zoey's mother. Believes Zoey owes her money. Though, if we're being truthful here, she believes Zoey owes her *everything*.'

'I heard Zoey's mum stole about a hundred grand from her, and now Zoey has the debt.'

'Oh, that's very possible, as gypsy debts cross generations,' Anna frowned. 'But you'd need to speak to Luana Flanagan about that.'

'Could she have done this?'

'Well, she's been around recently,' Anna said. 'I saw her.'

'What about the final one?' Ramsey tapped the middle card.

Anna turned it over, revealing a Jack of Diamonds.

'Young male,' she said. 'An unreliable or dishonest young person with light hair.'

She picked the card up, turning it around, placing it face-down onto the table before flipping it back over, revealing it was now a Jack of Spades.

'Or an unpleasant young person with dark hair,' Ramsey looked down at it. 'Both sound like terrible dance partners. But which one is it?'

'There are many men in Zoey's life,' Anna shrugged. 'Some of them might not have her best interests at heart.'

Ramsey leaned back, staring at the three cards facing him.

'Jacob?' he asked.

'Possibly. Maybe there's some other man in her life she needs to worry about.'

Anna flipped the card back over. Then, with a grin, she flipped the other two on either side, until all cards were face down again.

'You have another question?' she said.

'Yes, but it isn't card-trick based,' Ramsey asked. 'You used to do an act. I saw it once. You can remember things – like some kind of mentalism trick.'

'I still do it now and then,' Anna nodded.

'Did you see the people on stage last night?' Ramsey asked. 'The ones who checked the straitjacket and chains. If you did, and using whatever techniques you used to use, can you remember anything about them?'

Anna now leant back in her chair, watching Ramsey.

'You mean Chaz, Becky, Veronica and Biz?' she asked.

'Biz?'

'It's the name he gave. I'm not going to judge his parents today,' Anna waved a hand dismissively. 'I saw them all from the side of the stage. I used mnemonics to remember everything.'

'Would you be able to write them down for me?' Ramsey gave a winning smile in an attempt to win her over.

'Already have,' Anna smiled, reaching into a pocket and passing Ramsey a folded piece of paper. 'I knew someone would come by, and I knew eventually someone would click there were stooges in the audience. Veronica looked at the straitjacket. I'm sure that's who you're looking at here. She was in seat F-sixteen, in the stalls. There was a man named Biz, came from H-five.'

'I didn't think Zoey Park used stooges?' Ramsey checked the paper.

'I didn't say they were Zoey Park's stooges,' Anna smiled, groaning with stiffness as she finally stood up. 'Find her phone, Ramsey Allen. Nobody saw it in the theatre when they looked for her and a person like Zoey wouldn't be without it.'

'Do you know where she could be now?' Ramsey asked.

'She grew up on the streets,' Anna replied. 'Lived her life

in Covent Garden. If anyone's going to ground, they'll go somewhere they know.'

She walked past Ramsey, patting him on the shoulder as she did so.

'I've given you everything I can, Ramsey. It was good seeing you. I really hope you've kept up your skills better than that half-assed pinch I saw you give Jacob.'

'I still remember a thing or two,' Ramsey smiled. 'Many of which you taught me.'

Anna Lever stopped at the door, pausing as Ramsey rose.

'Is there anybody we should be careful about?' he asked.

'I've given you all you need,' Anna said as she walked out the door. 'You just need to finish the trick.'

Ramsey frowned. *What did she mean by that?*

He looked back at the pack of playing cards, in particular the three cards still face-down in a line of three-card monte, the backs slightly bent to allow easy laying down onto a board or table.

Reaching down, he paused before turning the first card.

'You've taught me most of what I know,' he said to himself. 'Also you know me better than myself, so I'm guessing you answered the last question before I asked it.'

Sighing, he flipped the card over.

It was a Joker. Unlike most packs that showed a jester as the image, the Bicycle deck had a King of Spades riding a bike as the Joker image, looking to the side as he did so.

The King of Spades.

In cartomancy, this meant a dark-haired selfish and ambitious man.

Frowning, Ramsey flipped the second card.

Another Joker.

Sighing, knowing what it was before he even turned it,

Ramsey flipped the final middle card and was not surprised to see a third Joker staring up at him.

'Joker,' he said. 'Or is it Joe Kerr? What have you *not* been telling us?'

Placing the cards on the top of the deck, Ramsey patted them nostalgically, before leaving the dressing room.

———

7

CHINESE CURSES

Of all the people in Finders to be sent on this mission, Tinker Jones hadn't expected that would be *her* that was sent into Chinatown to look into the Tsang curses.

She wasn't an expert on curses, but she knew a few of them, and from what she'd guessed, it could be one of three types of curse. The problem was that Jimmy hadn't bothered to explain what it was, and so now they were even further back than square one.

Luckily for Tinker, she had someone who could explain it to her.

The Tsangs had their base in the back room basement of a Chinese restaurant off Charing Cross, but Tinker wasn't going there today. Instead, she made her way to a Chinese tourism shop – filled with brightly coloured kites, "happy waving lucky cats" and bamboo scrolls; things a passing, uneducated tourist would believe were "genuine artefacts," including a lot of jade statues, plastic laughing Buddhas and plaster models of Terracotta Army soldiers – next to a noodle bar and a Chinese medicine shop.

Tinker glanced in the window briefly before entering the shop. There was an American couple trying to haggle with the old lady behind the counter, who seemed irritated at their actions, but was unable to explain this because of her lack of English. She was old, maybe in her eighties, no taller than five feet in height and with curly grey hair that looked as if someone had glued a Brillo pad to her head.

The American male looked at Tinker.

'You speak Chinese?' he asked. 'This woman won't give her a fair price for this.'

The "her" seemed to be his wife, in a baseball cap and fur coat – a style choice that really didn't work.

'Does it have a price tag?' Tinker asked.

'That's not how haggling works.'

'Also we're not in China, we're in Central London, so pay the bloody price or piss off,' Tinker suggested. 'To think a Chinese woman would haggle because of her heritage is not only racist, but reprehensible.'

The American's eyes widened at this, and Tinker knew he hadn't even considered this. Placing a ten-pound note on the counter, he quickly took the item, a pair of commemorative chopsticks in a box, and hurried out, his fur-coat-wearing wife behind him.

'Bloody hell, Tink, you saved me there,' the Chinese woman spoke now, a broad Scouse accent coming through as she did so. 'Thought I was gonna have to break cover.'

She came around the side and hugged Tinker.

'You want some buns?' she asked, nodding at the back room. 'Sonia just made some. She's out for the moment, she'll be back in an hour if you can hang about?'

'I can't, but I promise I'll come back later, Liú Yǔn,' she said.

The Liú in Liú Yǔn came from "willow," a tree often associated with resilience and grace, while Yǔn meant "cloud," representing something elusive or mysterious. Combined, the name suggested a woman with an enigmatic grace, who had endured much in her life, with wisdom to share. Tinker knew that was pretty much exact, and had known the woman for almost twenty years now, since going to school with her granddaughter.

'So, what do you need?' Liú Yǔn asked as she placed the ten-pound note in her pocket.

'Jimmy Tsang,' Tinker held up a hand as she spoke, expecting the outburst. 'Apparently he's been cursed.'

'Good,' Liú Yǔn spat to the side. 'Kenny and Benny were pricks, but that man is the devil himself.'

'I was hoping you'd know a little about this?' Tinker gave a little nudge. 'You being one of the Matriarchs of Chinatown, your ear is always to the ground.'

'Not when it's in fear of getting me run over,' Liú Yǔn shook her head. 'Tsang isn't a good man to work for.'

'I know, but he'd owe us and it'd be a good debt,' Tinker shrugged. 'All I know is he's been cursed. Said to a colleague of mine that someone placed it on him, and his family by default. All I'm asking is if you heard anything.'

Liú Yǔn paused, pursed her lips and then nodded.

'I heard some,' she said. 'I heard – and I don't know who did it, before you ask – that someone placed a "Binding of the Red Threads Curse" on him.'

Tinker watched Liú Yǔn for a long moment.

'Liú, you're going to have to explain that one to me,' she said.

Liú Yǔn sighed theatrically.

'The concept of the Red Thread originates from an

ancient Chinese legend,' she said. 'It suggests that the gods tie an invisible red thread around the ankles of those that are destined to meet one another, or help each other in a certain way.'

She waved at a shelf in the shop.

'We actually sell red thread here, funny enough,' she smiled, showing a wealth of missing teeth. 'Most often, it's associated with soulmates or destined lovers, but it can also apply to significant, non-romantic relationships.'

'What about curses?'

'The curse, in this case, could be a manipulation of this thread,' Liú Yǔn nodded. 'Jimmy might be told his red thread has been tied to an object of misfortune, meaning that wherever he goes, bad luck will follow.'

'How could we fix this?'

'You'd need to find this object, and untangle the thread to break the curse,' Liú Yǔn was already working through this in her head. 'A rival to Jimmy's throne might desire not only to remove him from power, but to ensure his life is filled with misery and misfortune.'

She chuckled.

'He should join the queue.'

'Liú ...'

'The curse could be a method to undermine Jimmy's confidence, cause dissent among his ranks, and make him more susceptible to mistakes,' Liú Yǔn offered. 'Sounds like it's started to work if he's come to you. If you don't believe in the curse, it won't work as well, but Jimmy's old school. He'll believe it, but only if he knows it's been presented the right way.'

'How do you mean?'

Liú Yǔn folded her arms.

'Red thread alone means shit all,' she said, the words sounding strange from her mouth. 'You need to make a show of it. Whoever it is doing it, they could employ a disreputable Daoist priest or Shaman to perform the ritual. This could involve using a physical red thread, which would represent Jimmy's life-thread. The thread would then be tied around an object of misfortune.'

'Like what?'

'Anything really, Tinker. This object could be a symbolic representation of failure, betrayal, or downfall. For example, it might be a coin from a bankrupt dynasty, a weapon that was used in a treacherous assassination, or a broken artifact known to bring bad luck.'

'Anything else?'

'The ceremony would involve chants, burning of specific herbs, and placement of the object in a secret location,' Liú Yǔn considered this. 'You could go ask old woman Xiùlán next door in the herb shop about that. But that's just the showmanship side. To fix Jimmy Tsang, you need to show him he's free of the curse. So that means breaking it.'

'How would I—'

'You would need to locate the object, and then once located, the thread would need to be untied by someone pure of heart or during a particular time, like during a specific moon phase, or with a counter-ritual.'

'From a disreputable Daoist priest or Shaman?'

'If you want,' Liú Yǔn chuckled. 'It's all bollocks, anyway. Just find who did it and why, tell Jimmy, grab one of the bald Harry Krishnas from Soho Square, have them dance about and cut a red cord. There you go, job done.'

'What about the people who cursed him?'

'That's up to you,' Liú Yǔn replied and, as she did so, her voice darkened. 'But know this, child. Jimmy Tsang is an opportunistic piece of shit. He's killing the community and blaming his cousin for it. He wants power and won't go back to Shanghai until he gets it. So anyone who has placed this curse on him? I'd say they had good reason to. So if you're the person looking to stop it ...'

Tinker nodded.

'Yeah, I see,' she said. 'I'll grab a bun later. Say hi to Sonia for me.'

Giving Liú Yǔn a last hug and leaving the shop, Tinker now stood outside, staring up and down the narrow China-town alley.

As much as she didn't believe in this, someone did. After all, they placed this curse on Jimmy Tsang for a reason.

The question was – could the favour they'd gain from Jimmy, added to the one Kenny owed already, make up for whatever vengeance would be laid down the moment Jimmy Tsang worked out who was going up against him?

This might be a question for bigger minds to decide.

Sighing, Tinker checked her phone, saw a message from Ramsey about three-card-monte or something, and turned and walked back towards Leicester Square station.

If she'd walked the other way, she might have clocked the young Asian man watching her from the doorway of the Chinese medicine shop. He was young, not yet out of his teens, and wore jeans, a white hoodie and a grey baseball cap with a manga character on, covering his shaggy black hair.

He noted Tinker's direction, checked once more where she'd come from, and then noted it down on a phone message, sending it on.

He didn't know if it was relevant, or even if it'd be worth anything. But if it was, he'd get a payday.

Because Jimmy Tsang always gave good paydays when it was good news.

8

OLD FOES, NEW FRIENDS

ARRIVING BACK AT FINDERS, RAMSEY FOUND THE PLACE BUSIER than usual. For a start, Davey was having an argument in the boardroom with Robert. It sounded quite loud and intense.

Ellie was in her office, watching through the glass with a small level of amusement.

'What's going on?' he said, as he joined her beside her desk.

'Apparently, Joanne Davey isn't used to the levels of forensics that we have here,' Ellie grinned. 'She's making this clear to Robert right now.'

'Do we have *any* kind of level of forensics?' Ramsey asked. 'Most of the time she's just examining locations or items. It's not usual for us to...'

He paused.

'Okay, so we have needed some major stuff every now and then,' he admitted. 'And she's only now realising we don't have what she needs.'

'No,' Ellie grinned. 'I think that's the problem.'

'Ah,' Ramsey said, watching as Davey angrily stormed out of the office.

'How am I supposed to find fingerprints when there's nowhere I can use to find fingerprints?' she snapped, marching away down the corridor towards her own office.

Robert walked in, looking a little flustered.

'She's right, you know,' he said. 'When we had Raj do it, he would use the police's equipment. I suppose it's a bit off to expect that Davey could just wander into Temple Inn and borrow stuff, and the jobs she's been on while I've been... well, away - have been child's play for her. We ought to bring some things in before she starts cutting up lifelike figures in rooms surrounded by glass.'

'Where's she gone now?'

'To work out what she can do with the portable kit she has in her car,' Robert shrugged. 'Which, considering who she trained under, probably has more equipment in it than most provincial police stations.'

He looked at Ramsey.

'Good work with the witness,' he said.

'In fairness, it was an old friend,' Ramsey shrugged.

'Everyone in London seems to be an old friend of yours,' Robert smiled at this. 'We've taken the information and passed it across to Casey.'

'You've put Casey on this?' Ramsey raised an eyebrow as he looked back at Ellie. 'I thought he wasn't being used unless it was important.'

'Facial recognition is important,' Ellie shrugged. 'Also, your friend's line about hunting Zoey's phone made me wonder where it was last found.'

'And?'

'Long Acre, just north of Covent Garden, which again

matches with what your informant told us,' Ellie leant over her chair's arm to ruffle the head of Millie, sitting beside her. 'I sent Tinker down to see if she could find it, after she finished up in Chinatown. She phoned back telling me she'd found it in two pieces, broken and dumped in a side alley.'

'So, what you're telling me is, Zoey Park deliberately broke her phone – or somebody took it and broke it for her?' Robert said darkly.

'We won't know until we get more information, and that involves CCTV. Casey's having a check around.'

'Team's back together, it seems,' Ramsey grinned. 'You said he found his ...'

His smile faded as he trailed off, looking out of the office window, towards to the entrance lobby of Finders.

There, standing, waving a warrant card at Sara, the receptionist, was Kate Delgado.

'What the bloody hell is *she* doing here?' he snapped, about to turn and head towards the door. 'She has no right—'

He paused however, as Ellie held up a hand.

'Don't get angry. You'll upset Millie. I knew Kate was turning up; I called her.'

'You bloody what?' Ramsey turned in utter shock. 'You called the police, and you called *her*? The Piccadilly Theatre's in the West End! It's not the wheelhouse of Vauxhall police!'

'True, but Delgado's changed Units,' Ellie explained. 'Whitehouse has left an unpleasant taste in everyone's mouth right now. She's on secondment to Charing Cross and Soho. Which means, if anything, Delgado could have come in and claimed some kind of seniority on the case, but she didn't.'

'Joe said not to get the police involved,' Robert, also obviously not involved in the conversation to bring Delgado in, grimaced.

'Joe could also be an unreliable narrator, and a suspect in the case,' Ramsey added. 'Anna seemed to think he was connected—'

'Anna gave you a playing card,' Robert snapped back. 'How the hell does that say Joseph Kerrigan?'

'Three jokers,' Ellie said. 'On a man whose stage name is Joe Kerr. You can see where the lines get drawn. I know this is personal for you, but we look at all angles here.'

Robert went to reply about coincidences and conspiracies, but stopped himself as Kate Delgado walked up to the door and, surprisingly, brushed a strand of her long blonde hair from her face and knocked before entering.

'Reckless,' she said. 'Allen, Mister Lewis.'

'DI Delgado—'

'*Acting* DI. Don't go there, please, it's not official yet.'

'Thank you for coming,' Ellie nodded, rising.

'Thank you for giving me new information on the case we've recently gained,' Delgado said. 'I'm hoping this level of communication will be something we'll see a lot in the future.'

'If it's relevant to your Unit, sure,' Robert snapped, grumbling. 'Which apparently isn't Vauxhall anymore.'

Delgado turned to look at him.

'How are you doing?' she asked. Ellie couldn't be too sure whether this was actual concern or the realisation that she *ought* to ask.

'I had the equivalent of a mini-stroke when your *partner* beat the living shit out of me,' Robert replied icily. 'So forgive me if I'm not all full of niceties.'

Ellie placed her hand on his shoulder.

'She's not Mark,' she whispered. 'Delgado didn't know what was going on.'

'So she says,' Robert glared at Delgado. 'Before she apparently ran from the Unit like a scolded dog. You called her in, Ellie. I want no part of this.'

With this, Robert turned and stormed out of the office, most likely going back to his own, further down the corridor.

Ellie looked back at Delgado.

'He's got a point,' she said. 'The last time we worked together, you had a boss.'

'Mark Whitehouse is no longer part of the force and is currently awaiting trial,' Delgado said coldly. Ellie got the impression this wasn't the first time she'd had to state this, and if she'd changed locations, it was probably her daily explanation.

'Is he going to trial?' Ramsey asked. 'Because, let's be honest, last I heard, he was trying to gain some kind of plea deal.'

'It's above my pay grade, and no longer my Unit,' Delgado shook her head. 'I wish I could help – he made a fool out of me.'

'He tried to kill Robert,' Ramsey replied matter-of-factly. 'But we're *all* so worried about your feelings, Kate.'

'Kate? So *personal*, Ramsey?'

'Well, you did say not to use your title.'

'Actually, if you want to help with relationships between us, we could do with some help with a couple of things,' Ellie held up a hand to stop any more back and forth.

'Go on.'

'For a start, could borrow some of your forensics people? Our expert needs to check a straitjacket. Obviously, all information will be shared.'

'We can arrange that,' Delgado nodded, already pulling

out her phone and typing a message. 'Unless Joanne Davey wants to start shouting at my people, at which point—'

'She trained under Rosanna Marcos,' Ellie grinned. 'She has a high level of expectation. I'm *sure* your people would reach it. In the meantime, we'll do our best to keep her reined in.'

'How did you know about this, anyway?' Ramsey asked Delgado, frowning. 'I was under the assumption this was off the radar.'

'It was until about two o'clock,' Ellie said. 'When somebody placed a YouTube video up entitled "Where in the World is Zoey Park?", showing the end of the show. You can see the promoter explaining that due to technical reasons, the show has now ended, and the audience are all asking what's going on as they're encouraged to leave. With no exciting, end of show reveal of where she was, afterwards people started to ask.'

'It landed on my new desk with a suggestion we work it out before the press start sniffing,' Delgado continued. 'We checked in with her partner, Joseph Kerrigan, and he wouldn't speak to us. He just kept telling us to contact you. At that point we knew it was trouble.'

Ellie gave a slightly sheepish shrug at this.

'We aim to please,' she said softly. 'So currently the police are ...'

'Treating it as suspicious until we learn something else,' Delgado said, before turning and walking to the door. 'Plus it gives me an opportunity to try to mend old wounds.'

'Wounds you created,' Ramsey muttered, loud enough for the DI to hear.

'If we hear anything, we'll let you know,' Delgado ignored him, looking back at Ellie. 'I'd appreciate the same back.'

'You could have phoned this in,' Ramsey muttered. 'You didn't have to come here.'

Delgado paused, considered this and turned back to him.

'I can detect lies better when they're face to face,' she said.

'Oh, we're lying to you now, are we?'

Ignoring Ramsey's comment, and without saying goodbye, Delgado left the office, walking off down the corridor.

'Even when she's trying to play nice, she still comes across as an authoritarian dick,' Ramsey muttered.

At this, Ellie couldn't disagree.

'Come on, let's see what the Wunderkind has discovered,' she said, patting her thigh for Millie to follow.

ELLIE AND RAMSEY WALKED OVER TO A SIDE OFFICE, A TAPED piece of A4 on the glass window stating "TEK SUPPORT" in marker pen.

'He knows that's not how it's spelt, right?' Ramsey raised an eyebrow.

'I think it's a trendy way to say it,' Ellie shrugged as she knocked and entered to find Casey Noyce sitting behind a bank of monitor screens, like some kind of teenage stockbroker checking from screen to screen as he tapped on his keyboard. He was thin, still in that teenage "gawky" stage of his growth, with shaggy black hair over a navy blue hoodie with "FRENCHIE" written on it. Ellie didn't know if this was a brand of some kind, so simply coughed to gain his attention.

Looking up, he smiled at Ramsey.

'Wondered when you'd turn up, Grandad,' he said.

'Less of the "Grandad", lad,' Ramsey muttered, but it was

good-natured. 'I'll have you know that one of the people giving us information today made me look like a small child.'

'Been talking to coffins again?' Casey said, the smile on his face pausing as he looked down at Millie, now scraping a paw against his desk drawers. 'Aw come on! You know she's not allowed in here! All she does is beg!'

Ramsey frowned, confused as Ellie looked innocent.

'Casey has beef jerky in his drawers,' she explained. 'He made the mistake of giving her some once. Now it's the magic beef drawer.'

Casey responded by pulling a bag out of the drawer, passing Millie a small piece and then hiding it elsewhere.

'It won't work,' Ellie shook her head. 'She's a trained sniffer dog.'

'Sure, if it's only snacks she's sniffing out,' Casey grumbled.

'What have you got?' Deciding to move on from the current dog-related topic, mainly because it involved giving Millie treats, and he'd already had a couple of bollockings on that after his "dog sitting" put a kilo extra on the spaniel, Ramsey wandered over, Ellie beside him.

'I've been looking into Ramsey's suggestion that she climbed onto the roof,' Casey waved them around the desk so they could see the screens.

'There. This is Google Maps,' he said, tapping a roof on the screen. 'It's on satellite view, which means that you can see the buildings rather than blocks. If your witness claims that Zoey Park escaped via the roof, there's only one area she could have gone.'

He tapped again on the flat roof.

'We're north of Piccadilly Circus,' he said, showing this on the map. 'She would come out onto the roof by this door on the southern corner, and then she has three options. She can't go forwards; there's no building, just a big fall onto Denman Street. To the left, or her right as she comes out, is Sherwood Street, which doesn't have a way down. To the right – which is her left – is a path towards Charing Cross road, over *The Queen's Head*, around the stage door area and, if there is still scaffolding there, onto the buildings around Ham Yard.'

He tapped a building, the side of which had a fire escape. He then zoomed in on the street, the map turning into a street viewpoint.

'From here, she can get down to the courtyard inside, and then she's got a variety of destinations she can go,' he said. 'At this point, I'm using historical pings from her phone before she tossed it at Covent Garden. I think from the looks of things, she made her way quickly to Leicester Square and then walked down Long Acre to Covent Garden, where she broke the phone.'

'CCTV?'

'Working on it,' Casey said. 'Hopefully, I'll have something soon.'

'So, Zoey Park ran from a West End theatre and headed straight to Covent Garden,' Ellie said. 'Do we know what time she arrived?'

'Estimated time, I would say based on the show ending around ten, and the confusion she'd have on the roof once up there, you're looking at her arriving there probably half-ten to quarter to eleven in the evening.'

'Too late for shows,' Ellie mused.

'Too late for most things,' Ramsey replied. 'Why would she be going there?'

Ellie tapped at her cheek as she thought this through.

'Maybe we need to go and have a chat in Covent Garden,' she said. 'Do we know where Joe is right now?'

'I would have said work, but I think today he's probably looking for Zoey as well,' Ramsey added. 'Which might not be that great an idea, based on Anna and the game of the three jokers.'

'That could mean him, it might not. But either way, he's known at the Garden, and at the moment, he's our best opportunity to get the performers there to answer any questions we have, especially about who might have known about her owing a hundred grand to Luana Flanagan.'

'Tinker's there now,' Casey added, looking up. 'At least for the moment, let's see how she does before anything else?'

Ellie paused, frowning at her teenage colleague.

'That's quite restrained for you,' she said. 'Which makes me suspicious. What's going on?'

Casey went to protest, but instead slumped slightly, smiling, knowing he was caught out here.

'I have a bet with Davey,' he said. 'Closest time to Tinker punching someone out wins. I thought this could be a learning opportunity for her.'

'Or a chance to make money,' Ellie sighed. 'Ramsey?'

'I'll go to the Garden, find Tinker, ask about Flanagan,' he smiled.

'Actually, I might need you to look into Jimmy Tsang's enemies,' Ellie said. 'Tinker dropped an email to me, saying something about Shaman and curses involving red thread?'

'I can look into that too,' Ramsey said. 'It's around the same area.'

He looked back at Casey first.

'Anything on the four stooges?'

Casey used his mouse to pull up another window, a list of names scrolling down.

'This is the list of ticket sales for last night,' he said. 'As you can see, it was three-quarters filled.'

Ellie looked closer.

'How do you have this?' she asked in surprise. 'Surely, data protection—'

'Probably best not to ask,' Casey grinned. 'Let's just say the system they used is a little ... antiquated and ... well, someone like me ...'

He tailed off, his expression one of triumph, reaching for the mouse.

'Do you get credit card details?' Ramsey asked, his eyes twinkling as he stared at the screen.

'Not for the reasons you're thinking, old man,' Casey slapped Ramsey's hand away. 'I get the last four numbers of the card. Everything else is asterisked out, which is about usual, but it means I can get information.'

He pointed at another screen. This one had a layout of the stalls of the Piccadilly Theatre.

'This seat here, for example, D-nineteen. That's Michelle Childs. She bought two tickets. These here, N-eight and seven, they were bought by someone named Gary Monroe.'

'And our four?'

Casey pointed at the two seats.

'Veronica was F-sixteen, right? That's the seat there. I think "Biz", here in H-five is short for Bisley.'

'Any reason?'

'Yeah. The artist Simon Bisley basically uses "Biz" as a cut-down version of his name.'

'I didn't think you were into art,' Ramsey gave a slight smile.

'Comic art,' Casey grinned. 'Simon Bisley is the *man*. Does incredible painted covers. I bought one at a Comic-Con last month.'

'Expensive?'

'Oh, hell, yes,' Casey smiled. 'But luckily my mum reckons she's negotiated a better hourly rate with you for my services, so I thought I'd be okay.'

Ellie shook her head.

'I seem to recall you managed to get a nice windfall after the Lumetta case,' she said. 'How many grand does one of those bottles go for now?

Casey looked innocently at her.

'I don't know what you mean,' he replied, straight-faced. 'But we are upping my salary, right? My mum would be very unhappy if she learned you weren't looking after me.'

'That's a question for Robert,' Ellie sighed. 'Maybe we'll be lucky, and his brain injury means he's forgotten who you are.'

'So, this Bisley in seat H-five, I'm guessing you can find his details, get a name and address?' Ramsey changed the subject.

'I'd love to, but there was no Bisley that booked seats,' Casey shook his head. 'Before you say I got the name wrong, there was no Veronica either. The other two, though – Charles "Chaz" Bailey and Becky Lynch? Their details are on the list.'

'So, two out of four are findable.'

'But the wrong two,' Casey replied, scratching the back of his neck. 'Look.'

He tapped a few more buttons, and on the screen, fifty of the seats in the stalls turned red. The positioning was random; most of them were two seats next to each other, most likely a couple who had booked for the show. But they were spread evenly out, the entire first eight rows.

They included seats F-sixteen and H-five.

'What am I looking at?' Ellie asked.

'All of these tickets were booked by the same credit card,' Casey replied. 'It was a two-for-one night, so fifty tickets came in at thirty pounds each, rather than the usual sixty. But you're still looking at a grand and a half, probably more with fees paid on the card to spread the audience out.'

He tapped two of the chairs with his finger on the screen.

'This one is Veronica. This one is Biz.'

Ramsey stroked his chin.

'Someone else stacked the deck,' he suggested.

'How do you mean?'

'Look at it this way,' Ramsey replied, staring at the screen. 'When somebody calls people out of the audience, they'll go random. It's the only way it works to an audience, unless they have their own stooges, at which point they'll find a way to get an audience member who they know. They'll throw balls into the audience, or bounce a beach ball, something that looks random, but is, in actual fact, quite simple to rig. This is different.'

He tapped at some of the red chairs, mostly at the sides near aisles.

'When you pick a stooge,' he said. 'You find somebody easy to move. There's no point in picking someone in the middle of a row, it takes them ages to get out, causes disruption and takes attention away from the trick. So, you pick someone within the five or six seats to the left or to the right, or even down the middle if there's an aisle.'

'That's pretty much all of these,' Ellie said, nodding. 'Somebody has been stacking the chances of being picked, making sure that their people – ringers they brought in – are used.'

Ramsey nodded as he looked back at Casey.

'Do we know whose card this is?' he asked.

'I'm working on it,' Casey obliged. 'Usually, the cards are quite easy. The data on it links to somebody who's actually booked, and who's attended. So, Mr. So-and-so, they've bought a ticket for himself and his wife and turned up to see the show? We have them. This isn't the same. It's a corporate card, I think, and they're a little harder to get through.'

He shrugged, sitting back as he looked up.

'It's not impossible, though,' he said. 'I will get through. I'm just saying it could be a little harder.'

Ellie stared at the seats on the screen.

'I want the details for Veronica and Biz,' she said. 'I want to have a very serious word with them. Do anything you can, yeah?'

'I will,' Casey nodded, serious now. 'They would have had to pick up the tickets and been accessed into the system with their full names. With that and CCTV, both of which Robert's sorting now ...'

'How the hell is he doing that?' Ellie exclaimed.

'I think he's lawyered up,' Casey grinned as he passed Millie another piece of jerky. 'After all, they don't want to be known as the theatre that lost their biggest star, either. Asking for two names is far easier than asking for an entire audience.'

'When you get them, send them to me,' Ellie straightened. 'Ramsey? Hang around for a moment. I might need you with me when these names turn up. Casey? Good work. I think we might have a plan right now.'

Tinker hadn't spent time in Covent Garden as a tourist in a long time; usually it was a place to walk through on the way to somewhere else, but for once, she could pause, take in the atmosphere, watch the street performer on the main piazza outside St Martin's Church, and take a breath.

It was early afternoon, and the half-term had meant a far greater proportion of children with their parents out today. Tinker grinned at one as she looked up at the scary, army-coat-wearing woman, but the grin faded as she looked across the piazza, over to the front kerb, beneath the balcony of the Punch & Judy pub.

Slowly, so as not to disturb her, she walked over to the young woman sitting on it, watching the show, which today seemed to be an Australian with a terrible mullet, on a unicycle, juggling fire torches.

Before the woman could say anything, Tinker plonked herself down beside her, looking at her with a smile.

'Hello, Zoey,' Tinker said. 'You've got a lot of people looking for you right now.'

9

ZOEY PARK

ZOEY LOOKED UP AT TINKER, HER EXPRESSION UTTERLY emotionless. Tinker had expected her to bolt and run, but there was an eerie calmness to the woman as she shrugged, staring at Tinker with a mixture of suspicion, curiosity, and interest.

But one thing that Tinker realised she wasn't showing was any kind of surprise.

'You don't seem that fazed to see me,' she said.

Zoey nodded, looking back at the performer on the square now, currently talking to a member of the audience.

'I knew someone would come and find me eventually,' she said. 'I did my best to hide, but at the same time, I know that technology finds me. I'm guessing you're police?'

Tinker raised an eyebrow.

'Why would you think that?' she asked, looking down at her olive army coat.

'I saw I was mentioned on TV, "Where on earth is Zoey Park?" or something like that, and guessed the police would take an interest,' Zoey chuckled. 'I'm getting press I couldn't have *paid* for a week ago. People are wondering if it was some kind of staged stunt just for that – I bloody wish I'd been smart enough to think of it. So, if you're not the police, who are you?'

'Tinker Jones. I work for the Finders Corporation. You may have heard of us? We've been on the news. Ellie Reckless is my boss.'

Zoey leant back a little as she looked at Tinker again, now realising that perhaps this wasn't the person she was expecting.

'No, never heard of you,' she shook her head.

'That's fine,' Tinker said. 'I'm happy with that. We have a client who asked us to find you and one who—'

'Who sent you?' Zoey's response was abrupt and nervous, as she looked around the piazza. 'Are you alone? Is there anybody else here? Are you watching me?'

'Whoa, whoa, whoa, calm down,' Tinker held a hand up. 'The only reason I'm here is because I was following your broken phone. No other reason. Also, I'm alone. Nobody else even knows I'm here.'

Zoey calmed a little, but was still nervous as she looked around.

'So, who sent you here?'

'We don't usually give out our clients,' Tinker replied. 'But it was your partner.'

'Jacob?'

'No, no, not business partner, your relationship partner. Joe.'

At this, Zoey went to rise, her face paling. However, as she moved, Tinker placed a hand on her arm. It wasn't a strong grip, but it was secure enough to say, "Wait."

'Look,' Tinker said. 'You don't know me, and I get that.

But you have to understand something about Finders and Ellie Reckless. We're given cases by clients, and half the time those clients turn out to be absolute pricks. Or they're using us to claim some kind of alibi, or using us as pawns in games they don't even know how to bloody well play. Either way, when half of your clients turn out to be the bad guy, you take all of your jobs with a pinch of salt.'

Zoey relaxed a little, and Tinker removed her hand.

'What I'm trying to say is, your boyfriend – or whatever he is – Joseph Kerrigan asked us to find you. If you have a problem with that, if you're running from him, then we bypass him, and we look after you. Do you understand?'

'Why did Joe want me found?'

'Something to do with a doll with a knife stabbed into the chest?'

At this, Zoey did a double-take at her.

'A what?'

'Yeah, of course, you probably don't know about this,' Tinker leant back, placing her hands on the coolness of the kerb. 'So, Joe came home from whatever he was doing last night to find your duplicate doll in his bed, with a blade stabbed in its chest, one of your magic show blades, and a message that said, "do what I say, you bitch – or the next knife goes through you." He then had a phone call from Jacob, asking him if he knew where you were.'

'Ah,' Zoey nodded. 'That would have been ...'

'Yeah, after you'd done your own disappearing trick,' Tinker grinned. 'With Jacob worried about your safety, and a doll with a blade in it, Joe kind of knee-jerked a little. He told us he couldn't go to the police because there was a chance you might have done something illegal, and this might be why you're being chased. That's all we know.'

She paused.

'Actually, that's not quite true. We know you escaped the theatre on the roof, made your way down to Charing Cross, came down Long Acre to here and threw away your phone, staying somewhere overnight. We also know that you've been working with Anna Lever, who's an old friend of one of our team. She made it quite clear that you might have a problem with Luana Flanagan, who you may be in hock to for a hundred grand. How am I doing so far?'

Zoey gave a weak smile.

'Ten out of ten for investigation,' she said. 'But you're right, Luana wants my head on a plate right now. But I didn't screw her over, I swear.'

'Do you know who did?'

'If you ask anyone in Ireland, it was my mum,' Zoey sighed. 'Apparently it was a calamitous state of affairs ending with a hundred grand's worth of ... well, more an item she wants back.'

'What sort of item?'

'I actually don't know,' Zoey shrugged. 'I just know she thinks Mum took it. But it's probably just an excuse for her to attack me. She's hated me and my family for years.'

'That's usually how it happens,' Tinker frowned. 'But listen. Joe asked us to find you, not Luana. The chances are, she's gone to her own people to do it. Think about it, if I can find you quickly, so can they. In fact, they might even be here right now.'

'Oh, she's got people here,' Zoey nodded. 'Several of the performers have worked with her in the past. Her family deals drugs to a lot of them. You know, coke to keep them pepped and some puff to bring them down when they get too excited.'

'There's a lot of drugs here?'

'Not all the performers take, but some do. It used to be a lot worse when I was here,' Zoey continued. 'I mean, I'm in this strange situation now where I'm not famous enough to be recognised by people, but famous enough to find old friends don't want to help me right now as I'm "too big for my boots" and their rejection might find me some humility.'

Tinker looked around the piazza as Zoey finished.

'Why the hell did you come here anyway?' she asked. 'I mean, let's be serious. It's not exactly the place to go if you're looking to be hidden. Not only are you well known in the area, it's also not that secret, secluded, or filled with areas you can hide.'

'You'd be surprised,' Zoey said. 'But, to be honest, I was hoping to catch hold of a friend of mine. I got here last night and she was able to put me up and keep me hidden, but she was gone by the time I woke up. She had left a message saying to come see her when she was doing a show.'

She waved at the Australian, now on a unicycle that was ten feet high.

'As you can see, though, she didn't turn up.'

Tinker felt a shiver slide down her spine.

'Your friend didn't turn up for her spot?'

Zoey shook her head.

'No,' she replied. 'She arrived this morning to put her name on the list, but after she set the time she disappeared, and then called in to security a couple of hours later to say she was probably not going to make it back in time, and if she missed it, to pass it on to the next act. By then it'd apparently gone over by half an hour, so her dropping out brought everything back under schedule.'

'Would she usually turn up for her spot?' Tinker continued.

Zoey nodded again, and Tinker had that feeling – the "someone walking over your grave" feeling – that things weren't quite working correctly here.

'Would your friend have known Luana Flanagan?'

Zoey shook her head – not at the question, but more where she knew the question was going.

'She wouldn't have done that,' she said. 'We've known each other for years. She's probably late. It's why I'm hanging around.'

'Yet on the day you're told to meet her, she doesn't turn up.' Tinker looked at her watch. It was ten minutes past three in the afternoon. 'Again, would your friend have known Flanagan?'

Zoey went to argue again, sighed, and then looked away.

'Most people do, so I'm sure she does.'

Tinker stretched her back, rising from the kerb as she did so.

'Then we need to act as if the entire area is hostile,' she breathed. 'If your friend informed on you, it might not have been deliberate. She could have told someone who told Flanagan ...'

It was meant to reassure Zoey, but she could already see on the woman's face that Zoey Park had realised the truth. Her friend had informed on her, and had been told to stay away from her own street show, probably even paid double what she'd make in it, to do so.

Zoey followed Tinker to her feet, but then paused, staring across the piazza at the edge, where people were entering the pedestrian area from the road. Tinker followed her gaze and saw two young men walking towards them. They were in their twenties, wore green and brown bomber jackets respectively, and looked like muscle. The kind you didn't really want to bump into.

Especially if you owed money.

'Oh shit,' Zoey hissed.

'Do you know them?'

'I know that tall blond guy's Liam, and the redhead is Sean,' Zoey looked around to see if any others were in the area. 'They both work for Flanagan.'

'Well, I think we don't need to suspect that your friend sold you out,' Tinker sighed. 'This pretty much confirms it.'

The two men were examining the crowd, searching through the audience at the front of the church, checking the show rather than looking at the piazza. So, as yet, they hadn't seen the two women, possibly more likely expecting to see Zoey on her own.

'Why are they looking over there?' Tinker asked, looking back at the front of St Martin's Church.

'It's where the performers wait before their shows,' Zoey replied. 'They probably think I'm waiting there, looking for someone ... and alone.'

'Then we should go before they—'

'Zoey!' The tall blond man, previously identified as Liam, half shouted as he started towards them, finally spotting his target. 'You'd better wait there!'

His accent was Irish, not that strong, however. The kind of Irish you get if your family came from there, but you yourself grew up in London.

'Liam, you don't want this,' Zoey said. 'You know this isn't me.'

'Ma Flanagan says you gotta come back with us,' the other man, known as Sean, added.

'Ma Flanagan can go whistle,' Zoey snapped back. 'You know damn well I don't have the bloody thing. She's doing this to try to get my contract—'

'Claudette has signed away all performance rights,' he said. 'She did it last night, after that terrible, terrible accident on stage. You could have died.'

Tinker glanced at Zoey, watching the woman as she bit her lip, holding back her anger.

'Fight or run?' she asked.

'I don't really want to draw attention,' Zoey whispered. 'It's bad enough people are talking about me on YouTube. But if these wee shites start anything, I'm not backing down.'

'Then we run, for the moment.'

Tinker grinned at Liam, walking towards him.

'Now, mate,' she said. 'Perhaps we should have a bit of a chat.'

'Yeah?'

'It's not nice walking up on a lone woman in the middle of a public place. There are a few movements around that stop that these days. You'd be cancelled on social media if it got out. Although you look like the kind of bloke who doesn't really care about that. You're more a "toxic masculinity" type, right? Not caring if she's alone?'

'She ain't alone, though, is she?' Liam replied, a smirk on his face. 'Whoever the hell you think you are—'

'I'm someone you don't want to get to know,' Tinker squared up, preparing herself for a confrontation. 'I'm someone you should turn around and walk away from.'

'Oh, you are, are you?' Liam gave a mock horrified expression. 'I will, for sure. Walk away. In a moment. Right after I give you a bit of a slap and move on.'

He went to bat Tinker; he wasn't even trying hard,

expecting more likely that Tinker was just some performer friend who was playing a bit of bravado, who'd back away the moment a hand came up. But Tinker had been waiting for this, grabbed him at the wrist and twisted it, pulling him down to a knee.

'As I said,' Tinker repeated loud enough for Sean to hear as well. 'Turn around and walk away.'

'Can't do that,' Liam groaned. 'Flanagan—'

He said no more as Tinker let go of his hand, using the sole of her foot to push him over, stumbling backwards into his friend. In the same movement, Tinker spun, grabbing Zoey's arm, and with a yell of "run", started into the crowded mall behind them.

They darted towards the Jubilee Market, the clamour of traders and tourists disguising their rapid footsteps. The historic iron and glass structure loomed above, and Zoey's breath came in ragged gasps as they weaved through the stalls, Tinker's hand a vice on her arm.

A glance back revealed the relentless pursuit of the two Irish men, their faces set in grim determination. Tinker's mind raced as she glanced around, formulating a plan.

'Split up!' she commanded, pushing Zoey towards the London Transport Museum. 'Meet me at the Royal Opera House!'

The push was unexpected though and Zoey stumbled, crashing to the floor, face planting herself onto the cobblestones.

'Shit, are you okay?' Tinker pulled Zoey up – she'd caught her temple in the fall, but there was no blood. Zoey, terror in her eyes, nodded and disappeared into the crowd. Even though they'd only just met, it looked like she trusted this new woman with her life right now. Tinker veered right, sprinting towards the cobbled streets outside the Jubilee Market, turning sharply into a narrow alley, her back pressed against the cold brick wall, her breaths shallow but controlled. As Liam, furious at being outsmarted, rounded the corner, she struck, her fist connecting with his jaw.

He staggered back, a snarl distorting his features.

'For feck's sake!' he hissed. 'It's nothing personal!'

'Walk away.'

Liam shook his head and charged.

ZOEY, HEART POUNDING, MADE HER WAY TOWARDS THE ROYAL Opera House. She could hear shouts behind her; Sean was closing in on her, knocking aside tourists in his hurry to catch her, eyes sharp, and steps relentless. Panic welled inside her, but she steadied herself, spinning around and, with a false bravado, pointing at him, her index finger outstretched.

'Stop or I shoot!' she shouted.

Sean actually did so, and Zoey wondered if she was going to get out of this, but then he started to laugh, pointing back, making the same "finger gun" as she was.

'Are we playing cowboys now?' he asked, continuing on.

'I'm serious, Sean, back off,' Zoey replied nervously, straightening the arm. 'You know what I can do.'

'You're not some kind of wizard,' Sean said, chuckling. 'I think I'll take my – *Jesus!*'

The last expletive was shouted as, seemingly from the tip of her finger, Zoey Park fired a small ball of flame into his face. Seizing the moment as he staggered back, hands to his eyes, blinded and batting away any fire, Zoey slipped into the shadows of the Garden, leaving Sean, bewildered and scanning the area in vain, his eyes still half blinded with bright light.

BACK IN THE ALLEY, TINKER WAS TIRING AS SHE SPARRED WITH Liam, each movement becoming more laboured. As much as she was all for equality, she was wishing he'd offered to take it easy on her; she was military trained, but he had the style of the streets, fighting dirty when he could with the moves of a bare-knuckle fighter, and his grin widened, sensing victory.

That was his mistake.

Tinker, with a last surge of energy and determination, landed a swift kick between his legs, catching him off guard. He crumpled to the ground, clutching at himself as he whimpered, and Tinker, leaning against the wall for support, caught her breath before taking a punt at his head, her boot connecting with his skull, knocking him unconscious to the floor.

'Should have walked away,' she said. 'Now you can crawl.'

Battered but not beaten, she emerged onto Bow Street, a renewed sense of urgency propelling her towards the Royal Opera House. She spotted Zoey in the distance, a small figure waving frantically.

'Did I see right?' she asked. 'Did you throw a bloody fireball at your guy?'

'Flash paper,' Zoey grinned, showing a ring-shaped contraption on her finger. 'One shot only, I'm afraid.'

Tinker nodded at the side of Zoey's head, where a slight bruise was forming under what looked to be a minor graze.

'Sorry about that,' she said. 'We should get it cleaned up. I know somewhere we can take you to do that.'

Tinker started north, away from the Royal Opera House.

'We'll work out what happened back at the office—'

'No,' Zoey pulled at Tinker's arm. 'Look, no offence, but you've proven you're not on Flanagan's side for the moment, but Joe hasn't, and he's the guy who sent you.'

'I don't get it,' Tinker placed her hands on her hips, watching behind Zoey in case Liam and Sean returned. 'You've been living with him for months. What changed?'

'I found out he'd been lying to me last night,' Zoey started walking away from Covent Garden, but on her own steam. 'He didn't meet me at a Christmas party by chance. He was sent to me by his step-mum.'

Tinker knew the answer before Zoey even said it.

'Luana bloody Flanagan.'

'Bingo. Give that woman a rubber chicken,' Zoey nodded. 'It seems the woman who's been trying to kill me sent her own stepson to seduce me. What does that say about your client now?'

10

STOOGES

AFTER CHECKING THE DETAILS OF THE BOX OFFICE PICKUPS, AND
with the knowledge of the seat location they were looking for,
it hadn't taken long for Casey to eventually find the full name
and home address of Veronica Carter, and with this information both Ramsey and Ellie had made their way over to it.
Weirdly, it was in a house in Shoreditch, only half a mile
from the apartment that Ellie lived in, and she took the
opportunity to pop in and pick up some treats for Millie in
the process.

Ramsey chided her for overfeeding the Spaniel, but it was
most likely a backhanded dig after he'd been accused of over-
treating her.

Veronica wasn't at home, but her husband, Jerome, was
thrilled to explain to the two people on his doorstep, holding
a cheque for her, where she was. Ramsey had gone in under
the assumed identity of a representative of an insurance
company, explaining that because of a claim against a corporation that had happened earlier in the year, Veronica, as one

of many people inconvenienced on the day in question was now the beneficiary of a two-thousand-pound grant. The only problem was it had to be handed to her personally.

Unsurprisingly, this wasn't a problem, and Veronica's work address turned out to be the Wunderland theme park, which was a pop-up experience on the south bank of the Thames. It was something the city had been trying to create for years now, a form of "Edinburgh Festival" in a contained area, with both afternoon matinee and evening performances happening for the next three weeks.

'Is she there every day of the festival?' Ramsey had asked.

'Oh yes,' Jerome replied. 'I don't see her for weeks when she's working on it. Usually from one in the afternoon until midnight, working the VIP bar more often than not.'

'So, she was there last night?' Ramsey asked, frowning.

'Yeah. Is there a problem?'

'No, not at all,' Ramsey smiled. 'I was there myself last night. If I'd known, I could have given her the letter then!'

He gave a little laugh, which seemed to reassure Jerome and this now decided, they left, heading back towards the south bank.

Arriving at the main entrance of the Wunderland theme park, however, Ramsey realised that getting into the VIP tent, and therefore the bar, was going to be a little more difficult than they expected.

The location itself was in Jubilee Park, close to the Hungerford Bridge and the London Eye. It was an expansive grassy area, which for the moment had become a funfair, complete with small Ferris wheels, Bunko booths, and even a Waltzer, where you could "scream if you wanna go faster." The entrance was free; after all, whoever was hosting the Wunderland amusements wanted people to come in, and many of the people entering were here because they'd bought tickets for the shows. These were in the middle section, which was cordoned off, where a small theatre tent had been placed for the various circus shows and cabaret artists to perform, a large poster showing a list of the day's performances. Next to it was a VIP tent with a bar.

There was a steady stream of people walking in and out of the VIP area, but Ramsey noted the two security guards at the gate were checking their wrists, and the ones who were being allowed in had some kind of silver wristband, while the others were being politely told to piss off.

'We need to get a silver wristband,' he said, looking around.

Ellie, however, was already on the phone with Casey. After a moment, she thanked him and disconnected the call.

'Apparently, you can't get VIP passes,' she said. 'It's mainly for guests of the performers and special invitees. We might have to wait till she's on a break.'

'Or we just go in and speak to her,' Ramsey smiled, walking away from the main entrance along the side and reaching into his pocket. 'I've never let rules bar me from a party before, and I'm damned if I'm letting my first failure be in a field.'

'You're going to climb the fence, are you?' Ellie smiled. 'I thought you were a bit old for breaking into festivals. Also, it's a park, not a field.'

'Oh ye of little faith,' Ramsey smiled, holding up an Apple air tag and showing it to her. 'We're going to use this.'

With a practised throw after a quick check no one was watching, Ramsey lobbed the air tag over the fence, sending it deep into a quieter area of the VIP space.

'You're going to have to explain what your plan is here,

apart from the fact that you've just thrown away an expensive air tag,' Ellie shrugged.

'Watch and learn,' he said, pulling out his phone and walking up to the two security guards at the gate.

'Excuse me,' he said, his accent suddenly becoming even more "plummy British Gentleman" than usual, 'I was hoping you could help, as I need to go back in.'

'Wristband?'

'I did have a wristband. I took it off, though.' Ramsey smiled apologetically. 'I thought I wasn't coming back in, and it itched terribly. My daughter—'

He nodded at Ellie.

'—was meeting me outside as she didn't get one. I was a guest of Mat Ricardo. He just finished his afternoon show?'

Ellie was impressed by this. She hadn't even noticed who performed that day. But then she realised that the guards probably didn't know either. All they cared about was the wristbands.

'Well, what's the problem?' the one on the left asked, already bored with this.

'I was in here about an hour and a half ago,' Ramsey said in a soft and polite way. 'I left my iPhone in here. Look, this is my granddaughter's phone and you can see here...'

He showed his phone, and on the screen was a "Find My iPhone" app, showing a map of the immediate area with *Granddad's iPhone* marked on it in the spot where the air tag had landed.

Now Ellie understood what Ramsey had done.

He had named the air tag *Granddad's iPhone* and tossed it into the back of the VIP area. So, as far as the guards were concerned, the iPhone was there.

'I was just hoping that I could run in and grab it, before someone more unscrupulous takes it?' he asked. 'It shouldn't take long. It's down between those tables there. I mean, you could go and find it if you want, but it's only going to take me ten seconds. I did come in earlier on, I was talking to the chap at the bar over there. He'll vouch for me.'

'It's fine. Don't worry about it,' the older man said. 'It's coming to the end of the afternoon session, anyway. So you pop in, get your phone and come back. Yeah?'

'Thank you so much,' Ramsey smiled.

With that, he pulled Ellie with him past the guards.

'Call me impressed,' she said.

In the VIP area, Ramsey made a point of walking towards the air tag and picking it up, before veering off and heading towards the bar. There were only three people serving, and the bar was now quiet with most of the shows for the afternoon now over, and the evening performances were yet to start. These were two men and one woman, which made it far easier to work out who to speak to.

'Veronica?' Ellie asked, as she stepped up to the bar.

The barmaid, a woman in her fifties with short dark hair pulled back into a slicked look and wearing a black shirt over trousers, stared at her suspiciously.

'Yeah.'

Ellie didn't usually do this, but for some reason, she felt there was a need.

'I'm Ellie Reckless,' she said, pulling out and opening her old warrant card. On it showed Ellie's face, her name, and "Detective Chief Inspector." It was a role she hadn't had for a very long time, but the warrant card was enough to give an element of authenticity to her statement. What she hadn't done was say 'I'm DCI Reckless', for that would have been false and could have got her into actual trouble when someone invariably learnt she'd done this.

Veronica nodded, understanding the meaning of the warrant card.

'What do you want?' she asked.

'I understand you were at Zoey Park's show yesterday,' Ellie asked. 'We've been brought in to look into her disappearance.'

'Oh, it was nothing more than a trick,' Veronica replied quickly, glancing about, as if worried someone may have overheard the reasons for her absence the previous day. 'It was all staged, right?'

'I get that,' Ellie replied. 'But you are technically one of the last people to see her.'

'I didn't really see her,' Veronica shook her head. 'I was brought on stage to check a straitjacket.'

'How was it that you were there?' Ramsey asked.

Veronica straightened, squaring her shoulders, and Ellie could see she was defensive.

'We know you didn't buy your ticket,' Ellie added. 'You were part of a conglomerate of fifty tickets bought by a firm. I was curious if you'd won it in a prize or something like that?'

'Oh,' Veronica smiled now, it was a weak, cautious one but her body language showed she was relaxing. 'Yeah, I-I won it, in-a in-a phone competition.'

'Really?' Ellie replied with mock enthusiasm. 'How lucky for you. Did your husband go with you?'

'No, it was only one ticket.'

'That must have been annoying,' Ramsey said. 'Was he okay with you going?'

'Of course.'

'That's strange. When we spoke to him earlier, he said you were working last night.'

Veronica paused again, the new information showing this was more than a passing chat.

'It wasn't his thing. Plus I wasn't on shift yesterday.'

'Then you were lucky enough to be picked to go on stage. How wonderful,' Ellie continued, ignoring the answer. 'Tell me what happened when you went on stage.'

'Nothing much. Like I said, I took the straitjacket, I looked at it. It was a straitjacket. I've not got much experience with the things, but you know, you see them on TV and you know what they look like?'

'Straitjackets,' Ellie nodded. She was about to continue, but then Ramsey stepped forward.

'At what point did you cut the key and the cord?' he asked as if it was the simplest thing in the world.

'I'm sorry?'

'Hidden in the wrist, there was a key attached to some thread. The only person who touched it before Zoey went up into her trick was you. The only way it could have been taken off was if it had been cut—'

'Now wait a second,' Veronica shook her head. 'I didn't cut anything, I swear to you.'

'You didn't sabotage the trick in any way?' Ellie leant forward, and at this, Veronica's expression changed, becoming more calculated and relaxed.

'Look,' she said. 'I'm not just your person off the street. Yeah. I've been involved in carnivals, performances, that sort of thing for a long time. Used to be a magician's assistant when I was a teenager, did some solo work too; I know how this works. If she had a key on that straitjacket, I would have seen it. There wasn't one.'

'We were told that she had a—'

'Oh, if you're gonna tell me about the little flap that she could open? It was there,' Veronica nodded. 'I saw it. But I wasn't gonna say anything. The only reason I saw it was because I knew it had to be there. She expected a normal member of the public to examine it, who wouldn't have noticed. But I can tell you now, when I looked at the flap, and mind you it was only a glance, there was a tiny switch under the cloth, but it wasn't connected to anything that I could see and there wasn't a key there.'

She straightened.

'If somebody took that key or cut a cord, it wasn't me, and it was done before I got there.'

'Did you speak to her?'

At this, Veronica paused.

'No,' she eventually said. 'She was in the middle of her patter. We didn't have time for a conversation.'

Ellie nodded, passing over a business card.

'If you think of anything, please give me a call,' she said. 'It's helped a lot that you've been able to tell us this.'

'It just says your name and your number,' Veronica frowned. 'Not that you're police.'

'Did I ever say I was the police?' Ellie smiled, but stopped as Ramsey patted her on the shoulder.

'Time to go,' he said.

Ellie glanced back at the gate to the VIP area, where the two security guards were now taking a very deep interest in the two people by the bar.

'Thank you,' Ellie said, turning back to Ramsey, who was

blocking her from the view of the two men, motioning for her phone.

Passing it across, the two of them walked back to the door. Ramsey was waving Ellie's second phone in his hand as if it was a triumphant success.

'Thank you so much,' he said.

'I hope you weren't trying to buy another drink,' the guard said.

'Oh, no, not at all,' Ramsey said. 'In fact, I was thanking the woman at the bar, who'd seen the phone and was keeping an eye on it for us.'

The security guards, apparently happy with this, nodded, as Ramsey and Ellie walked out into the main area of the Wunderland theme park.

'If she didn't cut the cord, then where did the key go?' Ramsey asked. 'Had to be taken beforehand. Still, it does answer one question, though.'

'What's that?' Ellie asked.

'If Veronica *had* cut it while checking, it would have gone either into her hand, or it would have fallen onto the floor,' Ramsey said. 'If it was the latter, then someone would have found the key. As nobody did, I'm guessing it had to be the other way.'

'You were told by Jacob that only the crew that placed it on the stand and Zoey touched the straitjacket,' Ellie said as he walked out of the main entrance. 'How reliable do you think he is?'

'If you'd asked me that before I saw him today, I would have said he was a one hundred percent reliable source,' Ramsey stroked his chin as he replied. 'But now I'm not sure. What we need to know is who bought these people's tickets? And did they all think they won a competition?'

He looked back at the VIP area.

'Because no matter what she said there, she *knew* she didn't win this as part of a competition. She *knew* she was there to sabotage a trick.'

11

THE YOUTUBE GUY

'YOU ARE BLOODY KIDDING ME,' NICKY SIMPSON SAID AS HE opened the door to find Tinker and Zoey Park standing on the other side of it. 'What the bloody hell are you doing here?'

'Good to see you too, Nicky,' Tinker smiled. 'We were hoping we could use you as a bolthole for a few hours.'

'Me, a bolt hole?' Simpson grinned. 'Usually, you're trying to find things out about me, not ask me to help you with your Quixotic plans.'

'Well, after we learned the truth, let's just say you're more of an ally these days – an asset to be used if need be,' Tinker shrugged.

Simpson stepped back, allowing the pair of them into his Battersea apartment, above his fitness club. He had done well since the news of his father and his grandfather had come out in the press a few weeks back, and had made damn sure his side of the story – how he had been the unfortunate, blackmailed face of the Simpson crime empire while his childhood best-friend and assistant kept a close eye on him, killing all his rivals without his knowledge, and leading him unknowing into the seedy world of his family – was out for everyone to see. It was the stuff of stories, and had given him a lot of press and promotion, something that Nicky Simpson, YouTube guru, a man with abilities to gain a sale from *anything*, used to his advantage.

Now, he found that cleared of the crimes he'd committed, ones he'd been guilty of but now had been slid over to his grandfather he still had that element of "bad boy danger" that people liked, whilst at the same time could state his innocence to everything that had been done. It was quite ingenious, actually. He had the "East-End hard-man" brigade that had previously spoken out against him, saying at the time he was nothing more than an effeminate twat, now standing up to be seen defending him. He was a South London kid made good, even when his own family had it out for him.

It was all bollocks, of course.

Tinker and Ellie both knew that there was no smoke without fire, and that Nicky Simpson had been involved in a lot of unorthodox and dodgy opportunities. But, as far as the courts were concerned right now, he was innocent – a plea bargain given to the police to explain about his family, allowing him to walk free of all charges.

This was, of course, all due to Ellie's help, as once she realised he wasn't the man she wanted to hunt down, he became just another client with a dodgy past and a problem, and there was a favour still owed, freely given at a time of their choosing.

Tinker wondered if Nicky Simpson wanted that favour spent right now – there was one thing to know you owed Ellie Reckless, and want it removed altogether, but another thing to know your favour could be used as security against something bigger down the line.

Whatever she thought about the man, Tinker knew Simpson always played the long game.

'Do you want me to call Ellie and get her to use the favour on this?' she asked, playing on the hunch.

Simpson smiled at this, holding up his hands in mock surrender.

'You've gone straight for the big guns,' he said, almost admiringly. 'Must be important and time sensitive. No, I'll let you in. I've got a slow day today. I've done my TikTok for the morning and I've got a YouTube this evening, but I'm not doing as much as I used to. I'm still working out my book tour.'

He nodded at Zoey, and his eyes widened slightly.

'Bloody hell. I saw you on *Britain's Got Talent*,' he said.

'And I've watched you on YouTube,' Zoey held a hand out. The two of them shook hands and Tinker wondered if she had made a mistake in bringing Zoey here. The look in Zoey's eyes was definitely one of carnal interest. It was no surprise to her that people found Nicky Simpson attractive; he was, after all, a good-looking specimen of a man, muscled and tanned with long, wavy hair and the slightest hint of stubble that made him look less messy, and more "sexily dishevelled." She didn't know how Nicky Simpson leant, sexually though – maybe he was more interested in her abilities as a performer, or wanted to talk to her about fashion ideas.

Either way, Tinker didn't really want to be involved in any conversations with Joe Kerrigan, when he learned how the woman he was asking them to find had now shacked up with a gangster's grandson.

Although it was an upgrade from "stepson," she supposed.

'What happened to your face?' Simpson walked over to a counter and pulled out a first aid kit.

'Your friend Tinker threw me onto a road,' Zoey smiled.

'She does that,' Simpson waved for her to come over as he opened up an antiseptic wipe. Once she was beside him, he wiped at the graze, Zoey wincing a little as the antiseptic stung. This done, he placed a plaster over the minor wound. It had a bumblebee on it.

'Really?' Tinker asked.

'I like bumblebees,' Simpson shrugged. 'I can pull it off if she wants.'

'It's fine,' Zoey looked back at Tinker. 'It's not like I'm going anywhere public in the near future and a plaster is a plaster.'

'So, what's the problem here, anyway?' Simpson asked, walking over to the bar. 'Who's up for smoothies?'

'Smoothies?' Zoey looked surprised at Tinker, who shrugged.

'It's a thing,' she said. 'He has macrobiotic things and stuff in them and doesn't really drink alcohol. That I know of anyway.'

'Fine,' Zoey smiled wolfishly at Simpson. 'I'll have whatever you're having.'

'Some answers, then,' Simpson replied, his smile fading as he turned to face Tinker. 'You wouldn't have come here if you weren't desperate. You would have gone back to your offices, or the diner, or to Ellie's apartment, the boxing club filled with overweight wannabe Krays or even your – I don't know what is it – bunker with an army bed at the side, in a shed full of flayed faces, in a field filled with shallow graves of enemies? I really don't know what you do, Tinker, when you leave the office, to be perfectly honest.'

'That was deliberate,' Tinker smiled darkly. 'I don't want you turning up at my mansion.'

At this, Simpson laughed, genuinely amused and impressed at the response, and Tinker nodded at Zoey.

'Someone tried to kill her last night,' she said. 'So we're keeping her out of the way. We were thinking the last place someone would look is a place that has no connection to her whatsoever, and so here we are.'

'Well, you've done wrong there,' Simpson said, shaking his head sadly. 'We *have* got a connection.'

'Have we?' Zoey seemed surprised at this.

'Yeah. You use Lenny Clarence as your editor for your videos, don't you?' Simpson passed across a smoothie to Zoey.

'Um, yeah, I think so. I haven't done a few for a while.'

'Yeah, he does my YouTube videos, mentioned you as a client once,' Simpson continued, looking back at Tinker. 'Wow, six degrees of Kevin Bacon and we've gone down to one.'

Tinker shook her head, annoyed at the chances of this happening. Although with Nicky Simpson being an influencer Z-Lister and Zoey probably hanging in the same circles, there had to be some kind of crossover.

'Is this going to be a problem?'

'I wouldn't have thought so,' Simpson grinned. 'The place is pretty much secure from attack – you know, from my past life as an oh-so-innocent gangster's grandson – so nobody will bother you here unless I allow it. To be honest, I've been considering changing editors, anyway. This could be a good reason to let him go.'

'Problems?'

'More ways of doing things that differ from how I like to do things,' Simpson shrugged. 'You know how YouTubers clap their hands before they start a video? Some YouTubers keep it in?'

Tinker didn't, but she nodded anyway; if she said no, she was painfully aware he would give her a long and boring lecture on "how this was a reason for doing something."

Zoey, however, hadn't read the memo and blurted out, 'Why would they do that?'

'It's so they can line up sound and face,' Simpson replied. 'They don't have clapper boards. They're just on their own, filming on an iPhone on a tripod, but a clap of hands gives a good timing for the editor to know *that's* where the sound goes.'

He smiled at Tinker, aware she wasn't interested, and enjoying every moment.

'Because the files will come with a sound file and a video file. Sometimes out of sync.'

'How is this relevant?' Tinker asked.

'Glad you asked,' Simpson still grinned, finally passing her a macrobiotic smoothie of her own. She hadn't asked for one, but she sipped it anyway. It actually wasn't bad.

But she would never let Nicky Simpson know this.

'Lenny has this annoying little habit when he does his edits, he puts a little sound cue in. There's a couple at the start of Zoe's ones, too.'

'I thought you only saw me on *Britain's Got Talent*?'

'I *also* saw you on that. I saw some of your uploads, mainly the close up stuff. I was checking Lenny was worth hiring. What it meant though is it's almost like he's signing his work,' Simpson's eyes narrowed. 'He says it's for the same reason, to match audio and video up, but it's just annoying because the first thing people hear when they see my videos is this one-second beep of four tones. I've asked him not to do it, but he reckons it's the software, or it's something else, but as yours also has the same thing before I gave him better software, I'm aware it's obviously a Lenny thing.'

His face darkened slightly and the Nicky Simpson Tinker truly knew slipped out for a moment.

'It shouldn't be a Lenny Clarence thing when it's a Nicky Simpson thing,' he said. 'I'd rather he just kept me clapping my hands. But now there's an excuse to get rid of him. I assumed he'd probably done the same to you.'

Zoey shook her head.

'To be honest. I've never noticed it,' she said. 'But then I've never really watched my videos, either.'

Simpson raised his eyebrows at this.

'You don't? I watch everything.'

'That does not surprise me,' Tinker grinned.

Ignoring her comment, Simpson looked at Zoey.

'How long do you need to stay here for?'

'A couple of hours until we can work out something better,' Tinker said. 'Last time I spoke to Ellie, we were being chased through London by possibly armed thugs who wanted her to see Flanagan—'

'Flanagan?' Simpson sat down on one of his kitchen counter stools, the smile now gone. 'Are you talking about Luana Flanagan?'

'You know her?'

'Of *course* I know her! When I was doing a deal with the Lumettas about opening up buildings in Dublin, Flanagan's name came up. She's a player in the area. She pretty much works all the towns from Dublin up to Dundalk – Drogheda,

Navan, even Blackrock. But she's not anything major. She's just carny folk, you know? She's *Zippos Circus* levels of danger.'

'Well currently, *Zippos Circus* levels of danger is fatal,' Tinker replied. 'Because we think Flanagan is the one who tried to burn Zoey alive on stage last night.'

Nicky Simpson looked Zoey up and down, decided it obviously hadn't happened, and smiled.

'Sounds like her style, but I only met her once or twice,' Simpson sipped at his smoothie as he considered this. 'She thinks she's the Queen of the bloody whatevers, but even she's got higher ups, and they've wanted her gone for a while. So let me get this right, Tinker Jones. You decided to bring Zoey Park to me because I'd be the last place they would look – without checking if I had any connection with the woman who was hunting her, or with anyone she worked with. You're doing really well with this bodyguarding job. You really should make a career out of it.'

'Can you hold her for a second? While I go and contact Ellie?' Tinker asked.

'Honestly, I'm fine,' Zoey interjected.

'She can stay as long as she needs. It's not often I have bona fide celebrities here. But this is on one condition,' Simpson replied.

'What's that?' Tinker inquired.

Simpson looked back at Zoey.

'You do a trick,' he said. 'With a cigarette in your hand. I think you're using a thumb tip. But I've never seen where you hide the thumb tip afterwards, because you don't have it on you when you finish, and you have a little flash of flame, too. I'd love to know how you did that. *That* is my payment for letting you stay.'

'I can deal with that,' Zoey smiled. 'You let me stay here, I'll show you the trick.'

'She uses flash paper,' Tinker said with a smile, making out she knew the intricacies of the trick. 'I thought you'd have worked it out.'

Zoey chuckled at this, relaxing a little as she pulled a small contraption from her finger. It was a small ring, flesh coloured, with a tiny flint on the underside.

'She saw me use this earlier,' she said, holding it up. 'You wad a little ball of flash paper in your hand and, as you flick it away, you also flick the flint to get a spark. Takes time, but you get it.'

'I know flash paper,' Simpson nodded. 'Highly flammable, though, right?'

'It's a paper or cloth made from nitrocellulose, which burns almost instantly with a bright flash, leaving no ash,' Zoey replied. 'Its first major use was guncotton, which was used as a replacement for gunpowder. It's very volatile. I never have more than a sheet with me, because if it went up, it could really burn something down.'

'Do you use it in your show?' Tinker asked, mainly with a professional curiosity as to the explosive levels of the paper.

'Yeah, lots,' Zoey shrugged. 'It's a staple of a magic show. We keep it in a secure location under the stage, where it can't overheat or anything.'

'What would happen if it overheated?'

'It'd ignite,' Zoey replied, as if this was the most normal thing. 'With the amount we have, it'd burn down the theatre.'

'But it wouldn't leave a trace?' Simpson leant closer.

'You can stop with your arsonist fantasies right now, Nicky, or I'll take your new friend away,' Tinker smiled.

Simpson shrugged.

'Purely a professional interest,' he smiled.

'Well, I'd appreciate it if your "professional" interests weren't helping you learn how to burn down buildings for insurance,' Tinker said. 'That's a life you no longer want, remember?'

She walked to the door.

'I'll come back to you as soon as I know anything more.'

But Simpson wasn't bothered with Tinker now, deeply engrossed with Zoey as she explained about thumb tips, stubbed cigarettes and flash paper. Sighing, Tinker walked out into the corridor, taking a moment for herself.

There was something off here. It wasn't just that she was in the bachelor pad of Nicky Simpson. For a start, Zoey seemed more relaxed than someone on the run would be. As well as that, Tinker couldn't work out how she had the dumb luck to find Zoey minutes before Flanagan's people did.

It was almost as if someone was leading her to Zoey, and then making sure they ran.

But why?

Ellie had sent some messages, updating Tinker on their side of the case, and reading these, Tinker nodded to herself before placing her phone back into her pocket.

Walking back into the main living area, she saw Simpson still listening enraptured to Zoey – but again, something felt off. He glanced at her, and Tinker froze.

Nicky Simpson was enraptured by Zoey Park's story, but it didn't reach his eyes. This was an act, something to keep her relaxed, but he knew something she didn't, and Tinker wanted to know it right now.

Simpson held a hand up to halt Zoey, nodding at Tinker.

'Bad news from the boss?'

'Can I speak with you?' Tinker asked, nodding to the hallway. 'Issues with our previous connections mean I need confirmation on something before we can stay here.'

'Sure,' Nicky Simpson rose, giving a smile and a nod to Zoey before walking out of the living room and onto the balcony of his apartment. Tinker followed, making sure Zoey was still seated, giving her a "this'll only take a moment" wink.

'What aren't you telling me?' she asked, her voice low.

'I hear things, still,' Simpson replied. 'I know, for example, people are saying Zoey's mum stole something worth a hundred grand and passed it on to her before she died, some kind of priceless artefact. I didn't know who from, but I'm guessing it was Flanagan.'

'She claims it was more a calamitous state of affairs,' Tinker argued.

'You can hide her all you want,' Simpson glanced back at Zoey, seeing her turning on his flat screen TV and sitting back down. 'She's welcome here because she's fit as hell. But know this, Tinker. Until that debt is paid, she won't be free and not only does she know this, but everyone around her does. So why don't you stop treating me as an untrustworthy asset, and consider me an ally, by telling me what the hell is really going on here?'

'I will when *we* know,' Tinker sighed. 'Because currently, I think the only person out there who knows everything is watching your TV, and she ain't telling us anything.'

12

TASERED

ROBERT WAS SITTING AT HIS DESK WHEN JOE KERRIGAN stormed into his office, Sara the receptionist moments behind him.

'Sorry, boss, he got through—'

'How dare you summon me like a lackey!' Joe snapped, interrupting Sara who, at a nod from Robert, slipped back out of the office.

Robert placed his pencil down, took a deep breath, and rose from his chair.

'The partners decided to bring you back in, after I suggested it to them,' he said calmly. 'You are our client, after all.'

'Damn right I'm your client!' Joe snapped back. 'I came to you for help, remember? Zoey's out there and—'

'You lied.'

The two words were short and to the point, and Joe paused, opening and shutting his mouth a couple of times as he stared back at his onetime law school roommate.

'I'm sorry?'

'We at Finders have a care for our staff,' Robert rubbed at his head, as if trying to keep away a headache. 'Which means if we're given incorrect data, we need to rectify this as soon as possible.'

Joe barked a laugh.

'Tell me how I gave incorrect—'

'*Luana Flanagan. You should start with her. Right vicious bitch,*' Robert spoke now. 'You know, having a really good memory can be a curse, but sometimes it's a blessing. You remember telling us this?'

Joe nodded.

'Let me remind you of more,' Robert's voice was rising in anger now. '*No, I only go on what I was told by Zoey. Luana knew Zoe's mum and it was one of the reasons Zoey got dumped in a foster home. Zoe's mum was Circus folk. Worked for Luana in Ireland.* I wrote it down in shorthand just to make sure I had it all.'

'You don't need to go on,' Joe sighed. 'What about it?'

'You lied.'

'Now you listen here, you sanctimonious little—'

The sound of Robert's fist striking the desk in anger paused Joe where he stood.

'No, *you* listen!' Robert shouted, his voice rising as he shook in fury. 'You *lied!* You came to me as my friend and lied to my face!'

Joe didn't speak, and for a moment his expression went from shock to surprise, to understanding.

'Look—'

'When Ellie asked you if you'd met Luana, you said no!' Robert shouted, wincing as a pang of sudden pain ran through his temples. 'But surely you'd have met her at your *father's wedding?*'

Joe licked his lips as he went to reply, but Robert wasn't finished.

'I vouched for you,' he said, his voice cracking with emotion. 'I vouched for you because you were my friend. I owed you. You called that in. But you lied to me! You used me!'

'Robbie, I was doing this for her—'

Robert held a hand up to stop Joe, pointing at his dirty blond hair.

'You see this?' he asked, indicating a white streak in the parting line. 'You might think that's stress of the job, or even approaching middle age, making me prematurely white, but it's not. It's trauma, Joe. Trauma when a surgical team had to shave my head and crack my skull open so they could remove pieces of skull from my brain. Pieces placed there when a *friend* tried to kill me with an iron bar!'

His hands were gripping the edge of the table now, and he was looking at the floor, his face flushing as he continued.

'Mark Whitehouse,' he continued. 'I'd known him for years. Believed him to be trustworthy. When I learnt he was the reason behind Bryan Noyce's death, I confronted him. You know what he said? "I was doing this for her." Then he hit me. Again. And again. All while I was unable to defend myself. He used me, lied to me, and tried to kill me – just like you're doing!'

Joe hadn't noticed the yellow X26 Taser in Robert's hand until he brought it up, having pulled it from his top drawer. Now, it was aimed at Joe's face, the blue cartridge holding the fifty-thousand watt charge waiting to be released.

'Now wait a damned second—'

'No!' Robert was screaming now, unhinged, tears streaming down his face, his eyes wide and not in the present anymore. He was reliving the beating in front of his eyes, and the taser wavered in his hand. 'I will not have it happen again! I'd rather—'

There was a commotion behind Joe, and Davey ran in through the glass door. She took in the scene quickly, and then ran in front of Joe, facing Robert.

'Boss, I know I've not worked for you that long, but I'm really hoping we've built enough of a bond for you not to want to taser me,' she said. 'It bloody hurts, for a start.'

'Get out of the way, Joanne. He's a liar.'

'I know he is, I saw Tinker's message about his step-mum too. But that doesn't mean you get to have all the fun shooting him,' Davey had her hands up. 'Please—'

Robert screamed out in a mixture of anger and agony and pulled the trigger – but at the last moment he pulled the taser to the side, the darts slamming against the window in the room's corner, as Robert collapsed to his knees, dropping the taser, weeping.

'I couldn't stop him ...' he whispered to them. 'I couldn't ... he kept hitting me ...'

'Jesus, he's more unhinged than I was told—' Joe started, but didn't finish the sentence as Davey spun on one foot to face him, kicking him hard between the legs with her other one, sending him also to the ground. However, this time she slammed him face first against the carpet, grabbing his wrists and cuffing them together behind his back.

'Walk a mile in this man's shoes and tell me he's unhinged,' she said. 'You have no idea what he went through. They tried to kill him. Tried. To. *Kill* him.'

Taking her knee off his back, she walked over to the collapsed and weeping Robert and, patting his back, reached over and picked up the Taser pistol, discarding the spent cartridge.

'Now, where do you keep the spares?' she asked loudly, but more to herself as she opened the drawers to his desk fully, rummaging in them. 'Aha. There you are. That'll do.'

She clipped something into the front of the taser and then walked back over to the still prone Joe, kneeling once more beside him, placing the X26 against his head as he found the right side of his face mushed into the carpet, feeling the two tines of the taser, cold and metallic against his left temple.

'You need to know a few things about me,' she whispered, moving her lips close to his ear. 'First off, I've been in private therapy off and on for years, because my sister Lorraine was murdered by a serial killer. I was nine years old. His name was Jacob Spears. They called him the Essex Ripper. You may have read about it. Almost twenty years ago, now. Lorraine Davey, Anna Callahan, Holly Bruce. All disappeared over a four-month period. They found their bodies in shallow graves dotted over north Essex, and all three had been attacked by an electroshock stun gun and then strangled.'

She pressed the Taser's tines into Joe's temples.

'They proved he killed Anna, but never proved the others,' she continued, her voice emotionless, as if telling a story. 'He served fifteen years for it. Then, two months later? He was tortured with an electroshock device, causing his heart to give up, and then hanged off the wall of what was once Newgate Prison.'

She looked up, remembering this.

'I didn't do it,' she said. 'But I knew who did. I told people I didn't want Jacob Spears dead, that I wanted him to rot in prison, but that was a lie. I wanted *justice*. You understand, right?'

Terrified, Joe nodded.

'I learnt forensics from the best so I could prove Spears was the killer, but now all I have is a dead target and all this knowledge. You know what that makes me, Joe? It makes me super good at faking murders and hiding bodies. So, here's what's going to happen. You gave my boss a breakdown, and I'm not happy with that. So, I'm going to fire this taser charge into the side of your head. It's not a recommended or typical use of the weapon, and it could potentially have severe consequences – especially if the prongs were to penetrate the skull and affect the brain. And they will, Joe. They will.'

Joe whimpered under Davey.

'When I fire, the electric shock could cause immediate and severe muscular contraction and pain, potentially leading to a loss of consciousness. You'll pass out. There's not even a hammer to cock. You wouldn't even know it was coming. If the prongs penetrate the skull and affect the brain, it could lead to permanent neurological damage. You could experience memory loss, impaired motor function, or other long-term disabilities. The shock might induce seizures or convulsions, depending on how it affects the brain. The electric shock could theoretically disrupt your heart's rhythm, leading to cardiac arrest, while you shit yourself. But let's be serious here. You're at best a vegetable, at worst dead.'

She half rose, the gun still against his temple.

'Then, I'll go into my office and grab my own one of these, kept from my time on the force. I'll set the scene, place it in your hand, which'll probably still be twitching, and shoot myself in the chest, making sure it's your finger on the trigger. Sure, it'll hurt, but I'll survive, and the scene will read as follows. You came in, were outed as Luana Flanagan's stepson who was setting up Zoey, you took my taser from me and shot me, and then Robert fired his own at you, tragically ending your life as you know it.'

'The police—'

'Will believe whatever I tell them. Even if Robert says it didn't happen that way, who's going to believe *captain brain trauma guy*?'

She paused, giving a moment for the words to sink in.

'Or you could tell me everything,' she said. 'Every damn thing. Why you came here. Why you used Robert. Why you lied to us. Who told you he was unhinged, and whether that was why you came here, because currently, buddy, you're shit out of second chances here.'

'I owed Luana money,' Joe whined. 'Over fifty grand. She was angry. She told me I worked for her now until the debt was paid.'

'Were you with Zoey at this point?'

Joe shook his head.

'That came later.'

'How was she when you started seeing Zoey?'

'She saw it as a chance to regain two debts. Plus take over Soho at the same time.'

'Did you know the attack was going to happen?'

'What attack?' Joe tried to look up, but the gun held him down.

'The one last night, in the theatre.'

'That wasn't an attack. That was a statement.'

'Who from?'

'I don't know. I wasn't there.'

Davey shifted her grip. There was a small chance Joe was being truthful here.

'Why come to us?'

'I'd seen your name in the news. Or, rather, Ellie's. I thought she could help – *nonononodon'tshoot* – okay, I was told you guys were coasting after solving the Simpson case, and Ramsey Allen had a debt owed to Jacob from years ago—'

'How did you know that?'

'Anna Lever mentioned it. Saw you all on the news. I thought I could use you, maybe find a way to screw over Luana—'

'You mean your step-mum.'

At this, Joe's face darkened.

'My dad bloody married her, not me.'

'Okay,' Davey relaxed a little. 'But it didn't hurt that Robert owed you.'

'No. Also, I'd heard he wasn't right after the ... well, after, yeah? I thought he'd take the case but he'd not be on the ball. I thought it'd be enough to divert everything away from why I came back into her life.'

'Your story of accidentally finding Zoey at a party, that was a lie wasn't it?'

A weak nod from Joe.

'I was told to get close to her,' he said. 'Luana was pissed she'd started calling herself the *Queen of Conjuring*, because that was her name from when she did the shows, and Luana believed it was a title that was handed down, not just taken like a trophy. Luana knew we'd met before and Zoey had just had a bad bust up with a street performer. I was to go in, get close, earn my debt back. Luana wanted her back out from under Claudette's clutches. She was trying to take over some businesses, needed to convince some old prick to step aside, but Zoey caused everything to go wrong there, and Luana was furious.'

'Let me guess, you fell in love?' Joanne pressed hard against the temple, the metal tines digging in.

'No, no, it was always business,' Joe blurted out. 'Yeah, the sex was good but it was just sex, yeah? No emotions from either of us.'

'Are you reporting to Luana?'

A nod.

'So here's the plan,' Davey sat up. 'You live, and you tell your step-mum that my boss wants to talk to her. Deal?'

'You're not going to kill me?'

Davey laughed, and it was here that Joe noticed someone else in the room, a teenage boy with shaggy black hair.

'What? In front of the children?' Davey asked, as the Taser no longer rested against his head. 'Be serious. Casey's my witness.'

'Besides, she can't use the Taser like that,' Casey nodded at the X26, and as Joe looked up, he saw the gun didn't have a fresh charge in it, and instead had a US-style, two-pin plug wedged into the end.

These had been the tines pressing against him.

'Yeah, I couldn't find a spare cartridge, so I made do with this,' Davey explained.

'It's in the base of the grip,' Casey replied helpfully.

Davey looked at the spare cartridge in mock surprise.

'You're right!' she exclaimed. 'How silly of me not to notice.'

She roughly sat the now weeping Joe up, facing him.

'Next time, it's real,' she said. 'Next time, you don't use us like the marks in your shitty card tricks. I know hypnotism, Joe Kerr. Like proper hypnosis. I can have you forget every important thing in your life, and I don't need to give your brain a fifty thousand watt stroke to do it. You understand?'

Joe did, and after having the cuffs removed, staggered out of the office, running for the elevator before the insane woman changed her mind.

'You sure that was wise?' Casey asked.

Davey shrugged.

'He pissed me off,' she said, walking over to Robert, helping him up. 'Hey, buddy, you remember when Ellie said you might have come back a little too early? I think you might have come back a little too early.'

Robert snuffled a laugh at this, and Davey gave him a quick hug, before realising she was expressing emotions, and backed away.

'I wasn't going to shoot him,' she said. 'I wanted the honest truth.'

'Would have been hard to do so with a plug in the end,' Casey smiled. 'Now, if we're finished with all the histrionics and drama, how about I show you some *real* detective work?'

13

FANCY CAMERAS

IN ACTUAL FACT, DAVEY HAD STAYED WITH ROBERT, MAKING sure he was okay for a moment, and Casey had returned to his "Tek Support" office to wait for her to arrive once Robert was settled.

However, shortly after Joe ran from the building, Ramsey and Ellie had returned, confused as to what was going on. After an explanation of why there were discharged tasers in an office, why Joe was no longer an impartial witness in the case and why Robert was having what looked to be some kind of breakdown, Ellie, concerned though she was, wandered into the office Casey had requisitioned as his own.

'So today's TED talk is about photography,' Casey was quite cheerful as he led them to his tablet beside the bank of monitors – as if he hadn't had enough screens in the first place – pointing at the screen where a frozen image of a bedroom was visible.

'The CCTV?'

'No, this is something else, I'm still working on that,' Casey leant over and tapped on his mouse. 'Someone did delete the CCTV when they put the doll in the bed, but it's not permanently removed, like they think. I should have it back by tomorrow. I was talking about this.'

On the screens now, the Piccadilly Theatre stage was visible. It was slightly grainy and obviously zoomed in.

Ellie looked at the screen.

'Is this that video? The one that Delgado mentioned?' she asked.

'Where in the World is Zoey Park,' Casey replied. 'It was taken during the show, and it's a video that shows the last trick and that trick only. Whether they were filming the rest of it, I don't know. But I've searched everywhere, and it seems to be the only video from the Piccadilly Theatre run of Zoey Park's show online. Probably because of takedown requests.'

He played it, and on the screen, the image burst into life. On it, Zoey spoke to the audience, waving up some random people onto the stage to check the items. On the screen, they watched as Veronica walked on, spoke briefly to Zoey, giving her name to the audience, and then examined the straitjacket. Ellie noted what Veronica had said to them in the VIP bar pretty much matched what they were seeing here; she didn't have much time to do anything. Even watching the video, you could see there was no way she could have tampered with the cords or stolen the key, but it did look like she said something quietly to Zoey – probably something like "I love your work."

The video was shaky and grainy, zoomed in from an upper level. They watched as the trick started, and then failed as the stage was filled with flames, then filled with fire extinguishers and smoke. After a few minutes of confusion, and of people running around the stage, a woman, most likely Claudette, came to the front of the stage to inform everybody that 'due to a technical situation, the show has now ended.'

The video stopped directly afterwards.

'So what did you want to show us?' Ramsey asked. 'We know there's a video out there. Delgado's seen it.'

'Yeah, but Delgado's just a standard copper,' Casey retorted. 'And I'm a savant.'

'You're an idiot savant is what you are,' Ramsey teased. 'Maybe without the "savant" part. Is that your new word for the day? We should try a different one. Modesty. Humility—'

'Ignore the old man and tell me what you found,' Ellie interjected, and Casey pointed at the screen.

'This is fake,' he said. 'Sure, it's a recording of the scene, but it's been made to look like it's been filmed on an iPhone or android system. The file itself is multilayered, something that smartphones don't usually do.'

'Explain?'

'Okay, so it's why, when you take a photo at night on a smartphone, it'll automatically make changes to the image, which they call "optimising" it, even if it makes it look false, or a bit crappy sometimes. On iPhones you can't even turn this off, and you can't edit it, as the software has done all this immediately and overwritten the coding, not given you the original. A professional camera, on the other hand, will give you everything you want in advance, and layer the file, so you can work on the RAW file in a photo editor, like Lightroom, or Photoshop. Likewise video.'

Ellie nodded.

'Okay. So someone used an expensive camera.'

'It's not just a camera,' Casey said. 'The angle they're at shows they're not in the stalls, most likely in the upper circles. I'd say the Royal Circle, as the Piccadilly Theatre is quite small compared to some of the big West End theatres.'

He swiped on his tablet.

'This is a popular site for people booking theatre tickets,' he explained as a new page appeared on it. 'The idea is people will go see a show, take a photo from their seats, and upload it here, so you can check the view from the seat you're considering buying. A good idea, right?'

'Absolutely,' Ramsey agreed.

'But what it also shows us,' Casey continued, 'is that if I'm on the front row of the Royal Circle, there're only two possible seats that would give the view this video has, and they are A15 and A16.'

He showed photos from the website of the two seat views. They were nearly identical.

'It's too close to say which one it is, but whoever filmed this definitely sat in one of those seats that night. They had a front-row seat, no obstructions.'

'You think this was deliberate?' Ellie asked.

'I know it was,' Casey replied, looking back at her. 'You see, I haven't finished yet. Look where Sara is.'

He pointed out of his office down the corridor to where the receptionist could just be seen.

'I've zoomed my iPhone on her,' he explained, holding it up.

'You're aware that's stalking, right?' Ramsey commented with a smirk. 'I mean, I know you're like a teenage boy and Sara's attractive, but ...'

'Shut up, granddad,' Casey snapped with a smile. 'This is a video taken of her from roughly half the distance they would've been from the stage.'

The image of Sara was zoomed in, and very pixelated.

'Not great quality, yeah? I've tried this on various phones. They all come out about the same,' Casey tapped the tablet screen, returning to the video on YouTube. 'The image here isn't pixelated. It's grainy. The Samsung Galaxy claims it's the king of zooming, but that's a digital zoom. If you want lossless zooming, that's ten times zoom at best. They've made it look as if it's been zoomed in digitally, but the zoom is actually better than it should be if that was the case.'

He then showed another picture of Sara. It was closer to the video image, but not that much.

'This was taken with a Sony RX 100,' he said, holding up a small compact camera beside him. 'I've been taking photographic lessons at school, so I have it with me all the time, and its video footage is quite good, HD four-K quality and a solid zoom distance. But even here you can see I can just about zoom in a little more than what you're seeing on a normal phone.'

'I don't get what you're telling me here,' Ramsey frowned. 'They did or didn't zoom in?'

'Depends on the zoom,' Casey held the camera up again. 'With a standard digital zoom, pictures captured by the image sensor of the camera are enlarged using digital signal processing. So, as the magnification level increases, signals to be processed also increase, and can reduce the image quality. However, more expensive cameras use a feature which allows images to be zoomed without losing picture quality. The central part of the picture's trimmed and enlarged without image processing.'

'So they used a big camera?'

'Exactly,' Casey smiled. 'A camera with a long lens that could zoom in to see everybody clearly. This video was made deliberately so that you could see the faces. If I used my iPhone to make this, you might not even have known it was Zoey on stage. The faces wouldn't be clear. The grading on this video is just enough to show that it's a distance shot, a zoomed-in photo, but not enough to hide their identities.'

'Which isn't normal?'

'No. More importantly, if you watch it, there's vibrations, a shudder as if they're holding a handheld phone, and it's taken this into consideration. The movement of someone next to him, you know, moving in their chair, which moves *his* chair, all these things that would make it shake or shudder a little? That's been added automatically here by AI or by some algorithm.'

'You're sure?'

'Yeah. It's not random. It's too mechanical. Again, it's a fake. Someone's made it look this way.'

Ellie straightened, considering the statement.

'So, what you're saying is that somebody sat at the front of an upper level, using the barrier to probably rest an expensive camera against, zoomed in on the scene, filmed everything, took it back to wherever and then put it through some kind of image-altering software to make it look like it's handheld, shaky, and grainy?'

'Yes,' Casey said. 'You can use a good deal of software add-ons and plugins to do this. After Effects could do it. Adobe has half a dozen things on its list.'

He grinned.

'But I know you like proof. So let me show you my own magic trick.'

He moved over to the bank of computers, pressing a button on the keyboard, and the video appeared once more in the middle screen, but this time it was held in another app, one that showed a timeline and different video and audio layers along the bottom.

'Here's the video,' he said. 'I've uncompressed it from the YouTube source, which is difficult to do if you rip it from the page, but if you can actually hack into the site itself and go into the original upload file of the person who sent this, you can do it quite easily.'

Ellie didn't really want to ask if Casey was saying he'd hacked YouTube, as he turned off one line of video. The grain disappeared, and suddenly the image was there in full 4K quality.

'And this,' he added, pressing another button.

The shaking stopped, and now the footage was stable as they watched the show on the stage.

'Only thing he couldn't do was screw around with the audio, as that came from the camera's internal mic,' Casey said. 'So the audio is pretty much exact. But here's the thing. You can't take a camera like this, with a massive zoom lens into a theatre. They don't allow filming during performances, and there's no way in hell that the theatre would let you do this. I contacted them and asked what their rules were, and they said if anybody with this camera had been seen – and if he's resting it in front of him, they would have seen it – he would have been evicted, which means he had to have only pulled it out for the final performance, knowing that by the time they got to him, he would be done.'

'Do we know who had those seats?' Ellie asked. 'Is it not another one of these random tickets bought?'

'No,' Casey shook his head. 'Here's the interesting part. Those two seats, they're part of the comp deal that Zoey Park has with the theatre, given to her every night for whoever she wanted. We don't know who was there last night because he didn't have to give a name. They just turned up and said, "I'm Zoey's comp guest", and were let in at the stage door.'

'That would be Arthur,' Ramsey said. 'I can go have another chat.'

'Or you could have a chat with your friend,' Casey said. 'The one who had your watch, because this booking could have been organised by her partner, Jacob Morrison, as he was probably the usual contact for this.'

Ramsey stroked his chin.

'Why create this fake video?' he said.

'Publicity,' Casey suggested.

'You kept saying "he," earlier,' Ellie frowned now. 'You said, "he did this," and "he filmed this." If you don't have a name for the person, how do you know it wasn't a woman?'

'Oh, because I pretty much know who this guy was,' Casey smiled. 'Did I not mention that when I told you how great I am? He started the video with this weird little tone.'

He moved to the slider at the very beginning of the video, where, in the first second of filming, three quick notes followed by one long note were heard in a space of half a second.

'It's a blink-and-you-miss-it moment. Most people, when they watch it on YouTube, wouldn't even click it was there,' he said. 'But because I was going through every single layer and checking, I realised that these four tones are on their own audio level. It wasn't from the stage. It wasn't from the show itself. This was placed in deliberately.'

He grinned.

'What do you know about text message sounds?'

'You press a button, and it beeps. The sound is usually for when you have to type a code, and the phone understands it because each number has its own specific sound.'

Casey nodded.

'So, before we had smartphones with QWERTY keyboards, we had numbers on our phones, with letters on our numbers.'

'The old phones. ABC, then DEF, and so on,' Ramsey nodded. 'Each number had three letters. You could make text messages by tapping the numbers the number of times to get the letter you needed. So "hello" would be made by tapping the buttons several times; if I remember right, it'd be four-four to get to "H", then three-three for "E", five-five-five twice, and then six-six-six for the others. Thirteen key presses for a five letter word.'

'Exactly,' Casey said. 'These are four text tones: the numbers five, three, six and three again.'

'Okay, but that gives us a whole load of possible outcomes.'

'It does,' Casey said. 'But then I started looking into the YouTube page. It's brand new, only got one post, which is "Where in the World is Zoey Park?" But it's connected to an account, and that account has several pages, which then links to *other* pages. I'm still looking into it, but I think this was done by a guy called Lenny Clarence, who's edited for about half a dozen YouTubers out there.'

'Why would you think it's him, apart from your amazing data abilities?'

'Well, there's the fact that I think he's connected to a particular creative collective, which this page is connected to,' Casey said. 'Then there's the fact that if you actually listen to the tones, the numbers also match L E N and then a long E. *Len-ee.* Lenny.'

'You're right,' Ellie said. 'It is Lenny Clarence.'

Casey wasn't expecting this and looked at her with a with

a confused expression.

'How can you be so sure?' he asked. 'I mean, I know I am, but you—'

'Just had a text from Tinker,' Ellie smiled, finishing the sentence. 'It seems Zoey Park and Nicky Simpson share the same video editor – Lenny Clarence – a man who starts his videos with a little tone.'

Casey slumped back into his chair.

'I don't know why I even bother,' he muttered, as Ellie chuckled, turning to Ramsey.

'Lenny Clarence works for Zoey Park. Last night he films a trick that goes wrong, using an expensive camera to get the detail before he then fakes it to make it look like it's some-body in the audience took it.'

'There's more going on here than we know,' Ramsey nodded.

'We have Zoey under wraps at the moment. But until we know what's going on, I want every answer we can possibly gain. Because I am *not* being used as the mark for a game of three-card monte. Anything else?'

'There's one last thing,' Casey said, nodding back at the door. But it wasn't the door he was nodding at; it was the office down the corridor where Robert Lewis now sat, still reliving moments that no man should relive. 'His so-called mate didn't tell us everything, even when Davey threatened him.'

'How do you mean?'

Casey rose, walking over to the landline phone on the desk beside his computer display.

'I found the company that bought the tickets,' he explained. 'It was a small offshore company linked to a larger company, which in turn was linked to a shell company and, one by one, I fell down the rabbit hole. You probably wouldn't have been able to find it using conventional search engines. But then—'

'Let me guess, when you're the king of the dark web, you have other things at your hand?' Ramsey asked.

Casey gave a large smile.

'You could say that,' he said. 'Either way, I eventually found that the tickets were bought by a company that was a subsidiary of Oberman Davies.'

'Oberman Davies? Where have I heard that name before?'

'They have a law firm in London,' Casey said.

'Jesus,' Ramsey muttered. 'It's the law firm he works for. He said it in the diner. "I'm an associate at Oberman Davies in Liverpool Street."'

'So Joe Kerrigan offered random people tickets?'

'That's the second part,' Casey said as he picked up a list of names. 'These are the fifty people that took the tickets. I've managed to find almost thirty of them so far, which is quite good. Twenty of them have got contact details, which I've also used.'

'Okay ... what are you not telling me?'

'I phoned a few up,' Casey began. 'Asked how they got the tickets. They informed me they won a phone-in competition – you know, one of those calls where you're up for a deal. You're told you're up for a prize fund, and good luck with that, but they also do a computer-generated monthly draw off which you gained a ticket.'

'So, each of these people believed they gained tickets to the show through some competition?'

'Yes.'

'So, does that mean this *is* more random than we thought?' Ramsey asked.

'No,' Casey replied, in the same singsong tone he had replied in the affirmative a moment earlier. 'I've been phoning them up, as I said, and I've noticed something. I thought I'd put it to the test. Humour me.'

He gave Ellie a number.

'This is Rupert North. He lives in Gravesend. Call him and ask about the tickets.'

Ellie tapped the number and put it on speakerphone. After a few rings, a man answered.

'Hello?'

'Hello, is that Rupert North?'

'Who's calling?'

'My name is Ellie Reckless. We're investigating the disappearance of Zoey Park at the Piccadilly Theatre last night. We understand you were there?'

At this, the man paused, and there was the sound of rustling in the background.

'Yeah, I was,' he said. 'Me and my wife.'

'Can I ask whether you paid for your tickets or whether you ...'

'Oh, we won them,' the voice replied.

'Really?' Ellie looked at Casey, who was motioning for her to continue. 'If you don't mind me asking, who did you win them from?'

'Oh, it was some telemarketing company we'd been talking to about having a carpet cleaned,' he said. 'They had like a prize fund that was going, and we were pushing for that. But their computer spat us out as a surprise gift. It was quite a surprise.'

'I bet it did,' Ellie said.

Casey motioned for her to finish the call.

'Well, thank you for your time,' Ellie said. 'Have a good

day.'

She disconnected, and Casey looked at Ramsey.

'What did he say?' he asked. 'Start from the moment he mentioned the telemarketing company.'

Ramsey began repeating the line Rupert North had said, but as he started speaking the words line by line, Casey pulled up a piece of paper, on which was written a handwritten statement.

Oh, it was some telemarketing company we'd been talking to about having a carpet cleaned. They had like a prize fund that was going, and we were pushing for that. But their computer spat us out as a surprise gift. It was quite a surprise.

'Okay, so that's either a new magic trick you've learned, or you found something else,' Ellie said, as Ramsey drew to a pause.

'Every single person I spoke to said this exact same quote,' Casey nodded. 'Word for word. Even the "like a prize fund" to make it sound more personable. Basically, every single person that won these tickets was given the very same thing as what to say if someone asked.'

Ellie pursed her lips as the anger flushed her cheeks.

'It's not as random as it seems,' she said. 'I'm guessing you're already looking for connections between them all.'

'At the moment, I'm not finding any apart from the fact that several of them have a history in a circus or in theatre, just like Veronica did,' Casey replied. 'Also, all of them, for some reason, were contacted and sent to the theatre last night by Oberman Davies.'

14

SPARRING

With Zoey now in Nicky Simpson's tender loving care and Tinker heading home to grab a well-needed shower, Ellie realised that nothing more was going to happen that day. Therefore, sending everybody home and making sure that Robert was in a better state than he was earlier, she took Millie and returned to her Shoreditch apartment.

She hadn't spent a lot of time there over the last few weeks; she'd found it slightly claustrophobic. An empty building with nobody around meant the walls seemed to stretch in on her. Millie, however, loved the apartment, especially the bed in the living room. And the one in the bedroom. And the one beside the entrance door where she could wait for flyers to come through the letterbox and attack them with gusto. As soon as they arrived, and once Millie had been fed, she wandered happily over to the bed, settled down and was asleep, snoring happily within moments. Ellie knew that within a couple of hours, Millie would wake up and demand a second walk, but until then, her time was her own.

She needed to get out.

Seeing Robert relapse in this way was something she hadn't expected, and she was surprised at how much it affected her. She'd been pretending in a way that Robert was better; she hadn't expected him to fall, she'd believed that he was improving. But it was more that she *told* herself this and ignored the fact that he wasn't ready to return to work yet. That was now certain.

But then there was this niggling fact that she'd have probably done the same thing if she was in his situation.

He had been lied to. And not just by Joe.

Ellie had done this to him, and he'd been building up to this ever since she'd persuaded him to step in and help her during the court case. Maybe the dream interview was right; maybe she was damaging her team in her crusade for personal justice.

She needed to get out of the house.

So, she threw on some running clothes and left the flat, deciding to blow off some steam.

Usually, when she went running, she'd pick a direction and just jog, but tonight she knew where she was going, as she moved eastwards onto the Bethnal Green Road, passing Korean BBQ and Sushi restaurants that morphed into locksmiths, tailors and the rather curious café and "cat emporium" that she'd still not visited, as the High Street now turned into housing estates and apartment buildings, before a new row of high street shops appeared, the landscape shifting and changing constantly within hundred-yard stretches.

It was another ten minutes running before she turned south down Morpeth Street, heading towards Bullard's Place and a familiar red-brick building, as the Globe Town Boxing Club rose ahead in front of her.

Checking her watch, she saw it was just past seven in the evening. The club would still be open. She hadn't been here for a while either, mainly because she'd been too busy.

No, that was a lie, she told herself. She hadn't been here because she didn't feel comfortable in the place anymore. Perhaps it was because Johnny Lucas was now respectable, or because it had become too easy for her to sit in a room with publicly reformed East End gangsters who still ran things when no one was looking.

Entering the gym, she breathed in the smell of leather and canvas, a smile tickling at the corners of her lips. It was a smell she had never quite got used to, even when money had come into the club and upgraded everything from the battered, paint-flaked walls to the posh-looking location it was now. It wasn't a Simpson's health club, a place which Ellie knew she could've easily wandered into tonight, where the machines were chrome and gleaming; this was far more a spit and sawdust kind of place, and that was exactly what Ellie needed right now.

A young man was folding up towels at the side, a boxer and part-time enforcer for Johnny Lucas.

'Evening, Leroy,' Ellie said. 'Where's Pete? Or the boss?'

'Boss is in his new job,' Leroy smiled, tacitly explaining that Johnny Lucas was at the Houses of Parliament. 'I think there's a bill he's voting on. I don't think even he knows what he's doing right now. Pete—'

He looked around.

'—I saw him earlier on, but God knows where he is now.'

'How's he doing?' Ellie asked, walking up to the ring.

'The boss or Pete?'

'Both really. I don't think being a Member of Parliament is exactly what Johnny thought it was going to be.'

Leroy snorted at this.

'I think he thought he could make changes he couldn't make as, well, him. Now he's realising that the only changes he could possibly make were if he went away from it all and became, well, him,' he smiled. "Do you need someone to spar with?'

'If you've got a few minutes? I have some frustrations I need to remove.'

Leroy grinned and threw down the towels, picking up a couple of pads and placing them on his hands. Ellie, in the meantime, picked up a couple of boxing gloves, medium-level ones used for sparring on heavy bags, and put them on.

He held up the pads, allowing Ellie to strike, nodding favourably as she did so.

'You've lost power from the last time I saw you fight. But that could just be because you need a warm-up,' he said, considering this. 'Are you not angry anymore?'

'Oh, I'm plenty angry right now,' Ellie said. 'But yeah, it's not the same anger that it used to be.'

She went through the motions. There was a drill that Pete had once taught her, and Leroy knew it as he barked out numbers, each one linking to a particular style of punch or swing. Ellie considered the fact that her anger had changed in the last few weeks. When she was fighting to save her job, her reputation, there'd been a frustration with the system, a ferocity gained from the fact no one listened to her. When she'd started at Finders and began her Don Quixote quest of saving people, the anger was more against the system, and had become more targeted against Simpson. She knew he was the reason for this, but couldn't yet explain how. With Simpson exonerated, his family accused, and a court case looming, Ellie was now in a situation where the anger had internalised into new areas. She was angry at what had happened to Robert, that Mark Whitehouse had been able to commit such a heinous crime to someone he once classed as a friend and then disappear without so much as a by-your-leave.

That Mark Whitehouse hadn't received justice for what he did was something that burned inside her.

That she hadn't seen it coming was something that shamed her.

'Watch it,' Leroy said, ducking back as Ellie swung wildly.

'Sorry,' Ellie paused. 'I didn't ...'

'You're letting your anger get to you,' he said. 'That's your problem, always has been, according to Pete, and Johnny, for that matter. You need something to chew on. You're like a dog with a rope.'

'Are you calling me a—'

'I'm not the one you're having a fight with right now,' Leroy held a hand up to head her off. 'You're fighting with yourself. You're annoyed about something you've done, and you want to be punished for it. But I can't do that for you, nor can Pete. Neither can the boss. Only you can decide what you want to do here.'

Ellie nodded, sighing, pulling off the gloves and leaning against the canvas ropes around the side of the ring.

'How do you do it, Leroy?' she asked. 'I mean, you come from the streets. You've had a shit life. From what I know about you, anyway. Your mum died of an overdose. Your dad disappeared when you were a kid. You got brought in by the Lucas brothers when Johnny was still classed as "brothers." You have everything in the world to be angry about. But you're just so relaxed.'

'I'm angry, Ellie,' Leroy said, placing the pads down. 'But

what can I do about it? You get dealt a hand, and it's up to you to see if you can make that hand better or worse. The more you work, the more chances you have to swap the terrible cards out and get a better hand.'

Ellie went to reply, to make a joke about card magicians, or something along those lines, but then paused as the door to the Boxing Club opened and a new person entered the room.

She was tall, muscled and had short blonde hair hanging over clear blue eyes. She was in her fifties but looked to be late thirties or forties. She was power in a human form, a coiled tiger ready to pounce, and Ellie recognised her instantly.

Luana Flanagan, flanked by two men, both burly, bearded, and from the same Irish stock as she was, standing slightly behind her as if blocking the entrance from anybody leaving.

'I'm looking for Eleanor Reckless,' she said, a slight lilt to her accent. 'I heard she was here.'

'How would you have heard that?' Ellie asked, turning to face the woman. 'I didn't tell anybody I was here.'

'Maybe the angels up in heaven decided I should know,' Luana smiled, but it was a dark, humourless one that made her look more like a shark with a sense of humour.

Leroy glanced quizzically at Ellie, and she shook her head. She knew he would've stood beside her, but she didn't think this was going to be a fight.

'You caught me in the middle of a sparring session,' she said. 'If you wait fifteen minutes, I can give you some time.'

Luana looked over to the men who stayed by the door, pulling off her jacket, leaving her sweater on. This done, she walked over and climbed into the ring, picking up the pads that Leroy had dropped.

'I'll spar with you,' she said.

'Look,' Ellie smiled, holding up a hand. 'I don't want to hurt you.'

'You think you could lay a hand on me?' Luana Flanagan laughed. 'Sweetheart, I was a bare-knuckle boxing champion at nineteen. I was the Queen of Louth by the time I was twenty-one. I might be older, these bones might be creakier, but don't for one second think that I'm as slow as you think. I was the Queen of bloody Conjuring.'

Ellie sighed and put on her gloves.

'Fine,' she said. 'I'm just going through the motions.'

'No, if we're going to do this, we'll do it my way,' Flanagan smiled, holding up her pads in a variety of positions. 'This is one, this is two, this is three, this is four. I call the number; you strike.'

Ellie moved into a fighting stance.

'So, what brings you here?' she asked.

'Heard you were looking for me,' Flanagan said. 'One, two, one, one.'

Ellie followed the numbers, hitting high, hitting low, and swapping feet as she did so.

'You are a person of interest,' she said. 'I won't lie. But coming out at this time of night is a bit more personal—'

'Oh, you made it personal,' Flanagan snapped in reply. 'You made it damn personal when you placed a taser to the side of the head of my stepson.'

Ellie chuckled at this, punching twice at the pads in quick succession, taking a measure of pride in seeing the surprise at the force on Flanagan's face.

'Joseph Kerrigan,' she said. 'Worried about him? Or worried about the debt he owes not being paid?'

'Family is everything. Blood is everything. Two, one, two-two.'

'But he's not blood, is he? He's stepson at best,' Ellie performed the moves, striking hard, forcing Flanagan to step back a little. 'Basically? He lied to us, hired us under false pretences, didn't give us the information we required, and then attacked my boss. He was restrained and yes, my employee might've been a bit enthusiastic about how she gained information from him. But there was no Taser. It was a discarded gun. There was no cartridge inside it. In fact, the only thing she placed into the end was a two-pin plug.'

'I heard,' Flanagan replied. 'One, three-three, one. It's the only reason you're still standing right now, love.'

'Tell me,' Ellie asked. 'Why would your stepson hire us to find Zoey Park and tell us you're the prime suspect?'

'Because he hates me,' Flanagan shrugged. 'Always has. He wasn't happy I married his dad. My previous husband had been strongly urged to leave me.'

'Oh? By whom?'

'Masked men with guns,' Flanagan said casually, as if this was a normal thing.

'And you listen to masked men with guns?'

Flanagan chuckled at this.

'Always,' she said. 'It was a message, and I knew who it was from.'

'Someone bigger than you?'

'There's always someone bigger than you,' Flanagan replied carefully. 'You'd be clever to remember that. Anyway, when I met Nino – that's Joseph's father – I decided to give it a second chance.'

'I heard Zoey Park owes a hundred grand to you.'

'Does she?' Flanagan chuckled. 'Child, you don't know anything about what's going on here. Zoey doesn't owe me "a hundred grand." Add that on top of what she owes me, and you wouldn't even see a difference to the total. That woman and her family have taken more from me than just money.'

'Like what?'

Flanagan paused, pulling off the pads.

'I was a magician, you know,' she said. 'Back in the day. We'd work the circus. Travel with the carnivals, moving up through mountains, bouncing back and forth between North and South. We'd go to the Kilkenny races and perform wherever we could. I was good, child. I was very good. Sleight of hand, nimble of mind. They called me the "Queen of Conjuring."'

'Isn't that what they call Zoey?'

At this, Flanagan's eyes narrowed, and they glittered malevolently.

'Zoey Park *took* that name. She wasn't supposed to,' she replied. 'I told her not to claim that title. She knew it was mine and mine alone. She promised me on her mother's life that she wouldn't take that title. But she went back on it. She lied to me.'

'That can't be the only reason you want Zoey so badly,' Ellie replied, leaning against the ropes, watching Flanagan carefully. 'Stealing a name is something that gets a slap on the wrist. Not an attempted murder.'

'You think *I* did that?' Flanagan asked incredulously. 'If I wanted her dead, I'd have a dozen different ways sorted out within an hour. You'd never see her body again. I wouldn't do it on stage in front of people. If that was a message, that was a message from somebody else.'

'Now who would that somebody else be?'

'You tell me,' Flanagan replied. 'That woman hasn't been answering my calls for quite a while now.'

'Yet you still knew where to find her today.'

This surprised Luana Flanagan, as her face crinkled into one of confusion.

'What the bloody hell is that supposed to mean?' she asked.

'Your two men finding Zoey at Covent Garden this afternoon,' Ellie replied. 'Luckily, my woman was there and was able to get Zoey out.'

Flanagan just carried on staring at Ellie as if she was speaking a completely unfamiliar language.

'My men?' she asked, glancing back at the two bearded muscles by the door.

Ellie walked over to the edge of the boxing ring. She picked up her light runner's jacket, reached into a zip pocket, and pulled out her phone, scrolling to a message from Tinker.

'Two large lads. One called Liam, one called Sean.'

'I've got large lads who work for me, and I've probably got a Liam and a Sean, but I don't know who these two were, and I didn't send anybody after her today,' Flanagan replied haughtily. 'You might not believe me, but I swear on a gypsy's curse.'

Ellie frowned at the passion of the statement.

'You're upset with her for taking your name, and you want a percentage of royalties to repay some massive debt she owes you,' she said. 'The accident that happened at the Piccadilly Theatre ended with Claudette giving you the rights to the show, so surely you can see how this aims directly at you.'

'Claudette didn't give me anything,' Flanagan shook her

head at this. 'We'd been negotiating for weeks. I heard she went out there and said that the show was over, but she went to ground shortly after.'

'Do you know where I can find Claudette?'

'Why the hell would I know where she is?' Flanagan asked, and Ellie could see she was starting to tire of this conversation. 'Look. Zoey's mum? She stole from me. She got her just deserts.'

'I heard she died of a drug overdose,' Ellie replied coldly. 'You think that's just deserts for the item she stole?'

'Yeah. It was in my family for years, generations even – at least since the sixteen hundreds – the very chain the Irish hero Cú Chulainn wore to bind himself to Clochafarmore, the stone where he died. It was passed to my family hundreds of years ago, and it's been there ever since. Zoey's mum took it from us during a tour in Limerick and passed it to her daughter's care.'

'So, all this is over a piece of chain?'

'That "piece of chain" is history,' Flanagan replied. 'We've asked repeatedly for it back.'

'So you sent your stepson after it?'

'Joseph? Nah, I sent Joseph no place he didn't want to go. That boy is a law unto himself,' Flanagan almost laughed at the thought. 'But I wanted that chain back. It belongs in our family. It's priceless.'

She paused, calming herself, realising she was talking too much.

'Find me that chain, Eleanor Reckless, and I'll show you why someone tried to set Zoey Park alight last night. But I can tell you now, it wasn't me.'

With that, Flanagan turned and started walking towards the door.

'Where can I find you if I need you?' Ellie asked.

Flanagan paused.

'At the Kensington Hotel,' she said. 'It's not hard to find.'

This said, Luana Flanagan walked out of the boxing club, leaving Ellie alone in the ring.

Ellie continued to lean against the cabled ropes of the ring; she couldn't work out what was truly going on here. Zoey Park and Joe Kerrigan were convinced that Flanagan was after them. Tinker even believed that members of Flanagan's clan tried to take them in Covent Garden, but Flanagan denied everything.

Was there something else at play that hadn't been seen here? Or was this more of a magician's misdirection, so Ellie looked in the wrong direction?

Either way, she now had an apparently priceless artefact to find.

Turning to Leroy, she gave her widest, most welcoming smile.

'I don't suppose I could borrow your car?' she asked.

15

MAHJONG TABLES

After Ellie had called it a day, Ramsey had made his way back to his house, changing into evening attire and heading out for the night. He wasn't a social animal by nature. Well, not anymore anyway. But he still liked to visit a couple of his favourite casinos and grab something to eat with a friend or two when the opportunities arose. As the years passed on, the friends dwindled, mainly due to incarceration or worse things, and Ramsey's taste for the tables had faded with them.

Now, he preferred to watch, play a couple of games of cards, and then leave. The casinos he used were well aware of his onetime addictions and had agreed to only allow him to spend or lose one hundred pounds in a sitting, as he felt this was a number he could adequately lose and not miss.

More often than not, he broke even. It was the action of gambling, rather than the hunt for money, that kept him going these days.

This time, however, he decided to attend one of his favourite casinos on a more work-related basis. After a small dinner in a bistro just off Berwick Street, Ramsey wandered into the Jasmine Casino. He hadn't been a patron of many casinos of late, especially after the last time he had gone to a casino while on a case. That time, in a small Mayfair casino he knew, off-the-books, Tommaso Lumetta had found him and he'd almost lost his ability to use his hands after being dragged into the kitchen, and a discarded meat cleaver – a sharp-edged chunk of metal with a heavy, flat reverse side – being slammed down onto his fingers.

Luckily, it had been on the flatter side. However, he had been beaten badly and left shaken.

But the Jasmine was a smaller, more intimate location, on the lower ground floor behind the kitchens of a Chinese restaurant. To get to it, one had to know the maître d', pass through the restaurant itself, down some side stairs, through a metal door, and into another world decked out in the style of a 1920s Shanghai speakeasy. This was all part of the act to make one feel part of something special, so that when one inevitably lost money, they would feel that at least they'd had the experience and didn't feel completely left out.

He didn't feel in the mood for blackjack tonight, and roulette was still too much of a game of chance. So instead, he sat down at one of the mahjong tables. He'd learned the game many years ago and, in no way was an expert, but he enjoyed it enough to put some money down.

After a moment, another man sat next to him.

'Mister Allen,' Kenny Tsang said, his voice slightly husky, his chest wheezing. Ramsey glanced to the side to the man who now sat beside him.

As tall as he ever was but with less fat on his frame now, Kenny Tsang was the cousin of Jimmy and was, at one point, with his brothers Benny and Donnie, one of the crime lords of Soho. He ran the centre of London, and it was only an assassin's bullet, causing his chest issues, that took him out of the game. The last Ramsey had heard, Kenny had been in prison, but his solicitors had got him out a few weeks ago. He also recalled that Kenny owed Ellie a favour. As far as anyone was concerned, he left the game a long time ago and, for the last few weeks, had been living the life of a man of luxury, most likely living off the illegal gains he had made over his years as part of the Tsang empire.

'Kenneth,' Ramsey nodded. 'I was hoping to find you here.'

'I wondered if this was business or pleasure,' Kenny smiled, waving for a drink. He didn't need to call out what he wanted. The staff here would have had it ready for him ten minutes before he even arrived. 'Did you want to speak somewhere more private?'

'Please don't take this the wrong way, Mister Tsang, but the last time I was taken somewhere more private in a casino, I had my hands crushed,' Ramsey interjected.

Kenny smiled, as if considering a long-forgotten, wholesome image.

'I heard about that,' he said. 'It's a shame there was no CCTV footage. I was looking for something to play at my Christmas party.'

Ramsey chuckled. He knew it wasn't a threat. Kenny was old school.

'I'm here about your cousin,' Ramsey said.

'I have nothing to do with Jimmy,' Kenny responded. 'After Benny was murdered, and I almost died, I stepped away from that life. Jimmy was the logical choice to come in after us.'

Ramsey nodded at this. The death of Jeffrey Tsang, the

heir apparent to the Tsang Empire, had been a shock but had also been part of a gangland war involving land grabbing; a war in which Ellie and her team had assisted the City of London Police in stopping.

Funnily enough, it was where Ramsey had met Joanne Davey for the first time, as she was working for the police unit that helped them.

'I get that,' he said. 'But I'm not here about criminal activities. I'm here about a curse.'

At this, Kenny placed his mahjong piece down on the table and looked back at Ramsey.

'A curse?' he asked, almost wide-eyed, before chuckling. 'Ramsey Allen coming to me with curses. What does the mad old fool think he's got? A chicken foot? Some kind of weird cat's eye?'

'We believe it's something to do with red thread.'

'You're wrong,' Kenny replied. 'The red thread isn't a curse. It's a story for lovers.'

'Your cousin seems to think that he's been tied to something terrible,' Ramsey shook his head. 'Tied to some cursed object or similar. Some rogue Shaolin Priest or Shaman has done some ritual to cause him harm, and he's under the belief, misguided or not, that they're going to keep continuing to do so.'

'So, you're here to see if I've got a company with a stake in red thread?'

'I hadn't considered you a suspect,' Ramsey replied calmly. 'I was hoping you could tell me who currently not only has an issue with your cousin, but has access to a priest.'

'We don't call them priests,' Kenny said, leaning back on his chair. 'They're not so much religious or spiritual when they do the curses. It's more like a voodoo practitioner—'

'Voodoo practitioners are known as Voodoo priests,' Ramsay corrected. 'So technically, if you're doing it like that, then they are—'

'Don't do that,' Kenny held a hand up irritably to halt Ramsey. 'Don't correct me before I finish. What I meant to say, Mister Allen, is that a Voodoo practitioner, or as you say, a priest, is all about the show. Anyone can be a Voodoo priest. Sure, there are people out there who train or learn under the tree of some other great magician, but that's all they are, smoke and mirrors. I've seen people hexed by Voodoo priests and every single one of them has died, or had what was cursed on them happen. Do you know why that is? Because every single one of them *believed* in that bollocks, Mister Allen.'

He shifted on his seat.

'Every single one of them believed that they'd been cursed to die. It was almost like their bodies listened to their brain and gave up.'

Ramsey said nothing, listening to Kenny spout off.

'That's the problem with belief, Ramsey,' Kenny Tsang continued. 'If you believe that somebody has the power to do something bad to you, then when something bad *happens* to you, you'll believe it's because of that power. My cousin the gangster is told bad things will come to him. Of course, they will. He's a gangster. He hurts people. Yes, it's only fair that at some point, someone will cause him damage. Did you ever read the prophecies of Nostradamus?'

Ramsey wasn't expecting the question, but nodded.

'As a kid in school,' he said. 'I remember there being a big thing about it in the eighties as well.'

'Sure,' Kenny said, placing another mahjong piece. 'I don't remember the eighties as much as you do, not being one hundred and ten. But the point I'm trying to make is, Nostradamus was a soothsayer, a prophet of sorts. But his prophecies were so vague that anybody could take anything with hindsight. People said he accurately foretold the Second World War. But a hundred years earlier, people were taking the same prophecies and claiming it was the Napoleonic wars. But, if you believe those prophecies, you'll find a reason for those prophecies to come true. Our brains are made in such a way to find patterns in clouds, to find answers. Pareidolia, for example, is a psychological phenomenon that causes people to see patterns in a random stimulus, like the Man in the Moon. It's also why people believe in gods and ghosts and divine ancestors.'

'You don't?'

'I had my moment to see the light, and I saw nothing.' Kenny took a drink from a server, nodding to let her know that she'd done well. 'Jimmy though, he believes everything. He's got like a dozen lucky cats in his office and put a shrine in the room behind. He rubs the belly of Buddha every morning, even though he hasn't been a Buddhist since he was nine. He wears a dozen different religious artefacts on his body – crosses, Stars of David, even Egyptian ankh – all to stave off evil eyes and warnings. He's well known for it; the spiritual equivalent of a hypochondriac. If someone has told him that a red thread has been placed on him to curse him, then he'll believe it. But he'll believe it more if he believes that the ritual that did this was something big and bombastic. The kind of thing a magician would do.'

Ramsey noted this silently.

'If you're about to ask if stage and sorcery are different things? I would tell you that all magic is the same,' Kenny said. 'But my opinion is different from a dozen other people in this room. Take the dealer of this mahjong table, for example.'

He looked up at a young woman facing them, no older than twenty-five, with strawberry-blonde hair pulled back, and the expressive face of an Eastern European.

'Do you believe in magic?' he asked.

'Of course,' she said. 'We all believe in magic where I come from.'

'Do you believe in curses?'

She nodded.

'The evil eye painted on a door, the thought of Baba Yaga watching—'

Ramsey held his hand up, looking back at Kenny Tsang.

'I get what you're saying,' he said. 'Yes, it might be bollocks. It doesn't stop the fact that someone has told your cousin that he's been cursed, and therefore your cousin believes he's *been* cursed. If we don't find out who did it, or at least show him we've managed to break this curse, he's going to go to war with everyone until he finds out who did it.'

'My cousin has never needed a reason to go to war,' Kenny chuckled. 'There's a reason Benny and I kept him out of the room when we had meetings. We left him in Shanghai for just that.'

'You left him in Shanghai because he was a psychopath. Do you miss it?' Ramsey asked, watching Kenny carefully.

Kenny went to reply and then stopped, smiling.

'You almost caught me there, Ramsey,' he said. 'But ask yourself, would you like the answer I gave you?'

He rose from his chair, motioning for Ramsey to cash in his chips and follow. Ramsey did, and they walked through the casino towards the main entrance.

'I didn't retire from this world,' Kenny said, his voice

darker now. 'The world retired me. I wasn't ready to walk away. But a gunshot to the chest made the decision for me. I was outed, shown to be weak, and Jimmy slipped in when no one was around. Would I come back? In a heartbeat. Am I annoyed that Jimmy took my position? Absolutely. I feel I owe it to my brother Benny to make good on what we did. Am I sad Jimmy seems to have some spiritual conundrum? Not really.'

Kenny looked away, thinking of something else.

'Why are you on the case?' he asked.

'I've already said, Jimmy asked us.'

'Yes, but why you?' Kenny finished his drink, placing it on a counter. 'I could give you a dozen people in my phone book alone that are experts in all this mumbo-jumbo bollocks. Why come to your people, led by a woman he doesn't like? A woman who beat him, apparently, at chess?'

He chuckled.

'Do you know the number of people that wish they had filmed that game? The ones who've had to sit and pretend to lose to this effluent prick over the years? I think she even won with a gun to her head.'

'She's a woman of many surprises,' Ramsey said, ignoring to mention the fact that when she had beaten Jimmy Tsang, she had had help from a dozen different people.

'Let's just say, though, she made him look stupid and that's usually enough for a death sentence,' Kenny replied. 'The favour I owe her, I know that hangs over his head. One thing Jimmy is, is all about traditions and rules. Honour, oaths, and all that sort of thing. But he wouldn't have come to you unless somebody *told* him to.'

'He made that clear to my colleague when he ambushed her outside our offices.'

Kenny nodded at this as if expecting the answer.

'So this isn't so much about the curse, Mister Allen, but why the curse aimed him at *you?*'

Ramsey watched Kenny. There'd been something off for the entire time. Although Kenny seemed to be unknowing of this curse, he was strangely accepting of it.

'This is your family,' he said. 'Your cousin. I know it's not a cousin you like, but it's still somebody going against the Tsang empire—'

'Everybody goes against the Tsang empire,' Kenny said. 'We have a dozen people every week trying to take the West End from us. In our heyday, Benny and I would fight two different people a day. It could be anyone. If somebody is stupid enough to think that *this* is the thing that takes him off the board, well, good luck to them.'

'You working with anybody at the moment?' Ramsey asked, finishing his own drink and placing it next to Kenny's. 'You said you didn't want to be retired, and now your cousin is finding an opportunity that might remove him. Are you by chance having discussions with other people about life after Jimmy?'

Kenny didn't reply, simply looking around the casino.

'I've always liked this place,' he said. 'The airs and graces are there for the tourists, but once you come through the door, what you see is what you get.'

He looked back at Ramsey, sizing him up and down.

'You've never been that way, have you? You dress like an English gentleman, but you still speak with the gutter accent of an East End squaddie. I liked that about you. It gives me the impression that you're looking to better yourself. But it shows you're just like all the others.'

'I could say the same about you,' Ramsey replied. 'As you

said earlier, I've known you for years, and I remember when you were just a chef. No, wait. You weren't even a chef, were you? What do you call the people who sit in the back of a Chinese restaurant cooking crap for people who don't want to eat it?'

Kenny nodded.

'Yes, I was that, so *touché*,' he said. 'Yes, I want back in, and yes, I want my cousin gone. But I didn't place this curse on him.'

He looked back at the casino to emphasise the point. 'If I was a gambling man, I would think you should look at whoever's making a pass at the West End right now. Who wants Chinatown? The casinos? The theatres?'

He paused.

'There was something I heard,' he said. 'I don't know if it's relevant to your thing. There was a theft a couple of decades ago. An Irish artefact, in a box about yay big.'

He made a motion with his hands to show a box that would be roughly a foot by foot in diameter.

'Apparently, it was connected to the stone some bog-sodden Paddy hero died upon. Very much a cursed object. It was in a private collection and got stolen, but I hear it raised its head again,' he shrugged. 'If such a cursed object was connected to Jimmy, maybe through his own connections to Ireland, he would believe very strongly that this was a curse worth worrying about.'

'Who owned the stone?'

'I don't know,' Kenny said. 'I didn't really go that deep into it. But I'm sure a company like you, with all your resources, could find out.'

He leant in with a grin.

'Or, for a favour asked of me, I could find out for you,' he smiled. 'Anything for a friend.'

Ramsey smiled in return.

'That's a question for the boss,' he said. 'Can we rain check on that?'

'You'd better hurry, because there's a bloody storm coming,' Kenny replied darkly. 'And my cousin is smack-bang in the middle of it.'

16

SWANKY HOTELS

LEROY HADN'T LENT ELLIE HIS CAR, BUT WHAT HE HAD DONE was offer to drive her where she needed to go. Which turned out to be the Kensington Hotel.

Asking Leroy to wait for her, Ellie walked towards the Kensington Hotel's main entrance, its brick facade a testament to its age and sturdy endurance. The tall, white-framed windows spoke of history, yet were clear and well-maintained. Entering through the glass doors, she was met with a lobby that balanced opulence with wear; marble floors, though not gleaming, held their own under the muted overhead lights. The walls sported mirrors that, while not ornate, added depth to the space and, to the left, in a seating area guests chatted in comfortable armchairs around a fireplace, their murmured conversations blending with the subtle hum of the city outside. Here and there, fresh flower arrangements livened up the space.

The reception desk stood prominently ahead, its dark wood contrasting with the brighter tones of the room. Staff members attended to guests, their motions efficient yet unhurried. Above them, an old clock added its steady ticking to the room's ambient noise.

Taking everything in, Ellie moved with purpose towards the reception.

'Hi,' she said, forcing a smile. 'I'm really sorry, but I'm hoping you can help me.'

The receptionist looked up at this strange woman, still in her running gear.

'Are you a guest, ma'am?'

'No, I'm a private investigator,' Ellie smiled. 'I've been sent by a woman to find out if her husband is having an affair. He's quite a prominent politician. You would know him if you saw him on TV, and we believe he's been having his relationships in this hotel.'

'I couldn't possibly talk about that, ma'am,' the receptionist started, and Ellie held her hand up.

'No, I get that,' she said. 'The problem is the press are about to go live with it in about an hour, and unless I can prove it wasn't in this hotel two days ago, you're going to have people camped out on your doorstep and it's going to give you a lot of bad press.'

The receptionist nodded to a man behind her who wandered over. He was tall and wearing a suit, a slight hint of a moustache under his lip. He looked twelve, but was probably in his late twenties.

'Can I help you?' he asked. 'I'm Charles, the duty manager.'

Ellie repeated her lie and reached for her phone.

'We have a clue,' she said. 'It's nothing major. But it might be something you can help with. He'd written a love letter to his, well, I suppose you'd call her his mistress, on headed notepaper. I think it might be from this hotel, but I'm not sure.'

It was a hunch, but one Ellie was happy to play. The message stabbed onto Zoey's fake figure had been from some hotel or restaurant, as the headed paper was a hell of a clue to that, and had been quite personal. There was every chance that Flanagan had written it before it was used, maybe even before sending people to Zoey's apartment. If she did so, it would have been taken from hotel paper in a place where she was staying – which was currently here.

'As you can see here,' she said, zooming in on the torn header. 'We can't make out the hotel.'

The duty manager leant closer, looking at it.

'That's not us,' he stated, reaching to the side, and pulling up a sheet of A4 headed paper. 'As you can see, this is our logo here, and whereas this in your photo is a shade of teal, we are now more of a mauve in our logo ...'

He trailed off, stroked his attempt at a moustache, held a finger up for Ellie to wait, and then walked out through a backdoor into the offices behind the reception desk.

After a couple of minutes, he returned with a pad of A5 paper.

'This could be it though,' he said, placing it down, and Ellie looked at the pad. The logo of the hotel was there, and it was similar to the one he'd shown her, but it was exact to the one that had been torn in the image.

Someone had definitely used hotel paper from this hotel, but what he said next killed her current theory.

'We had an upgrade in the New Year,' he explained. 'This was the old livery. It used to be that every hotel room would have a pad and a pen. But when we changed everything back in January, these got removed. I've only got these in the back because it's old stock and we use it when writing notes that don't need to be seen.'

'So, anybody who had been a guest at the hotel up to the New Year could have used this paper?' Ellie asked.

Charles nodded.

'The weird thing, though, is the tear. As you can see by these pads, they're glued at the top with a gum. You can tear each sheet off without any issues. Whereas this seems to be more deliberate ...'

'As if they wanted us to find the logo but not find it too easily,' Ellie finished the sentence. 'I don't think the affair is happening in your hotel after all, but I have a reason to believe that somebody wanted us to believe it was. Can I take this pad?'

'We've got loads,' Charles said. 'I hope you find whoever it is that's playing silly bastards with our stationery. But please, we'd prefer it if our hotel isn't mentioned.'

'I'll make sure that's the case,' Ellie said. 'Could you do me a favour?'

She took a piece of paper off the top of the pad, wrote a message down, and folded it.

'You have a guest staying here, Luana Flanagan. Could you make sure she gets this?'

Charles nodded, taking it and placing it folded in his inside jacket pocket.

'I'll do it right now,' he said. 'She's always been an honoured guest.'

Of course she has. Ellie took the pad, nodded to both the receptionist and the manager, and then started towards the lobby of the hotel, walking back to the car where Leroy was waiting.

She paused, however, as a new arrival was entering. In

her fifties, her dark hair curly but pulled back into a ponytail, she wore a Ted Baker overcoat with a Mulberry bag on her shoulder. Ellie recognised her immediately; it was a woman she recognised from a video named "Where in the World is Zoey Park?"

'Excuse me,' Ellie asked, pivoting from her exit, and now stepping in front of the woman to block her. 'Are you Claudette Storm?'

Claudette paused, looking at Ellie.

'I am,' she said. 'Have we met? You look familiar.'

'I don't think so,' Ellie replied as she smiled. 'My name's Ellie Reckless—'

'You're the cop for criminals!' Claudette exclaimed in delight. 'I saw you on the Peter Morris show. That was a bit of an ambush, wasn't it?'

Ellie winced. The interview hadn't been the best of career moments, but she had really hoped that nobody had seen it.

'Sorry,' Claudette smiled, realising she'd caused discomfort. 'I work evenings, so my television is mainly daytime. Peter's a bit of a slimeball, but he has excellent guests, present company included. What can I do for you?'

She waved towards some chairs beside the window in the lobby. Ellie smiled gratefully, accepting one.

'We've been hired by Joe Kerrigan to find Zoey Park,' she said, ignoring the additional fact that they had found her. 'I understand you were her manager.'

'I *was* her manager?' Claudette was surprised by the past tense. 'I think you'll find I *am* her management. In all forms.'

'Oh,' Ellie frowned at this. 'We were given the assumption that you'd sold the rights to the show to Luana Flanagan.'

'I see,' Claudette nodded now. 'It's true, Luana has bought controlling rights in the show, but I am still the agent and manager for Zoey Park. When she returns from whatever nervous breakdown she's having, I'll be her manager again.'

Ellie wanted to mention she didn't think this would be so cut and dry, considering the history Luana Flanagan and Zoey Park seemed to have, and so she simply nodded as if understanding.

'I wondered if I could ask a couple of quick questions,' she said. 'You know, before you get to wherever you're going.'

'I stay here when I'm in London,' Claudette said quickly.

'Really?' Ellie leant back, looking around. 'That must cost a fortune. It's a six-week show.'

'I'm not here for all the shows,' Claudette interrupted. 'I only come down once or twice a week. I do have other clients, you know.'

'Of course,' Ellie held up her hands in surrender. 'It's just luck you were here for yesterday's show.'

'What were your questions, Miss Reckless?' Claudette leaned back in the chair, waving for someone at the bar to come over and take her drinks order.

Ellie leant forward.

'Luana Flanagan,' she said. 'I understand she's now bought the rights to the show, but I've also been told she had a history with Zoey.'

'Luana Flanagan has had a history with most people in Zoey's life,' Claudette said conversationally. 'Myself included.'

Ellie looked up at this as a server arrived and took an order for Claudette. She noted Claudette hadn't offered a drink to Ellie, and when the server looked at her, she simply waved her hand and shook her head.

'I used to be a performer, too,' Claudette smiled wistfully once the server had gone. 'Many of us are. You know the saying, if you can't do it, teach it? Well, in theatre, if you can't get the jobs, become an agent.'

She looked out across the lobby, and Ellie wondered whether she was looking to see if Luana Flanagan was watching.

'I performed all over the world,' she said. 'Cruise ships, repertoire. I was good. I sang, I danced, I did a little magic.'

'Did you work with Luana Flanagan?'

'I did a few things with her,' Claudette nodded. 'That's how I got to know Zoey's mum. You know Mary Park was a performer, right?'

'Yes,' Ellie said. 'We've been given information about Zoey's mother.'

'Tragic tale,' Claudette continued. 'Literally drinking herself into the grave. I've never really been able to visit Bunratty without shedding a tear since then.'

She composed herself quickly, looking back at Ellie.

'Anyway, when Zoey gained some traction, she needed representation. I was an old family friend, and so she asked if I could help.'

'I'm assuming the ten percent commission didn't change your opinion at all?'

Claudette shrugged.

'I'm an agent. I do my work. I get paid,' she said. 'I wouldn't expect anything less. Also, these days, it's fifteen.'

'Good to know,' Ellie replied as she considered her next question carefully. 'So you worked with Luana Flanagan. You must have seen the problems between Luana and Mary.'

'I know there was a falling out, but I wasn't around at the time,' Claudette replied.

'What about the problems Zoey has with Flanagan?'

At this, Claudia shifted uncomfortably in her seat.

'What problems do you mean?'

'We have reason to believe that Luana Flanagan has been telling everyone Zoey Park owes her money,' Ellie replied. 'Quite a lot. Something that could be classed as corroborated by the fact she now has a controlling interest in Zoey Park's show.'

'So *that's* it,' Claudette narrowed her eyes. 'You're quite a detective, aren't you?'

Ellie gave a little shrug.

'I try,' she said. 'Is it true Zoey and Luana had issues?'

'Again, I kept out of it,' Claudette looked uncomfortable talking now. 'It really wasn't my place. All I did was to facilitate the shows. Although Zoey had been a naughty girl from what I can tell, and when she disappeared in the middle of a trick, giving an anticlimactic ending, we had a few people demanding their money back. As you can imagine, we now have a bit of a debt.'

'Do you know how you're going to repay it?'

'It's not my debt anymore,' Claudette smiled. 'Flanagan bought the debt and, in the process, has taken over the show's rights. When Zoey returns, we'll up the prices a little. With luck, the press will have given her a bit of exposure and raise those ticket sales, which, to be honest, weren't doing great beforehand. If she doesn't come back, well, maybe I'll get Jacob to do a show instead. The boy's quite good. You know, he's wasted being the assistant.'

The server now arrived with her drink, and she gratefully took it, sipping at it as she looked at Ellie.

'I could make a fortune with you,' she said. 'Get you on the lecture circuit.'

'I'm fine, at least for now, but I appreciate the offer.'

'It's a good one,' Claudette passed Ellie her card. 'Consider it, please. I know Peter Morris was a bit of a prick, but you hold yourself well, and I think we could get you some TV work.'

Ellie took the card but didn't intend to contact her anytime soon.

'Do you think Zoey would have been happy with the deal you made?' she asked.

Claudette finished her drink, placing it on the counter beside her and rose from her chair.

'I think Zoey is lucky to have anybody on her side right now,' she said. 'I've heard the things she's been doing, playing witch doctor with curses and screwing around with people's items and money. It seems that you can take the girl out of street performing, but you can't take the street performer out of the girl.'

She looked out of the window across the road, but Ellie could tell that she wasn't staring at it. In her mind, she was likely staring at a small child, someone she'd known all her life.

'I worry she's becoming her mother,' she said. 'I don't want that end for anyone, let alone Zoey.'

Realising where she was, and returning to the present, she looked down at Ellie, who now stood to match her.

'Consider the offer,' she said. 'But when it comes to Zoey, there's nothing I can do until she returns.'

This stated, Claudette now left the lobby, leaving Ellie alone. Deciding to exit before the servers thought she was paying for the drink, Ellie left the hotel, and walked over to the still-waiting Leroy, climbing into the passenger seat.

'I charge by the hour, you know,' he said, putting aside the Kindle he'd been reading.

Ellie grinned.

'Can you take me back home?' she asked, giving a winning smile.

Leroy raised an eyebrow.

'I'm not into funny business,' he said. 'This isn't like some Hallmark film romance where the young boxer makes good and meets the sexy ex-detective ...'

Ellie laughed.

'You're safe there,' she said. 'Just get me home.'

Leroy grinned, starting the car as they carried on towards London.

'Hold on. What did you mean, *sexy ex-detective?*' Ellie asked.

There was no response.

17

CURSES

JIMMY TSANG SAT BEHIND HIS ORNATE WOODEN DESK IN HIS Chinatown office and stared at the woman in front of him.

'Tell me that again,' he said, slowly, coldly, as if not wanting to believe the words she had just spoken.

'It is everything I said, sir,' the woman said. She was European, with strawberry-blonde hair pulled back, and a waistcoat over a shirt, the logo of the Jasmine Casino embossed on it. 'It was spoken in front of me. There were witnesses.'

Jimmy leant back on his plush leather chair, stroking his wispy chin beard, considering this. The Jasmine Casino wasn't owned by the Tsangs, but they used it often and, over the years, had gained a small network of loyal friends and servants. The dealer had been working there for six years now, for three of which she had been working for Benny and Kenny.

When Jimmy had come over, the first thing he did was find out who had spoken to Benny and Kenny, who they trusted, and paid them an extortionate amount of money to turn against them. He knew Kenny would want to return to his position at some point, and now Jimmy was here, there was no way in hell he was letting that happen.

But now, this new piece of news had chilled him to the bone. Kenny had been talking to the thief, Ramsey Allen, about family business. He had talked about curses. He talked about Jimmy and he talked about his thoughts on the Tsang empire he had helped build – an empire, it seemed, that Kenny Tsang wanted to return to. This, on the same day another of Ellie's crew, Tinker Jones, had been asking around about Jimmy in Chinatown.

Jimmy reached into his drawer and pulled out a wad of fifty-pound notes. It was easily one thousand pounds' worth, possibly more. He pulled half of them out and tossed them over to the woman standing in front of him. He knew that a good dealer could make close to what he was giving in a night, but at the same time, she had shown loyalty, and loyalty needed to be rewarded.

'Wait outside for a moment,' he smiled, his yellowing teeth strangely unsettling.

The dealer nodded, gave a small bow and took the money from the table where it had landed, before she left the office, leaving Jimmy alone with his bodyguard, Chow.

Jimmy stretched his arms out, feeling his muscles, tight from stress, loosen as he considered his next move.

'Do you believe her?' he asked Chow.

Chow, a burly, middle-aged man who had once worked for Benny as his personal bodyguard, nodded.

'She has nothing to prove, sir,' he said. 'She has no "skin in the game," as they say.'

Jimmy considered this.

'So her information is trustworthy?'

'I do not think that any information is trustworthy,' Chow replied. 'Unless given by the most trustworthy of sources. But when looking for any information that can be used, loyalty can be a valued friend.'

'So, what you're saying is she's telling the truth?'

Chow nodded.

'When she arrived with this troubling news, I asked to see the Jasmine Casino's security footage,' he said. 'We sent a man over there immediately. He called back half an hour ago, replying that Ramsey Allen and your cousin have both been seen at the mahjong tables. It makes sense that if they were together, they would be talking.'

'Was this a chance meeting?'

'Ramsey Allen has not been at the Jasmine for quite a while. It seems strange that he would arrive the day after you asked his company to look into your curse—'

Chow stopped as Jimmy rose angrily, backhanding him across the face.

'Don't speak of that in this room,' he snapped.

Chow, reddening not just from the mark on his cheek, stepped back and nodded.

'Apologies, Mister Tsang.'

Jimmy paced around the office.

'Kenny wants me out,' he said. 'I thought this was someone else. Maybe the Seven Sisters or Johnny Lucas finding a way to take what he used to own. Maybe the Simpsons, playing silly buggers. Even that mick bitch Flanagan and her boss. I never thought it would be my own family.'

He looked across at Chow, who stood silent.

'Go on then, tell me what you wanted to say,' he sighed.

'I worked for your cousin,' Chow replied, choosing his words carefully. 'I have to say, if I was going to pick anybody to be a rival of yours, it would have been Kenneth before all others.'

He looked around the office.

'Tsangs are bred to lead,' he said. 'You were never bred to follow. Your cousin Kenneth had this taken from him. It makes sense he would like it back.'

Jimmy didn't strike him for his words. Instead, he nodded.

'I must think about this,' he said, glancing at his clock. 'Take our dealer friend and get her a car. Wherever she needs to go.'

Chow nodded and walked through the door, into the waiting room outside. The order was nothing more than getting somebody else to do this, but it meant that for a few brief moments, Jimmy Tsang was alone.

He leant back in his chair. It was past the time he would usually go to bed, but this information had been important, and he'd waited to hear it.

Looking at his watch, he realised it was past four in the morning now. He decided to call it a night; he could find out what was going on with his cousin in the morning.

Rising from the chair, he stopped as a sound through the window could be heard.

It was the single caw of a crow, or maybe a raven.

Jimmy smiled at this. Chinese superstition said that if you heard a crow caw between the hours of three and seven in the morning, you would receive a gift. He wondered what gift he would get.

The crow cawed a *second* time.

Jimmy wondered if this meant he'd get two gifts. The English had a superstition about magpies, and he knew people that believed strongly in it, but also those who believed that if you saw one magpie, which meant "for sorrow," twice before the sorrow occurred, they would retroactively turn into "two for joy." Did this mean that with hearing two caws—

Three caws.

Jimmy walked to the window. The crow sounded close, too close. He couldn't understand how he could hear—

Four caws. Then, for a long, silent moment, nothing more.

Jimmy paused. Hearing one call was lucky. But four calls were not as much. Four was an unlucky number. Four was death.

Was the gift he was being given something he wouldn't want?

He shuddered, looking at Chow, now returning from the doorway.

'Did you hear that?' he asked.

'Hear what?' Chow replied, confused.

'The crow,' Jimmy stared at him. 'You must have heard it. It was very loud.'

'I'm sorry, I heard nothing,' Chow walked to the window. 'You heard a crow?'

'Why does that sound so strange?'

'Because we're in Chinatown, sir,' Chow said, waving a hand out of it at the lights of the restaurants and clubs, still open at this late hour. 'Crows never fly around here. Pigeons maybe, seagulls sometimes, but crows?'

'Are you telling me I didn't hear a crow?'

'Of course not, sir,' Chow replied quickly, his hand unconsciously reaching for his bruised cheek. 'I'm just saying I did not hear it. Maybe the ancestors believed you should be the one that heard the message.'

'Yes,' Jimmy said. He liked the idea that maybe he'd been singled out for a message by the ancestors. 'I need to grab my things and then we'll go home. Get my car ready.'

Chow nodded and once more left the office. Jimmy Tsang turned to walk into his back room. This was an area he could relax in when he didn't want meetings, when he didn't want the public face of Jimmy Tsang to be seen – a moment for the true Jimmy to relax. He had other warehouses and other meeting places around London and Shanghai, but, currently, much of his work had been centred in the West End. He needed a place where he could communicate with the ancestors, especially now with a curse placed upon him.

The back room was dimly lit, filled with various items from Jimmy's ancestry, and a slight, musky scent of burning incense. There were statues of dragons, phoenixes, and other mystical creatures, all depicting protection, wisdom, and luck; venerated ancestors watching over him. In the centre of the room was the shrine. An altar of sorts, dedicated to his ancestors. Photographs of his lineage adorned the area, with offerings of fruits, rice, and tea placed in front of them.

Jimmy slowly approached the altar, sinking down on a cushion in front of it. Taking a deep breath, he closed his eyes and tried to connect with the spirits of his ancestors. With the revelation of the betrayal and the curse, he needed their guidance more than ever.

Something was wrong.

He was tired, and hadn't paid attention as he arrived; now he opened his eyes again, looking around.

The mirrors in the room were turned around, and red sheets of paper had been placed over the statues, the ancestors, blocking their views of him.

He rose, feeling a queasiness in his stomach. When a death occurred in a family, all statues of deities in the house were covered with red paper, so as not to be exposed to the body or coffin, and mirrors would be removed from sight, as if you saw the reflection of the coffin in a mirror, you would shortly have a death in your family. A white cloth would be hung across the doorway of the house, and a gong placed on the left of the entrance if the deceased is male, and right if female.

He looked back to the entrance to the backroom, seeing a small gong on the left side.

This was a funeral room for a male.

This was a funeral room for Jimmy Tsang.

Quickly, he stormed across the room, pulling a sheet of red paper off the first of his ancestors – but then took a step back in horror. The statue was a dragon and had been bound in red thread. Beside it was an ancestral spirit tablet that had been broken in half.

Cursed.

Staggering back from the altar, Jimmy now pulled away the red paper from all statues; each of them was bound in red thread.

Cursed.

Running from the room, hurtling through his office, he almost barrelled into Chow, returning from the underground car park, likely to tell him his car was ready.

'Who's been in here?' he shouted.

Chow, looking around, frowned.

'You, me, the men—'

'No, the back room!'

'Nobody,' Chow shook his head. 'You said—'

But the words were now to empty air as Jimmy pushed past him, into the stairwell, where he headed towards the exit into the underground car park. It was a large, public one that ran under Chinatown, but at this time of the morning, it was almost empty. There was a car waiting, the engine running, likely pulled up by Chow and now waiting for the driver to return.

Jimmy opened the back door and stopped—

There was a bundle of red thread on the back seat.

'No, no, no,' he muttered as he started to run away, across the car park, towards the main entrance. He was ignoring the cries of the men behind as he clutched at his heart, feeling it beat hard and fast, unsure where to go …

A crow cawed.

Jimmy paused, stopping in the middle of the car park as he looked up at the rafters—

He didn't see the car that ploughed into him, bouncing him off the windscreen and sending him to the floor as it gunned its engine and drove off into the West End.

Chow ran over to the prone figure of Jimmy Tsang, staring down dispassionately at him.

'Call the police,' he said. 'And an ambulance, and then call Kenny Tsang.'

'Sir?' The guard beside him looked surprised at this, but Chow simply smiled.

'Yes. Tell him I believe there is a vacancy in the Tsang organisation again.'

18

FINGERPRINTS

AFTER RETURNING TO NICKY SIMPSON'S FLAT, TINKER HAD hung around for another hour or so, but eventually, tiring of the flirtatious attitude between Zoey and Simpson, she'd made her excuses and gone home for the night. Zoey had claimed she was fine where she was, and Simpson himself seemed happy to have the company. Tinker had picked up the information she needed from Ramsey and Ellie, and early the following morning, she'd returned to Battersea to make sure everything was okay with her missing magician.

Nicky Simpson opened the door in a dressing gown, a cup of what appeared to be expensive coffee in his hand.

'Morning, Tinker,' he said.

'Good night?' Tinker replied, sliding past him into the room.

'Very,' Simpson grinned. 'I would have invited you to stay and join us, but you never really struck me as a swinger—'

'Let's just stop there before I break your fingers,' Tinker interrupted. 'You'd better go with the fact that it would never have happened. Not even in your dreams.'

'I don't know,' Simpson said, walking back to his sofa. 'I have very vivid dreams.'

'Where's Zoey?' Looking around the flat, Tinker noticed Zoey hadn't left. Or, if she had, she'd left her clothes behind, which were scattered throughout the flat in the chronological way items are pulled off, one by one as two lovers head to a bedroom.

No. Scrub that bloody image out of your head, Tinker.

'She's asleep,' Simpson shrugged. 'She didn't sleep well.'

He gestured to the coffee machine, and Tinker nodded. She wasn't about to turn down excellent coffee, and she knew it'd be the best around – it fitted every other aspect of his personality.

'Would you like me to wake her?' Tinker asked.

'No,' Simpson replied. 'I think we need to have a little chat first.'

'About what?' Tinker inquired.

Sitting at the kitchen breakfast bar, Simpson took a sip of his coffee as the machine made one for Tinker.

'As you know, Miss Jones, I'm not a trusting person,' he began. 'Last night when Zoey decided to share my bed—'

'I don't want to know any more about that,' Tinker said.

'Are you sure?' Simpson grinned. 'It was quite strenuous. I didn't video or anything, but I could go through it, blow by blow ...'

'Just move to the part you want to tell me.'

'Oh, but this could be the part I want to tell you.'

Tinker glared at Simpson silently. Eventually, he shrugged.

'I don't trust people,' he continued. 'That is, I find it very hard to trust people, and as pretty as that woman is and as

good as she is at well, things you don't want to know about ...
I don't trust her either.'

He nodded across the apartment at his laptop.

'Around three in the morning, I was asleep, and she got
up to get a glass of water,' he said. 'She told me to stay where
I was, saying she was just stressed and needed a walk. But she
didn't just walk around, Tinker. She went to my laptop and
started browsing.'

'How do you know this? Did she leave the pages open?'

'Oh no,' Simpson replied, taking a moment to sip his
coffee. 'She did an excellent job of clearing the cache and
ensuring I'd have no clue. She even used incognito mode on
the browser so nothing came up when looking. Had I not
known, I wouldn't have suspected her at all.'

'So, without explaining the obvious, how did you know
she was on your computer?'

Simpson set his mug down, reached behind him to the
counter, and handed a cup of coffee to Tinker.

'I've a key logger on my laptop,' he confessed. 'In fact, I've
key loggers on all my systems. It ensures my staff aren't up to
no good.'

'Isn't having a key logger on company computers illegal?'

'You'd have to ask my grandad. He's the one into dodgy
dealings,' Simpson said with a dismissive wave. 'My key
logger recorded everything she typed.'

'When can I see this data?'

Simpson pulled a USB stick from his robe, revealing a bit
too much in the process, and Tinker averted her eyes. It
wasn't that Simpson wasn't attractive; it was just seeing his
"breakfast sausage" would be an unexpected sight, and something she'd look away from before he revealed too much.

Recovering with a smirk, Simpson handed her the USB.

'Don't worry, I'm wearing my Calvins,' he grinned. 'Give this to your tech-savvy twelve-year-old. I might not know all the details I'm looking at here, but from what I've seen, she communicated with a few people on a forum about magic-related stuff. She also sent a couple of messages, and checked her apartment's security systems, which is peculiar since she was keen on staying hidden.'

He sipped at his coffee some more.

'Either way, you'll find message board chats that'll clue you in on whatever the hell Zoey Park's currently up to. Because I tell you now, from my own experiences of public and private lives, the Zoey you're aiding *isn't* the Zoey Park that you're aiding. She's wearing a mask, she's good at it, and she didn't even let it slip when ... well, when we—'

'Nuh-uh-uh,' Tinker waved a hand at Simpson as she pocketed the USB. 'Don't want to know. What are your plans for today?'

'Filming for YouTube, doing a TikTok, and checking in at the gym,' he replied. 'I know you're about to ask me to babysit, but frankly, I'd prefer it if Zoey was gone in the next half hour.'

'No longer a conquest, so no longer interesting?'

'More that I see too much of myself in her.'

'I'll wake her, and we'll leave,' Tinker decided. 'That is, if we're done here? I know Ellie wants to chat to her.'

'You do that,' Simpson said, standing up. 'I'm off for a shower.'

'I thought you wanted Zoey out?' Tinker raised an eyebrow. 'She'd want a shower before she leaves.'

'Well, she could join me,' Nicky Simpson grinned. 'You too, if you fancy, as I've always had a thing for the grimy look.'

He didn't expect the right hook.

'She can shower at the office,' Tinker said as she looked down at the sprawled-out influencer. 'Thanks for your help, Nicky. Nice tightie whities.'

Simpson just rubbed at his jaw, looking up at Tinker with a look which looked to be a mixture of surprise, anger, pain, and arousal.

'Any time,' he said. 'But next time, don't bring a friend, yeah?'

DAVEY WAS AT FINDERS WHEN ELLIE ARRIVED, PACING OUTSIDE her office.

'You have your own office, you know,' she said as she unclipped Millie's lead and allowed the dog to run to her office bed.

'I wanted to have a chat with you before anybody else came in,' Davey replied. 'I've got some reports back from the forensics.'

'Are they ones I'm going to like?' Ellie asked with a smile, placing her backpack down beside the desk, pulling her laptop out as she did so.

'Probably not,' Davey admitted. 'Thank you for getting Delgado and Soho forensics to deal with me, but I'll be honest, I could have done better without them.'

Ellie frowned at this.

'Not up to your level?'

'More "told to keep an eye on me" by a certain Kate Delgado,' Davey said. 'If I'd realised I was going to be micro-managed, I would have stayed in Temple Inn.'

'It's short term,' Ellie grimaced. She'd hoped Delgado's

offer had been genuine, but now it seemed there were caveats attached again. 'We'll work out something for next time.'

'I'm already doing that now,' Davey replied. 'I've spoken to my old mentor, Rosanna Marcos. She reckons she's got some locations I can use.'

She looked at the door as if about to say something else, but wasn't sure how to say it.

'Where are we on this?' she asked.

'What do you mean?' Ellie asked as she sat down at her desk.

'I mean, are we still thinking that Luana Flanagan is the bad guy, or are we looking at other people?'

'Maybe,' Ellie watched Davey as she paced around the office. 'You have a theory?'

'I'll be honest. This is starting to feel a bit like a frame-up.'

'How so?' Ellie now opened her laptop as she waited for Davey to speak her mind.

'So the straitjacket is exactly as we thought. It's a bust, so there's nothing that can really give us fingerprints and DNA. It has a dozen different people a day touching it. The leather's the only place you could grab something off it, and the partial was near to nothing,' Davey began. 'The paper, now we've examined it is definitely the same as the stock that you found last night at the Kensington Hotel. Although I haven't done a full forensics – I don't think we need to go that far down the line – it's something that had to be picked up from there, and a while back. Not current. The blade is the thing I want to talk about.'

'The stage knife?'

'It's more of a juggling knife,' Davey made juggling motions with her hand, and then stopped as she realised what she was doing. 'It's large, it's hefty, it's sharp as hell, which is odd for a juggling blade, and it was rammed into the fake Zoey with a chunk of force.'

She finally stopped pacing and sat opposite Ellie.

'The doll itself had a maker's name and number on it, so I gave them a call,' she said. 'I wanted to find out what it was made of, to get an idea of the force that was needed to ram into the chest at that speed. Different types of silicone and foam can cause different levels of impact, you see.'

'Okay,' Ellie said, not sure where this conversation was now going.

'I found out two things while examining the blade,' Davey replied cautiously. 'The first is that the blade has no fingerprints on it apart from one, a partial thumbprint which, when checked against the records, was a confirmation for Luana Flanagan.'

'Flanagan's fingerprints were on the blade?'

'I didn't say that,' Davey waggled a finger. 'I said there was one partial thumbprint on the handle.'

'How is that different from what I just said?'

Davey pulled out a torch from her inside jacket pocket. It was a slim pen torch, about six inches in length, and she tossed it at Ellie, who automatically grabbed it in her right hand.

'Look at your hand now,' Davey said. 'You've gripped the handle of the torch in the same way that someone would have gripped this blade. If you're stepping upwards or stabbing downwards, either way, the grip would have been the same. You can see there that you've got a partial on your thumb, and under that you'd have a partial on all of your fingers. The grip on the juggling blade would have had the same, and for the blade to only show a partial thumbprint means that someone's either wiped it down and not done a good job, or they only had a partial thumbprint to work with.'

Ellie nodded. 'Do you think it's the latter?'

'I pretty much know it's the latter,' Davey smiled. 'Because there's degradation in the thumbprint to the point where I think it was taken from some tape and placed onto it this way. But that's not the only thing I found. There were apparently two of these made.'

'Two knives?'

'No, two fake Zoey Parks. They were worried they'd have a failure on one of them, so created a backup. The company said Zoey bought both but only picked one up for the show.'

'So, where's the other?'

'That's the interesting part,' Davey said. 'Apparently, it'd been paid for way back, but simply left in storage, in her lockup.'

'So we need to look in the lockup ...' Ellie trailed off. 'Shit.'

'Yeah,' Davey nodded. 'The same lockup Joe said had been broken into.'

'Do we know where it is now?'

'No,' Davey shook her head. 'But I reckon if you go to her lockup and have a look, you'll find a space where it was.'

'Who knew about this?' Ellie nodded.

'Honestly, could be anyone. But I would say it would be either Zoey, or the person who booked the order in the first place, Jacob Morrison.'

'Keep on with that,' Ellie replied, leaning back in her chair. She went to speak again, but paused as she saw Ramsey entering.

'You will not believe who's downstairs,' he said. 'Tinker's bloody brought Zoey Park herself.'

'Zoey Park is here?' Ellie was surprised by this. 'Maybe Nicky Simpson didn't want her in his house after all.'

'But yeah, either way the Queen of Conjuring, so to speak, has arrived,' Ramsey grinned.

'I saw you had an interesting night last night,' Davey said to him now. 'Didn't invite me.'

'Didn't realise that Chinese games of chance were your thing,' Ramsey replied. 'Next time I'm talking to a Chinese gangster, I'll definitely invite you.'

'Appreciated,' Davey nodded, and Ellie wasn't sure if she was mocking or not.

'So, Davey has some news and you have some news. I'm guessing Tinker has some news,' Ellie considered as she looked around. 'I think we might need to go have breakfast in the diner.'

'What about Zoey?'

'Zoey can wait in a room,' she said. 'I'm not too sure at the moment what the situation is.'

'And Robert?'

'He can bodyguard her,' Ellie sighed. 'I'm not having him involved right now. I think there's a lot of personal issues hitting here. Until we know what's truly going on, I think it's best we keep him out of it.'

'Is he going to like that?' Ramsey asked.

'Probably not,' Ellie replied with a slow smile. 'But if he's upset, he can tell me afterwards, not in the middle of a meeting.'

Tinker, at this point, was seen walking down the corridor, Zoey Park beside her. She seemed to have a small plaster adorned with a bumblebee on her temple, but Ellie decided not to comment on that.

'Zoey,' she said as she rose, walking out of the door to face the magician. 'A lot of people are looking for you.'

She gave her a smile.

'Do you like dogs?'

CAESAR'S WAS SURPRISINGLY BUSY FOR THE TIME OF DAY, AND Ellie and the others found they couldn't have their usual booth. Instead, they picked one close to the windows. It was the same size and fitted them in the same way the other one did, but Ellie wasn't happy about the fact it was beside the window. She felt a little more exposed than usual.

Ramsey didn't care. He was already picking his next meal and ordering it from Sandra. Ramsey had gone through the menu number by number, and was now on his second or even third time through. Tinker was rubbing her forehead, having already explained how much of a nightmare it was meeting up with Nicky Simpson again. Joanne Davey had politely ordered a coffee but still hadn't chosen any food.

As they sat down, Ellie was about to start when Casey walked through the door, placing his rucksack on the booth.

'Sorry I'm late,' he said. 'How are we doing? I understand we've got a magician upstairs.'

He grinned as he looked at Tinker.

'I also understand you've been having bedroom frolics?'

'Don't even start,' Tinker snapped. 'Not in the mood.'

Casey sat down, and Ellie started the meeting by telling them what Davey had already told her about the fingerprints and the straitjacket. Ramsey confirmed that there was no way one could hold a blade without leaving fingerprints. He used his knife and fork as examples before fiercely stabbing the sausage on his plate, looking at Tinker and asking if it reminded her of anyone recently. Tinker wasn't impressed, but she explained what Nicky Simpson had told her about Zoey Park's night time exploits and passed Casey the USB stick he'd given her with the key logger information.

Casey pulled out his laptop, opening it up and sliding the USB into the side port. As he was scrolling through the lines, working out how to decrypt them, Tinker pointed at the screen.

'What's that file?' she said.

'Oh, it's the video,' he replied, looking at Ellie before returning his attention to Tinker. 'You weren't here last night. It's "Where in the World is Zoey Park?" cleaned up.'

'Can I have a look?' Tinker asked. 'I've only seen the one on YouTube and it's grainy as hell.'

'Sure,' Casey said, spinning the laptop to face her and playing the video.

It was the same video everyone else had seen; Zoey in the middle of her trick, the flames rising, fire extinguishers spraying, and stagehands rushing in amidst the smoke.

'Stop,' Tinker said, her face darkening. 'Go back ten seconds.'

Casey did, and they watched the video again.

Just as the fire extinguishers were being sprayed and the crew appeared on stage, Tinker said, 'Stop. Play it again.'

'What am I looking for?' Casey asked.

'As I said, I saw this on YouTube,' Tinker said. 'But now it's cleaned up, I can see the faces better. There, pause.'

Casey paused, and Tinker pointed at the stage where the crew was rushing to put out the flames.

'That guy there and the one beside him,' Tinker said, tapping the screen. 'That's Liam and Sean, the two men that confronted us yesterday at Covent Garden.'

'Flanagan's men?' Ramsey inquired.

'That's what I was told. Now, I'm not sure,' Tinker replied.

Ellie leant back in the booth seat as Sandra approached with tea for Tinker.

'Are you sure you don't want anything to eat?' she asked Davey, who looked around the table and eventually nodded.

'Two slices of toast, please,' she said. 'And some butter.'

Sandra made a tsking sound with her mouth, as if annoyed that only toast was being asked for while Ramsey tucked into a full English, and walked off.

Ellie placed her elbows on the table and leant forward.

'Last night when Flanagan came to see me,' she began, 'I mentioned Liam and Sean. She claimed she hadn't sent anybody. Now you're telling me that the two men who came to find you were actually part of Zoey Park's show?'

She shook her head.

'That's too convenient.'

'I've got more,' Casey interjected, looking up. 'This was stuff I found yesterday, and the key log stuff will be for later. But last night, I did some digging and found a few things.'

'Go on.'

'So, Zoey Park was in a foster home when her mum died,' Casey continued. 'There were a few people there she'd mentioned to Tinker, when she talked about not enjoying being alone.'

'Yeah, Joe mentioned it when he talked to us.'

'Well, she wasn't alone,' Casey said. 'In fact, three of the people that were with her in that foster home were in the audience two nights ago.'

'They were "picked randomly" by this contest? You're kidding me!' Ramsey burst out laughing.

'That's not all,' Casey said, now turning to face Ramsey. 'I understand that when you went into prison, you left Jacob and his mum.'

'I don't see what that's got to do with this,' Ramsey interjected, his tone icy.

Casey raised his hand in a placating gesture.

'It's just when I looked into the records, Jacob's mother didn't cope well. She got involved in some small-level crime, dabbled in drug use, stuff like that. Jacob was taken away for a while.'

'Taken where?'

'When you were in prison, he was in a foster home.'

'Are you saying Jacob was in the same foster home as Zoey Park?' Ellie questioned. 'He told us he only met her a few years ago when performing.'

Casey nodded.

'Sorry, Ramsey. But he's been lying and I don't know when it started.'

Ramsey stared at the watch on his wrist, the same one he had taken the previous day.

'Is it just me or does it seem like they're trying to set up Luana Flanagan?' he pondered aloud.

'It can't just be about the name she stole from Flanagan, this "Queen of Conjuring" title,' Ellie mused. 'Luana Flanagan said last night that Zoey's mum had stolen an important Irish chain or something.'

'This,' Ramsey slammed his fist on the table, jolting everyone back, 'is about that bloody curse!'

At their confused and silent expressions, he placed his cutlery down to explain.

'Kenny mentioned a cursed item, an Irish chain linked to a family's tragedy. Something about tying things with a red thread? This is why Jimmy came to us, because he's been cursed, and it was apparently done by a magician—'

'And Zoey's a magician who might have a cursed Irish item in her possession,' Ellie replied.

'They're aiming that at us, just like Joe did,' Tinker nodded in agreement.

'It makes sense,' Ellie reflected, stealing a slice of toast from Davey as Sandra arrived with it. 'Someone, maybe Zoey, sends Joe to us, begging us to find her, providing a narrative where she's being pursued by Flanagan, while Jimmy is told to find us, knowing we'd work out the item was one owned by Flanagan. But why?'

'Kenny said the West End was being played for, and Flanagan's an obvious player,' Ramsey suggested. 'Maybe this is a way to take her off the board.'

'I think it's time to find all the answers,' Ellie determined. 'Luckily they're in a building five floors above us.'

'Can it wait until after breakfast, though?' Ramsey smiled. 'I'm really hungry.'

Ellie went to reply, but paused when the door to the diner opened and Kate Delgado walked in, a police officer behind her.

'I understand you have Zoey Park upstairs?' she asked as she walked over to Ellie.

'Good morning, Kate,' Ellie replied, watching the officer. 'Can I ask what's going on here?'

'Jimmy Tsang was hit by a car early this morning in an

underground car park near his West End office,' Delgado stated. 'We think Zoey Park was the one who did it.'

'How do you work that one out?' Tinker asked.

Delgado shrugged.

'Because we have CCTV footage that shows her driving the car when she did it,' she said. 'So, shall we all have a little chat?'

19

DOUBLE TROUBLE

'No, that can't be right,' Ellie replied, looking around. 'Last night she was at Nicky Simpson's.'

Delgado laughed at the statement.

'Oh, and he's such a paragon of virtue?' she replied.

'He's also a man who's so paranoid, he probably has cameras in every room in his house,' Ellie said. 'The chances are he knew exactly where she was at every minute of the day.'

'Well, that's a hell of an alibi to have,' Delgado chuckled. 'It's got to be a good one, because it's got to beat the image we have of her driving.'

She glanced at Casey, who looked queasy as he looked at his laptop.

'Your boy looks like he's gonna throw up,' she said.

Ellie glanced at Casey, who looked at her with an imploring expression.

'What?' she asked.

'I need to talk to you,' he said.

'Spit it out.'

He glanced at Delgado, and Ellie understood. *This was something he wasn't sure whether Delgado should know.*

'Look,' she said, 'if it's in relation to Zoey, we might as well just say it in front of the police.'

'I've got information,' Casey reluctantly nodded. 'I just had a friend of mine come through with the data from the security camera.'

'What security camera?' Delgado raised an eyebrow.

'Joe Kerrigan told us that Zoey's been having night terrors,' Ellie explained. 'They put a camera in their room, motion detected, to pick up if she walked around. To check on what she was doing. I think they were worried about whether she was sleepwalking.'

'On the night that the body was found in the bed – the fake body, that is – the footage had been deleted,' Casey added. 'We couldn't see who did it.'

'Which meant that it was somebody who knew there was a video camera watching them,' Delgado replied, looking at Casey. 'I'm guessing you've got some friend who could go into the hard drive.'

'Got a data scrubber friend who knows how these things work,' Casey nodded. 'They deleted the video but forgot to remove the cloud storage. So, there was a folder, and we just had to ...'

He trailed off, but the point of the message was made. Casey had hacked into the server, an illegal act that he was now confessing to the Detective Inspector.

Delgado chuckled.

'Don't worry,' she said. 'Breaking fifteen laws before breakfast is pretty much normal for your crew. I'm not going to have a go at you if you're able to help us with the crime.

Although we won't be able to use it in a court of law unless we can find a legal way of gaining it.'

'I can do that,' Casey replied eagerly, probably grateful he wasn't about to go to jail. 'The cloud server's there, you could get a warrant to see the stuff.'

'Is it stuff we'd want to see?' Delgado replied.

Casey looked at Ramsey and then Ellie, and then he turned his laptop around to show them the video that was now playing on his computer screen.

It was the CCTV of the bedroom. On it was Joe Kerrigan, talking on a phone.

'This is the CCTV we've already seen,' he said. 'Joe showed it to us to prove that he'd found the body.'

On the screen, Joe Kerrigan placed the phone down, turned to Zoey, and pulled aside the bedclothes to reveal the doll with a knife in it. Casey took his mouse, took his trackpad and scrolled back.

'This was about half an hour before he got home,' he said. 'About eleven-fifteen in the evening.'

On the screen, the bed was empty. No doll, nobody sleeping.

'What am I watching?' Ellie asked.

Casey nodded at the screen, silently telling her to shut up and watch. As they stared at the screen, there was a light appearing to the side.

'Motion Detector picks up light as well,' Casey said. 'The moment torch light hit that room, the camera turned on.'

On the screen, a black-clad figure walked into the room, torch in hand. They were slim, possibly a woman or a teenage man – definitely not the muscular types Luana Flanagan hired. The figure was hooded with a mask across their face, only their eyes visible. But they also seemed to know that there was a camera in the room, as they kept their head down, walked to the wardrobe, opened it, and pulled out the duplicate Zoey doll.

They brought the doll to the bed, positioned it, took a note, and then stabbed it into the chest. Ramsey gasped as it happened, looking sheepishly at the others.

'Sorry,' he said. 'It just ... it looks so lifelike.'

Ellie nodded as she looked back at the screen. The figure was now placing the doll into the bed under the covers, making it look like Zoey was asleep. Then, turning, the figure walked over to the video camera, glancing up at it as if checking it was on, or realising perhaps they'd be filmed, before hurrying out of the room.

'I think that's when they realised they were being watched,' Casey said. 'There's no more movement. The entire section was deleted, possibly before that person even left, which means they knew where the camera's hard drive was. But this is the bit I wanted to show you.'

He scrolled back to the point where the figure stared up at the camera, an HD image. The figure was close as they looked up at the recording device; the face was obscured, a hood covering the hair, and a mask covering the nose and mouth, but the eyes were clear. The eyes were visible.

And the eyes and the surrounding makeup were damning.

Without a doubt, Zoey Park was staring at the camera.

'This is impossible,' Ellie looked back at Delgado. 'She was on stage, we know that.'

'She did her final trick and disappeared,' Tinker added. 'Remember, we know she climbed onto the rooftops and ran, and we know she went to Covent Garden, but we only know that through her phone records, not through CCTV. What if

Zoey didn't go to Covent Garden, and instead returned to her house to set this up, while someone else took the phone, knowing we'd follow it?'

'It's a possibility,' Davey said, as she munched on a slice of toast. 'We don't know Jacob's whereabouts either. We just assume he was there. Anna Lever told us to check the phone, possibly knowing it'd lead us to Covent Garden.'

'As you noted, Zoey Park is upstairs,' Ellie said to Delgado. 'I think we should all have a chat.'

'Especially as we have another question to ask her,' Delgado looked at the group, checking each face in turn. 'Or were you aware Zoey Park did a Christmas show at the Kensington Hotel last year?'

Ellie shook her head mutely. She knew what this meant; Zoey could have gained a stationery pad from the hotel Luana Flanagan loved to stay at, but hadn't realised they'd changed their livery in the time between.

She looked across at Ramsey.

'You okay?'

His face had reddened, and his fists clenched, his food now untouched.

'You go speak to the magician,' he said. 'I'm gonna go speak to her assistant.'

'Are you sure?' Ellie looked at Tinker, as if silently suggesting she go instead, but Ramsey placed his cutlery together on the plate, dabbed at his mouth with the paper napkin and then rose.

'I'll be fine,' he said, sliding out of the booth seat, glaring at Delgado before leaving the diner.

'I don't think your man likes me,' Delgado commented.

'That's because he's got taste,' Ellie said, waving for the bill, before looking back at his plate.

'The bugger left without paying!' she exclaimed.

———

ZOEY WAS IN THE BOARDROOM PLAYING WITH MILLIE WHEN THE others returned.

She looked up, frowning as she saw the new addition to the team.

'Who's the woman?' she asked.

'Detective Inspector Kate Delgado,' Delgado replied. 'Met police, Soho division.'

Zoey glanced at Tinker.

'You dobbed on me?'

'Jimmy Tsang was caught in a hit-and-run last night,' Ellie replied before Tinker could speak, walking over to a chair and sitting down, facing Zoey across the table. 'They've got footage showing the driver was you.'

'That's impossible,' Zoey looked around, glancing back at Tinker, her eyes widening. 'I was with Simpson all night. You know that. I told you. You came and found me.'

'I also know that you disappeared from the bed around three in the morning,' Tinker said. 'Nicky noticed this when you'd gone on his computer.'

She shrugged.

'Maybe you were passing a message. Maybe he wasn't as lightly asleep as he thought, and you snuck out.'

'I didn't,' Zoey shook her head, her face defiant. 'I never.'

She looked back at Ellie.

'I'm being framed.'

'It does look that way,' Ellie nodded. 'But it's not just that. Your CCTV – the one you use for your night terrors? We found a deleted scene.'

'What do you mean, "deleted scene"?'

'She means the person who placed your fake body in the bed and stabbed it with a note deleted the video, but didn't delete it fast enough for us not to find it,' Delgado replied, ignoring the fact it'd been Casey that found it. 'Also, on the video, we can see, well, mostly see, that it was you.'

'However, we have the situation where it was done just after you disappeared from the stage,' Ellie said. 'So, we have an interesting conundrum. How is Zoey Park in two places at once? Were you actually running across the rooftops and heading towards Covent Garden where you broke your phone into pieces? Or was that a diversion as you leapt into a cab and went home to set up the fake doll, knowing that Joe wouldn't be back for another half-hour?'

Zoey's gaze flitted from person to person, looking for someone, anyone, who was on her side. Seeing none, she settled back in her chair, her face darkening.

'You all believe it was me,' she said. 'That Luana Flanagan didn't do this. You think I set up my own disappearance, that I faked the doll, that I—'

'Tried to kill Jimmy Tsang,' Delgado interrupted. 'Yeah, I do. I'd like you to come down to the station and have a word.'

'Now wait a second,' Ellie held her hand up. 'We've been working with you in good faith. We've been giving you information. I'd like a little in return.'

Delgado looked back at Ellie.

'When she was just missing, it wasn't a problem,' she said. 'But now she's a potential murder suspect.'

'Jimmy Tsang isn't dead.'

'No, but she tried to kill him and that's enough for me.'

Ellie rose from her chair, moving to stand between Delgado and Zoey.

'Zoey Park is our client,' she declared.

'I thought Joseph Kerrigan was your client.'

Tinker now moved forward as well.

'Joseph Kerrigan proved to be lying to us,' she said. 'We decided last night. Ellie's consultancy took Zoey Park as our client instead.'

'As such,' a new voice spoke now, and Ellie glanced around to see Robert standing in the doorway, 'if you want to arrest a client, you need to provide us with evidence that shows that not only was she there, but that she had the intention to kill Jimmy Tsang.'

'We've got CCTV—'

'That we haven't seen,' Robert interrupted. 'CCTV we've yet to prove was even her. So, until you provide that, I'm not letting her out of my sight.'

'That's not how the law works,' Delgado retorted.

'I know perfectly well how the law works. Are you arresting her?'

'She's a person of interest—'

'I said, are you *arresting* her?'

Zoey looked around the room and realised that she was on a losing streak. She slowly rose.

'It's fine,' she said. 'I'll go with her. Um, can I use your toilet first?'

'Sure,' Ellie walked over to Zoey, taking her by the arm and guiding her to the door. She pointed down the corridor.

'Second on the right,' she directed.

Zoey nodded and walked off, as Ellie returned to Delgado.

'You know, you were a piece of work when I worked with you,' she remarked. 'I truly thought you'd changed.'

'I'm just doing my job, Ellie,' Delgado replied. 'In the

same way that you're doing yours. If you don't think Zoey Park did this, then prove it.'

'That should be your job,' Ellie snapped back.

'It is,' Delgado acknowledged. 'I will, to the best of my abilities, investigate all angles of this. I swear to you. But currently, Zoey Park is the prime suspect for the attempted murder of a gangland boss who apparently believes he was cursed by a magician.'

'Look,' Robert said, looking at Ellie, 'she might be a jobsworth, but she's not wrong here. You have to give the police their chance to make things right.'

'I'm sick of relying on the police. It's not the first time they've screwed us over, and it certainly won't be the last.'

Delgado glanced back at the corridor.

'How far away is that toilet?'

'Come on, it's been a minute. Maybe she's having a nervous poo,' Tinker suggested.

'No,' Ellie countered. 'She's right. Something's wrong here.'

With Delgado matching her step, the two of them walked to the toilet doors. On the left were the male toilets, on the right the female toilets.

Opening one of the doors, Ellie leaned in.

'Zoey, are you okay?' she called out.

There was no response.

'Zoey?' Ellie walked in, looking around, but she didn't need to search the room. The bathroom was small; two cubicles only and a sink. Both cubicles were wide open.

There was no way Zoey Park could have hidden and not be seen.

'Shit,' she muttered as Delgado followed in, looking around as well.

'How could she have got out?' Delgado wondered, surveying the surroundings. 'You know this place.'

'She can't,' Ellie shook her head. 'The only way she could get out would be to go past us, and we have glass walls.'

'Then she found a new way out,' Delgado snapped, as she glanced at an office to the side. 'Whose office is that?'

'One of the partners,' Robert replied, walking behind them. 'He's barely here, and a lot of them hot-desk. but we have an office for him just in case.'

Delgado pointed at the far right of the office, where the window could be seen slightly open.

'That's a five-storey drop,' Robert said. 'There's no way she got down from that.'

Delgado ran through the office, over to the window, and peered out.

'There are handholds,' she snapped. 'A famed escapologist like Zoey Park could have done it.'

She turned to the officer beside her.

'I want everybody looking for this woman now. Get downstairs. Get out there. Find her. She's not far. She might even have fallen.'

She looked back at Ellie.

'If I find out that you knew she was going to do this ...'

'Oh, come on, Kate,' Ellie snapped. 'You know damn well this wasn't us. It's you coming in like a bull in a china shop and scaring her off.'

'Why do you always make it so difficult?' Delgado sighed before running off past Sara and into the stairwell that led downstairs, not even waiting for the elevator to take her to the lobby.

Ellie walked over to her phone, picking it up and texting Ramsey.

'What do you know that we don't?' Tinker asked. 'You're strangely calm for someone who just watched Zoey Park do a solo escape act.'

'It wasn't solo,' Ellie said, looking at Robert. 'Was it? You had plenty of time to give her a tour while we were waiting. I texted you to say Delgado and a couple of uniforms were coming up. Did you plan this because you still don't trust Delgado?'

Robert shrugged.

'I'm not really myself at the moment,' he said. 'I think I need to go lay down. I know you have this in excellent hands.'

As Robert walked off, Tinker glared at Ellie.

'Come on,' she said. 'You know something.'

'Casey,' Ellie said with a smile. 'You can get into Ramsey's iCloud account, right?'

'Sure, but I'd rather not—'

'It's okay, I just texted him to tell him you were doing it,' Ellie showed a response from Ramsey.

> Just don't go into the photos.

Casey nodded at this and started tapping on his laptop.

'What am I looking for?'

'Devices,' Ellie replied as she looked back at Tinker. 'What I know is that while Delgado runs around London looking for Zoey, we can pretty much work out exactly where she is.'

Casey turned the laptop around to show Ellie and the others – on it was a map of London. Travelling down Fleet Street was a little circle with '*Granddad's iPhone*' next to it.

'I don't get it,' Tinker asked.

'I placed a tracker on Zoey Park before she left,' Ellie said.

'An air tag that Ramsey used yesterday. While Zoey's got it in her pocket, we know exactly where she is.'

She sat down at the boardroom table.

'So until she gets where she's going, all we can do is wait,' she said. 'In the meantime, Davey and Tinker? Go look at Jimmy Tsang's office. See if you can see anything. Casey, work on the key logger Simpson gave us.'

'What about you?'

'I'm having a chat with someone who owes a favour,' Ellie smiled. 'It's about time we were told what's truly going on.'

20

GOING DARK

CASEY HAD FOUND WHERE JACOB WAS THAT MORNING BEFORE Ramsey had even left the diner, and unsurprisingly, it was the Piccadilly Theatre that Ramsey arrived at, only to find the stage door open.

He paused, confused, but then moved aside as people emerged through the doors; movers were bringing out boxes and crates.

'What's going on?' he asked, as one tall, black man, unconcerned by what he was asking, passed by and shrugged.

'Show's cancelled,' he said. 'Moving it all out. I think they're bringing "Bake-off the Musical" back. Zoey Park isn't doing shows anymore, and something else starts tonight.'

'This is because Zoey Park's missing?'

'We didn't watch the news,' the man grinned and walked off.

Ramsey bit his lip as he considered this. He knew that Claudette had sold some rights to Luana Flanagan, but he didn't know what. Maybe Flanagan had cancelled the show?

Either way, this explained why Jacob's phone pinging was currently appearing here at such a time in the morning.

Walking through the back corridors of the theatre, unchallenged by any of the people walking back and forth, Ramsey eventually walked onto the stage. There, he found Jacob folding up items and placing them in boxes.

Jacob saw Ramsey approach and turned to glower at him.

'You've got some nerve,' he started, but Ramsey held up his hand.

'I've come to apologise and give you back this,' he said, holding up the watch he'd stolen the previous day. 'It meant a lot to me, so I took it by instinct, but I didn't realise at the time that it probably meant a lot to you as well.'

Jacob nodded, taking the watch and staring down at it.

'It was the only thing that you left when you ... well, left,' he said. 'I remember you telling me once that it had been given to you by your father. At the time, I thought you were the closest thing I had to one.'

He placed it back on his wrist.

'Over time, it became like a lucky charm for me. Every good thing that happened, I was wearing it.'

'Were you wearing it when you met Zoey?' Ramsey asked.

'Yes,' Jacob smiled. 'So I can add that, I suppose.'

'Were you wearing it two nights ago when she disappeared?' Ramsey asked, and Jacob nodded, a shadow falling across his face.

'Yeah. Maybe it's not lucky after all.'

'What about when you *first* met Zoey?'

'At the auditions?' Jacob frowned now; this was the second time in a row Ramsey had asked this, and it felt different, wrong somehow.

'No, I don't mean your auditions. I mean the foster home,'

Ramsey said, his voice darkening, its tone now colder, less emotional.

At the comment, Jacob winced.

'You know,' he said.

'Yes,' Ramsey replied. 'I bloody well know.'

Jacob nodded, slowly. He paced around the stage as he considered his next words carefully.

'Mum had a bad time,' he began. 'You leaving, and us with no money. She'd been relying on your income, whatever it was, and when you were gone, there was none left. She'd racked up some debts, which I hadn't been aware of, probably because she was still trying to live the life of Ramsey Allen, gentleman thief.'

Ramsey didn't reply. He'd already spent his time feeling guilty about this.

'Go on,' he said.

Jacob shrugged.

'She started trying to do her own thing. She had met enough contacts through you in the year that you were together, and she went to them and asked for help. At first, they all were friendly and offered to assist in whatever way they could. What she didn't realise was that they were doing this because they wanted something in return.'

'What did they want?'

'No, nothing like that. It wasn't a sex thing,' Jacob shook his head. 'They wanted information on you. Some of them were owed money. Some of them just wanted you hurt. But Mum didn't give them anything. She couldn't. She knew nothing because you'd bloody disappeared. In fact, it was only about a year after you'd gone we learned you were in prison. But by then it was too late.'

'What do you mean, it was too late?'

'Mum, by that point, was on drugs. She was hanging around the wrong people and making pennies on the pound for the work she was doing,' Jacob said, his voice hissing with anger. 'Social services weren't happy about this. They came by a couple of times, said she wasn't looking after me properly. I was basically being left at home a lot, which was fine by me. Auntie Anna would take me to her shows and I'd sit in the back of small cabaret halls, watching her sleight of hand and stuff like that. Or if she was doing a street show, I'd be watching for the police at Leicester Square and calling out if anybody showed up. For some reason, the social services didn't think this was a good life for me, either.'

'So, they placed you into a foster home?'

'Yeah, for six months. Six months away from my mum, away from Anna, away from everybody,' Jacob nodded. 'I wondered if this was how you felt, locked away in your prison. I almost contacted you at one point. But I had my watch.'

Jacob looked out towards the auditorium, recalling a scene from his past.

'There was this kid,' he said. 'I called him Desperate Dan. Beefy, stupid kid. All brawn, no brain. Thought he was the bee's knees. His mum and dad, I think, were both in prison and he'd been dumped in foster care. He decided he liked my watch.'

He glanced down at the watch in his hand.

'Tried to take it off me. I don't think he expected me to fight back. I broke his nose. He broke my arm. Wasn't quite a fair trade, but it kept him off my back for a while. But then, after a month, he started again. This time, bringing friends.'

Ramsey didn't need to ask what happened. He knew the story was about to be told to him.

'Then Zoey turned up.' Jacob smiled. 'All piss and vinegar, with a strong Irish accent. Her mum had left her with a guardian who'd passed, and she'd been dumped in the system. I think we were the third foster care she'd been to. The previous two she'd escaped without a problem.'

He chuckled now as he remembered the moment.

'She turned around and put the fear of God into him. I don't even know what she did. All I know is, one day, he came along with his friends and beat the living shit out of me. The next day he came up to me and was super apologetic, offered me sweets to make up for it. When I told him I was gonna get my revenge on him, he pissed himself in front of me. Like literally urinated down his jeans in fear,' he said. 'He was that scared of what I would do. I never learned what Zoey did. But whatever she said, whatever she did, I never got touched again.'

A wistful look overcame the smile now, and he leant against the table as he continued.

'I remembered that,' he said. 'But then, just like that, I was gone. I went back home; Mum was better, until she died, years later. It was how Anna met Zoey as well. She visited Mum a couple of times and I had Zoey with me one time. I think it might even have been what got Zoey interested in magic again. Anna had heard of her mum, and she had definitely heard of Flanagan.'

'Then you lost track until the auditions.'

'Yeah,' Jacob shrugged. 'Chance encounter. My story about how she couldn't work out a trick I'd done was bollocks. That was just for the press. When she realised who I was, she immediately told me I was working with her, no matter what.'

He waved around the theatre.

'All this, all the awards and the fans and the hangers on? She doesn't have many friends. She doesn't trust many people. But I came from her past, you know? I was proven, somebody she fought side to side with back in the day.'

'Is that why you betrayed her?' Ramsey asked.

'How do you mean?'

Ramsey shrugged.

'I understand you're the person who provides the staff, the crew, whoever. You hire, you fire, you do all that stuff.'

'So what?'

'Liam and Sean,' Ramsey said. 'Zoey ran from them yesterday, convinced they were part of Luana Flanagan's gang. Yet we know they were onstage performing with you the night she disappeared. That's just by chance?'

'You found her?'

'We found her.'

Jacob looked as if he wanted to ask more, but eventually sighed and continued.

'I hired them, sure, but Claudette vouched for them,' he said as he frowned. 'She'd worked with them on a touring production.'

Ramsey went to speak but then stopped, sighing.

'Look lad, I don't have time for going around in circles,' he said. 'We were hired by Joe Kerrigan, and we since found out he lied. We found Zoey, but then learnt that *she* lied and now you're here lying to me.'

'What's this about, Ramsey?' Jacob asked now, narrowing his eyes. 'Because I swear, I haven't a bloody clue.'

'Zoey's in trouble,' Ramsey said. 'The police arrived as I left, Jacob. They reckon she tried to kill Jimmy Tsang last night. Do you know anything about that?'

Jacob didn't reply, simply staring at Ramsey.

'Did she curse him?' Ramsey continued.

Again, no answer.

'Do you know anything about some stolen chain from Luana Flanagan? A Celtic antique of some kind?'

Jacob didn't speak again, but his eyes twitched at the name; he knew about this, even if he wasn't speaking.

'A cursed item,' Ramsey continued. 'Sound familiar?'

'She was made to do the curse,' Jacob muttered, but then placed a hand over his mouth, as if to physically stop himself from talking.

'Who made her?' Ramsey asked. 'Flanagan? Kerrigan?'

'I'm sorry, Ramsey, but I can't say about that, but I can tell you it's not what it seems,' Jacob replied, and for the first time Ramsey could see the inability to reply was actually weighing on the man.

'I've heard that comment a lot recently,' he said. 'People lining up to tell me "it's not what it seems" is today's cool thing.'

'Sometimes they might be telling you it because it's the truth.'

'I heard Zoey's mum stole the chain,' Ramsey continued. 'Before she died.'

'Before my time.'

Ramsey clicked his tongue as he looked at the younger man. He knew this was as far as he could go here.

'If you find you can at any point, you call me, okay?' he suggested instead.

Grateful for the offer, or maybe just grateful he didn't have to continue down this line of questioning, Jacob nodded.

'So, did you sort out the stooges?' Ramsey continued

regardless, changing the subject. 'We were told you're the one that sorts all that out.'

Jacob nodded.

'Usually, yeah,' he said. 'But on that night, I was told to leave it.'

'Who by? Was it Zoey?'

Jacob shook his head.

'Claudette,' he replied. 'She'd been shifty all day. I went to arrange some randos – that's what we call the random people called up onto the stage – but she said she had it sorted.'

'Did you get to vet who she chose?'

'No,' Jacob admitted. 'But I recognised a couple of them. People from the foster home. They'd been there when Zoey was there. A couple from when I was there, even.'

'Didn't you find this strange?'

'Of course I bloody did,' Jacob snapped back angrily. 'I guessed it was some kind of event, a "this is your life" kind of thing for her birthday in a couple of weeks. I don't think she'd have even recognised any of them, apart from Dan.'

'Desperate Dan?'

Jacob smiled.

'More "piss legs" Dan,' he replied. 'My bully, Daniel Bisley. He's harmless these days. Thick as mince. She could have waved every bloody trick's secret in front of him and he'd never have worked it out.'

He shrugged.

'I didn't understand the point of it either,' he eventually replied. 'None of them spoke to Zoey, anyway. She spoke to the audience while they checked the items, I don't even know if she gave Dan a second glance.'

'But you did,' Ramsey replied, considering this as he looked around. 'Maybe this wasn't for her, but for you.'

'Why me?' Jacob frowned at the statement.

'You're just as much a part of the act as she was,' Ramsey said, working through the theory as he spoke. 'When you saw your childhood bully on stage, moments before the trick, did it distract you?'

'Of course not—' Jacob started irritably, but then he trailed off, thinking harder. 'Yeah. Actually, the moment he said his name, calling himself "Biz," I knew it was him. Same accent.'

'What did you do?'

'Honestly? I had to stop myself dumping a stage weight on his head,' Jacob replied. 'I was in the wings, prepping everything as they came on. Then the items were wheeled out, and I headed up to my spot on the gantry. But I couldn't take my eyes off him.'

'What were you doing when they came on stage?' Ramsey asked. 'I know you were prepping everything, but what *exactly* were you prepping as you were distracted?'

Jacob paled.

'I was setting the key into the straitjacket,' he said. 'I-I was behind, I wasn't as fast as I could be, so I got someone else to do it.'

'Someone you trusted to do it right?' Ramsey pressured.

At this, Jacob nodded dumbly, and Ramsey glanced over to the right of the stage, remembering a conversation from the previous day.

'I saw them all from the side of the stage. I used mnemonics to remember everything.'

'Oh, you crafty bitch,' he whispered. 'Jacob, answer me honestly. Was it Anna?'

Jacob was surprised at Ramsey's question, but nodded.

'How did you know?' he asked.

'Because everything is coming together,' Ramsey was pacing now, his mind racing. 'When Claudette arranged the stooges, would she have done it alone?'

'Unlikely, she'd have got someone else to do it, as that's what she always does,' Jacob was absentmindedly rubbing at his watch now. 'Are you saying Anna picked the names?'

'If she did, it'd answer a lot of questions,' Ramsey nodded. 'For a start, it'd give a plausible answer to how she knew the names – she gave them with ease yesterday, claiming it was years of mentalism acts that helped, but knowing the names before always helps better.'

He stopped pacing, counting his points off on his fingers.

'She was at the side of the stage, and she was in the right spot to help you when you were distracted by your childhood bully,' he explained. 'She knew who'd be picked and how it'd affect you. Then she offered herself as help—'

'And in the process doctored the straitjacket,' Jacob finished. 'But why? She loves Zoey!'

Ramsey looked up into the auditorium.

'The video that was made,' he asked. 'Did you see it?'

'Do you mean "Where in the World is?"'

'Yes, that's the one.'

Jacob nodded.

'I had it sent to me,' he said. 'Why?'

Ramsey pointed to the front of the Royal Circle.

'We know it was taken from up there,' he said. 'Plus we know it was taken with a very good long-range lens.'

This made Jacob's posture shift.

'How do you know that?' he asked suspiciously.

'We're very good at what we do,' Ramsey turned his attention back to him. 'We also know there's a very strong chance that it was Lenny Clarence filming the video.'

At this, however, Jacob laughed.

'Lenny? God, no,' he replied. 'No way in hell he's up there. Not only does the guy hate heights, he's agoraphobic. It's why he works as an editor for half a dozen YouTubers.'

Ramsey frowned at this.

'Are you telling me that Lenny Clarence wasn't up there two nights ago?'

'Look, he might have edited the video. Your people know that better than mine,' Jacob shrugged. 'But I can tell you without any doubt whatsoever that there is no way in hell Lenny made his way up those steps, into that seat, and sat on the edge filming.'

'Then who did?' Ramsey asked.

'Zoey gives those two seats out,' Jacob admitted, looking uneasy. 'They're empty. It's often agents or scouts that she wants to impress, a couple of TV execs, sometimes even friends of the crew. Nine times out of ten, Claudette nicks them and passes them on to friends of hers.'

'What about two nights ago?' Ramsey asked.

Jacob didn't answer, but it wasn't that he didn't want to. His expression showed he simply didn't know.

Ramsey nodded.

'We'll find out,' he said. 'Someone will be able to tell us.'

'Look, I wish I could help you,' Jacob replied. 'But I genuinely don't keep an eye on that.'

He stopped, thinking about the question.

'One thing I can say, though,' he said. 'I might not know who was booked in to film the scene two nights ago, but I can tell you who's been up there *before* filming scenes.'

'Go on.'

'Only a couple of times, but he's done some promotional filming for her,' Jacob looked like he was getting angry, as he looked to the side. 'Kerrigan sits in that seat and takes photos and videos, and he has an open invite that if those seats are open, he can come in any time and watch the show. So if it was anybody, I'd say it was him.'

Ramsey nodded. Joseph Kerrigan was a good option for this. But he also knew that "Joe Kerr" was performing at the same time as the trick was going on, which made it a bit of an alibi that couldn't be fixed.

Or could it?

The Brasserie Zédel was across the street. Could he have timed the two things together?

Ramsey considered popping over to the brasserie to ask as soon as he was finished here.

'I'll check into that—' Ramsey had been walking towards Jacob at this point, but a noise from above, the creaking of the gantry stopped him, and a sixth sense made him look up, leaping to the side—

As a heavy stage weight crashed into the stage between them.

Looking up again, Ramsey saw a figure on the gantry looking down on them. A figure he recognised.

'Get back here!' Jacob, also looking up, ran for the ladder to the gantry, hurrying up it as Ramsey saw the figure run off to the side, the opposite direction from Jacob. Who, a moment later appeared there.

'She's gone!' he cried down to Ramsey.

'She went that way!' Ramsey cried back, pointing off to the side.

'Impossible!' Jacob shook his head. 'There's no exit at that end! You'd have to jump!'

Ramsey looked to the end of the gantry, frowning. That

had definitely been the route the figure he'd seen had gone. But once more, she had disappeared.

Because without a single doubt, Ramsey knew that as he looked up, he'd seen Zoey Park staring down at him from under a hoodie.

The question was, though – *was she trying to kill him, or Jacob?*

21

MAMA

Maureen "Mama" Lumetta grinned from the settee of her Islington living room as Ellie walked in, led by a tall, muscled goon.

'I didn't think I'd see you for a while,' she said as Ellie sat down opposite her.

'You look well,' Ellie replied conversationally. 'Retirement suits you. If you really are retired, that is.'

Ignoring the comment, Mama Lumetta sipped at a small coffee, probably some kind of very expensive espresso, and eyed Ellie up and down.

'Are you here to demand one of your two favours from me?' she asked. 'Tell me I owe you, and command me to do something and fix things for someone else?'

'If I need to, yes,' Ellie said. 'But I hoped that you might just help me with some questions, this time.'

Mama Lumetta considered this.

'It depends on what the questions are,' she replied. 'I'm only considering this because Ramsey has been an absolute gentleman of late.'

Ellie smiled. It was known that Ramsey Allen had had relationships with Maureen Lumetta in their youth, and that, after the Lumetta gold case, he had spent some more time with her, escorting her to a variety of events – more as a chaperone than anything else.

But with Ramsey, you never knew how far the flirtation went.

'The Lumetta family worked a lot in Ireland,' Ellie started. 'I seem to recall you have links in Dublin, all the way up to Dundalk.'

'Also Italy, and London, and Liverpool, and quite a lot of places. Please speak more clearly, Miss Reckless?' Mama Lumetta laughed.

'Did you ever deal with Luana Flanagan?'

At the name, Mama Lumetta's eyes glittered malevolently.

'Ellie Reckless,' she said with a slight singsong to her voice. 'You've found a way to get me to help you without begging a favour, haven't you?'

Ellie leant back in the chair, watching the Italian matriarch.

'I'm guessing you're not a fan,' she said.

'Flanagan has caused me a fair share of trouble in my time,' Mama Lumetta shook her head. 'Gypsy pikey—'

'I didn't ask for name-calling,' Ellie interrupted.

Mama Lumetta nodded, somewhat acknowledging she'd crossed a line. Although Ellie didn't believe that Mama Lumetta, for one second, believed that she was feeling apologetic or guilty.

'She runs the amusements and carnivals and circuses and any kind of entertainment you might know,' Mama Lumetta explained. 'Musicals, theatre, the lot. If you had a performance of Riverdance in the nineties, you probably had to pay her a backend, or get Michael Flatley to sleep with her, something like that. Any touring production in the counties had to go through her union. Although "union" is quite a loose term. Recently, she's spent her time in London trying to become the next Bill Kenwright.'

'I don't know who Bill Kenwright is,' Ellie replied.

'Was. He passed away recently. Some say he was a legend in the West End,' Mama Lumetta smiled, not caring if Ellie didn't know who this was, either. 'Could take a terrible show and make it look amazing. Very good at turning shit into gold.'

'Better than you?'

'Let's just say she thinks she can go legitimate and become some kind of West End producer. Whoever she thinks she is though, she's nothing more than a common whore in a pretty dress who has delusions of grandeur, of being a gypsy princess and an actress. Why are you dealing with her?'

'Zoey Park,' Ellie shrugged.

Mama Lumetta went to speak, but then stopped herself, and then gave Ellie a dismissive shrug.

'Heard of her?' Ellie asked, sensing something was up.

'Doesn't matter, it's just another client, another poor lost sheep you're trying to save.'

'It's a little more than that,' Ellie replied coldly. 'Luana Flanagan is trying to kill her.'

She couldn't be sure, but for the first time during the conversation, Ellie saw genuine surprise, and what looked to be a hint of fear cross Mama Lumetta's face at this.

'Why?'

'Why do you care?' Ellie waggled her finger. 'It's just another lost sheep—'

'Do not treat me like one of your favour-owing henchmen,' Mama Lumetta snapped. 'I'm not Danny Flynn or Nicky Simpson.'

Ellie paused, nodding.

'I'm sorry, you're right,' she said, her voice emotionless. 'Those people would actively try to lie to me, or give me the truth because they wanted something from me. They wouldn't hide from me.'

'That's what you think I'm doing?' Mama Lumetta rose from the settee, walking to a side cabinet and pouring a generous measure of Irish Malt Whiskey from a bottle.

'I know it,' Ellie leant back in the chair. 'For a start you've now found something to do while you regain your composure, turning your head from me so I don't see the shock on your face.'

Mama Lumetta smiled as she turned back to face Ellie.

'I was always right about you,' she said. 'Do you remember I said you and your team could take over London if you so wanted, with the connections you had, and the favours you were owed?'

'I do,' Ellie nodded. 'I remember telling you I was saving the favours for something else.'

'So, how did that go for you?' Mama Lumetta raised an inquisitive eyebrow, almost mocking the comment. 'Was destroying Nicholas Simpson the answer to your problems in the end? Or did you realise there were others above him, waiting for him to fall?'

Ellie shrugged, not replying.

'But now you've removed the facilitator, and you've removed the bigger threat,' Mama sipped at the whiskey, returning to her seat. 'As I said back then, I've walked the road for many years now, and I recognise all the houses on it.

Now you've gained your revenge and have favours to spare. So why not consider the offer again, and become my successor? Nobody else has been chosen yet. Plus you know I like your consigliere.'

'I'm not sure he's happy being consigliere,' Ellie smiled. 'I think he thinks I'm his.'

Mama Lumetta cocked her head to the side.

'Wouldn't work,' she said. 'People aren't as scared of him as they are you.'

At this, Ellie was surprised.

'People are scared of me?'

'Please, false modesty is cringeworthy at the best of times, and you've never been one for that affectation,' Mama Lumetta placed the now empty tumbler on the table. 'The offer is there for when you come to your senses.'

'I appreciate it,' Ellie smiled darkly. 'Almost as much as I appreciate the skill in changing subjects you just attempted.'

Mama Lumetta glanced away and looked out of the window. Ellie couldn't work out if she was thinking back to a moment in her past, or trying to work out what lie to tell her, but after a few seconds, she nodded to herself and looked back at Ellie.

'I knew Flanagan back in the day,' she said. 'Before I lived in London. I was helping my little Matteo. He was young, just getting into the business. We'd been working in Dublin for years at this point and he was getting his foot in the door.'

'When are we talking?' Ellie asked.

'A few years after the turn of the millennium, so fifteen, maybe twenty years ago,' Mama Lumetta counted off her fingers as she spoke. 'He decided he wanted to get involved in entertainment. Temple Bar has a lot of footfall. There's a lot of bars and nightclubs and he reckoned he could make some money. But then he found that Flanagan had her own opinions on who should work and *not* work in the area. We had some issues. We turned up on her doorstep. She brought a ton of gypsy carnival folk to face us.'

Ellie nodded.

'I see. So you were never friends?'

'No,' Mama Lumetta gave a smile. 'I can tell you with no doubt whatsoever that we would never share a drink together.'

'Did you hear about her husband?'

'I know she's had two. The first one apparently was given an option he couldn't refuse.'

'Don't you mean an offer he couldn't refuse?'

'No, it was definitely more of an option he couldn't refuse,' Mama Lumetta said. 'You know, option one is keeping his testicles. Option two ...'

She trailed off, and Ellie didn't need to ask what else she meant, as Mama Lumetta continued.

'He was spending more time with us, trying to facilitate some way of working together. People didn't like that. Her family were annoyed and eventually, it was strongly suggested that he should go.'

'When she was fighting you,' Ellie asked, 'did you ever hear the surname Park?'

At this, Mama Lumetta pursed her lips.

'This is why you're working with the girl, Zoey. It's her mother, isn't it?'

'What do you know about her mother?'

'Mary Park was a performer in some shows Flanagan did,' Mama Lumetta held up her tumbler, and motioned at Ellie to get her a refill. Ellie would usually have told her where to shove the tumbler, but she wanted to know more. So, she took it from the older woman and walked over to the sideboard.

'She was there a few years,' Mama Lumetta continued. 'Woman and child. After she had the baby, though, she'd left the life, but Flanagan pulled her back in.'

'To perform?'

'No, to be a patsy, I believe you call it,' Mama Lumetta's face darkened. 'It's a bastardised version of the Italian word *Pazzo*, which means "fool," but you get the gist.'

She sat back on the settee, accepting the top up.

'I don't know why they wanted her there, but we watched her. We didn't trust Flanagan, so we kept an eye on everything and when she got rid of the first hubby, it was one of our own she moved in on. Nino Kerrigan. First generation Dubliner, but parents came from the old land.'

She stopped herself, holding up a hand.

'I digress. Anyway, Mary Park? The story was she stole from Flanagan.'

'We know about this,' Ellie nodded. 'It's some ancient chain that supposedly held some mighty Irish warrior when he was dying or something.'

Mama Lumetta started to laugh.

'If you believe that, you're more naïve than I thought,' she replied. 'The Celtic hero Cú Chulainn is who you're talking about.'

'It sounds like it.'

'You're talking about the mystical chain that held him to the rock while he fought his last battles,' Mama Lumetta smiled. 'It's odd though, none of the stories of him mention this mystical chain around him. People talk about how he tied himself with ropes, or leather straps. Things a soldier of the time would have.'

'So the story's fake?'

'Well, I'm no expert, and the stories could be based on factual battles – the stone he was claimed to tie himself to exists, but he's like an Irish King Arthur, you know? In Italy there's the Befall, or Santa Lucia. Steeped in folklore but actually based in fact.'

'King Arthur's real?'

'There are records of him in the Vatican library, so I'd say so.'

She sipped at the drink.

'The story might not be fake, but the chain certainly is,' she eventually replied. 'This claim that it's been in the family since the sixteenth century is nonsense. The Flanagans weren't even travelling around Ireland at that time. They were hiding from the English.'

'I thought as much,' Ellie nodded. 'Then why the fuss about the theft?'

'And you, pretending to be a detective?' Mama Lumetta tutted. 'Why would you do it?'

Ignoring the jibe, Ellie considered the question.

'If I have an item that, for hundreds of years, my family has claimed is legitimate, and now there's a chance it might be found out as a fake, or if I knew it wasn't legit and now someones's about to "out" this—'

'Go on,' Mama Lumetta leant forwards, her eyes glittering.

'Okay, well, if that was the case, I'd have it stolen. That way, even if it's found, I could claim the chain they brought back to me wasn't the original, and nobody would be able to prove I was lying.'

'Exactly,' Mama Lumetta said. 'We all knew about the chain. Flanagan even used it in her own escape act.

Which surely you wouldn't do with an item worth so much money? A chain worth a hundred thousand pounds, minimum. If that chain was proven genuine, it'd be worth *ten times* that to a collector. Look how much a story can add to an item's value. But there you are, dragging the bloody thing around county fairs for a trick gaining pennies ...'

She shook her head.

'Luana Flanagan knew people wanted that chain. People were hunting a debt that she owed, maybe something her previous husband had built up, before he was ... well, before he disappeared.'

Ellie made a mental note to check in on what happened to husband number one, as Mama Lumetta continued.

'With the theft, though, Flanagan altered that narrative. She told everyone the chain was stolen, blamed Mary Park, and then lived off the story for another ten years while passing the debt to her. She had bosses, higher up crime families she probably owed the same debt to, and this gave her some kind of breathing space to get out before they started asking questions.'

'You think she brought Mary in just to use her like this?'

'It's what I would have done,' Mama Lumetta sniffed dismissively.

Ellie stared at the woman opposite her.

'I was told that Mary Park died of an overdose in Bunratty, shortly after, most likely because of this debt,' she replied icily. 'Is *that* something you would have done?'

'What in God's name are you talking about?' Mama Lumetta's eyes narrowed at this. 'Mary Park isn't dead.'

Ellie felt a trickle of ice slide down her spine.

'What?'

Mama Lumetta cocked her head as she looked to rephrase this.

'I mean she might be dead now, it's been a while, but she didn't die in Bunratty.'

'How would you know this?'

Mama Lumetta smiled, and it was a triumphant "I know something you don't know" smile that instantly filled Ellie with anger at the woman.

'Because we were the ones that got her out of Ireland,' she said.

Ellie rose from the chair at this, and Mama Lumetta, amused at getting such a reaction, laughed.

'It's true,' she said from her seat, looking up. 'We got her out, changed her name, got her safe.'

'What about Zoey?'

'Never told. Mary's choice,' Mama Lumetta said. 'Mary knew the moment she made contact, Flanagan would know. Also, she was a pretty shitty mother at the best of times. She genuinely believed the home was the best place for her. From a distance, she watched over her, of course.'

Ellie was pacing now, mentally going through names in her head. *Had she met the mum? Was it connected to the case?*

Mama Lumetta was up now too, walking over to a shelf where a line of books rested. Pulling one out, she flicked through it.

'This is an old photo album of the time,' she explained. 'I'm sure I have one of Matteo and Mary together, hold on ... aha. Here you go.'

Ellie walked over to Mama Lumetta and stared down at the photo. It was a pub, a party of some kind, with a young Matteo Lumetta standing beside a pretty young woman.

A woman Ellie recognised.

Suddenly, everything fell into place.

'Thank you,' she said, already walking to the door. 'I'm classing this as a favour burnt.'

'Oh, no, it's fine,' Mama Lumetta replied, placing the album back. 'If it hurts Flanagan, you get this one for free. I'm guessing you know her, and she's alive?'

'Yes,' Ellie growled. 'But I can't confirm how long that'll be, because I intend to kill her myself.'

22

IRISH WITCHES

JIMMY'S BODYGUARD, CHOW, HAD BEEN WAITING FOR THEM when Tinker and Davey arrived.

He wasn't happy. But then Tinker assumed he never was. The last time they'd met, when Jimmy was playing chess with Ellie, Chow had been by the door when she entered, and even then looked like a bulldog chewing a thistle.

'We want to see the office,' she said. 'We were allowed—'

'You've been given permission,' Chow replied angrily. 'I don't know if that equals *allowed.*'

Tinker nodded. She understood why Chow was annoyed; his boss was in hospital. Or, more likely, he was annoyed Jimmy had *survived*, and Kenny couldn't take over. So, instead of walking past him, she stopped and squared up.

'Let's be clear here,' she said. 'You don't like us, and that's fine. But if we've got a problem, I want it sorted now.'

Chow stared up and down at Tinker.

'Your thief,' he said.

'Ramsey?'

'Yes. That's the one. He was with Kenny the same night that Jimmy was attacked. They met at a casino.'

'Which you know about, I'm guessing because ...'

'Because we watch Mister Tsang's cousins,' Chow said. 'All of them.'

Davey, who'd been standing beside Tinker, raised her hand as if waiting to be allowed to ask a question. When they both looked at her, she offered a smile.

'I looked into your file, Chow,' she said. 'Hope you don't mind, but it's an old habit from being a copper.'

At the word "copper," Chow flinched.

'I thought I'd seen you before, I couldn't think where,' she continued. 'It was all that business with Jeffrey Tsang and Cousin Benny.'

She let the names trail off, knowing Chow would understand. It was the murder of Benny by their nephew, Jeffrey Tsang; the same murder that ended with Kenneth being shot twice by Jeffrey, but surviving, leaving a vacancy in the Tsang empire. One that Jimmy then entered.

'What about it?' Chow asked.

'I remember seeing you there,' Davey said. 'I've a good memory for faces and yours is one you can't forget. You worked for Kenny and Benny, didn't you?'

Chow nodded but remained silent.

'Then when Benny and Kenny went, you changed your allegiance to Jimmy?'

'I serve the same family.'

'So here's a question for you,' Davey posited, folding her arms and facing the bodyguard. 'You say you serve the Tsang empire, which is nice. But which side of the Tsang empire? Kenny Tsang told our man Ramsey when they met, that he wants to come back, that he wants to take back what was his.

Jimmy, as far as he's concerned, made a hostile takeover in his absence. So, if Kenny decided he *did* want to come back, would you side with him? Or would you stay with your new master?'

'Mister Tsang is not my master,' Chow replied. 'He is my employer.'

'Ah, but that's the thing with employees,' Davey replied, leaning closer. 'You can work for *other* companies.'

She watched him carefully.

'When Jimmy stopped me, when I was walking the dog, he said "my man Chow will send more details." Yet we didn't get anything else from you, did we? Almost as if you didn't want us to solve it. Almost as if you had your own agenda.'

Chow didn't answer but simply nodded at the room.

'The office is yours to look at,' he said. 'The police have already looked.'

'I didn't think they wouldn't,' Tinker said. 'Was it Delgado?'

Chow gave a curt nod, and Tinker sighed, opening the door and entering Jimmy Tsang's office. Before Davey did, however, Chow stopped her.

'Mister Tsang heard crows,' he said. 'Four caws. Bad sign.'

'Crows in Chinatown?'

'I thought the same,' Chow entered the office now and walked to the window. There, to the side of the blinds was a small black speaker.

'Bluetooth,' he said. 'Rubbish music quality, but enough to make someone think there was a crow outside.'

'But it'd have to be done by someone nearby,' Davey looked back at him. 'An app on a phone.'

'There was a dealer from the Jasmine Casino here at the time,' Chow replied. 'She knows Kenneth Tsang.'

'You think she played crow caws to play with Jimmy's superstitious nature?'

Chow shrugged.

'Not my problem,' he said. 'Maybe Mister Tsang heard a real crow. I just thought you should know. Most of the Jasmine are paid for by Kenneth Tsang.'

This said, he left them alone, stepping back to the door like some bulky temple guard. The office itself didn't take long to go through, though. There wasn't much to see, and Tinker was aware that the moment Jimmy was hit by a car, someone would have been sent into the office to remove anything illegal or incriminating.

The door to the side behind the desk was more intriguing.

There was a line of police tape across it, likely placed there by an overzealous officer wanting to ensure his fellow officers knew something was inside.

Opening it, they walked in.

The room was a shrine. Ancestors and deity statues adorned the area, with an altar at the back. There were spirit tablets, one of which had been snapped in half, and the statues were draped in red paper, with some bound in red thread.

Chow had followed them in, and from his expression, Tinker could deduce this wasn't new to him.

'Do you know about the curse?' Davey asked.

'I know Jimmy believed he was cursed,' Chow replied. 'If that's what you mean.'

'Do you know who could have cast the curse?' Tinker asked, noticing Davey now examining the items, her latex gloves already on and moving through the altar.

'I believe it was the Irish woman, Luana Flanagan,' Chow

said. 'I've heard from others that she had procured a cursed item from her homeland that they used to bind to Jimmy.'

'Do you believe that?'

Chow paused for a long moment, then shook his head.

'No,' he replied. 'But it doesn't matter that I don't believe. What matters is that *Jimmy* did.'

'How did he know he was cursed?' Davey asked from the altar, examining a stone tablet. 'When you're cursed, you don't instantly think, "Oh, I must be cursed." Something must have been said for him to know this.'

'I get where you're going with this,' Chow nodded. 'Yes, Jimmy was informed that a curse had been placed on him. An informant came and told him what had happened.'

'And what was that?'

'That Luana Flanagan had attached a cursed item using an Irish Witch whose mother had originally gained the item. The term was "magician", but it can be used for many things.'

Tinker accepted this.

'Okay, so you know Luana Flanagan placed a curse. What did this informant tell you after that?'

'They told us that the curse had been placed by Luana Flanagan using Irish mystics at her command, and they knew somebody who could stop it.'

'So who was that?'

'Your boss,' Chow replied simply. 'We were told to contact Ellie Reckless.'

'To break the curse?' Tinker was surprised by this.

'No,' Chow almost laughed. 'Your boss might be powerful, but she cannot defeat ancestors.'

'I didn't think you believed.'

'I don't believe in the curse,' Chow replied earnestly. 'But I do believe mortals cannot define what happens on the astral plane. We were told that Ellie Reckless would be the best person to find the Irish Witch that did this, and get it removed. Yes, I was told to send you more information, and yes, I delayed this for my own reasons. But, before you managed to find her, however, the Irish Witch tried a more human way to remove Jimmy Tsang.'

'The car accident,' Tinker said.

Chow nodded.

'The car accident,' he repeated.

'Tell us about it.'

'I've already told the police.'

'But we're not the police,' Davey said.

'You said you were a copper.'

'That was in the past tense,' Davey corrected. 'Tell us what you told them, and I'll tell you how to break the curse.'

Chow considered the offer, then nodded.

'Zoey Park,' he began. 'She's more than a magician. Our contact explained she was the "Queen of Conjuring" – a gypsy mystic whose family was part of a long line of Irish Witches.'

'So, what? Zoey Park had the power to curse and to break it?'

'She worked on behalf of Flanagan to do this.'

'How do you know it was Flanagan?'

'I told you, we were informed. Her mother bequeathed cursed chains to her, and she used those as a debt to Flanagan.'

'No, I get you were informed,' Tinker said. 'But you've just also said Zoey Park was the one who did the curse, and Park and Flanagan don't like each other. Who told you that Flanagan was behind all of this?'

'A rival.'

'To you?'

'No, to Flanagan. Someone who wanted to make sure that Flanagan paid for her sins.'

'Could this rival have been lying to fulfil their own agenda?'

'It doesn't matter,' Chow made the slightest of shrugging motions. 'Jimmy believed, and that's all that he cared about.'

'Did your informer give a name?'

Chow looked uncomfortable at this.

'If she told her name to Jimmy, I would not know. I was not worthy enough to be in those conversations.'

'Would you recognise her if you saw her?' Davey asked, looking up.

'Yes,' Chow replied. 'I would indeed.'

Tinker heard a beep from her phone. Looking down, she saw it was a message from Ellie.

Reading it, her eyes narrowed.

'Can you hold on a moment?' she asked Chow, dialling a number. 'Casey, it's Tinker. Did you get the text?'

She looked at Davey, who was now looking at her own phone, her eyes widening,

'Great. Can you send me the photo of the person she just mentioned?'

Tinker disconnected the call and looked back at Chow.

'I think we might know who your informer is,' she said as she glanced over at Davey, who was back to looking at the statues. 'Anything?'

'This thread isn't anything special.' Davey looked back up from the broken tablet. 'I can dust for fingerprints, but the police have already done that. Apart from seeing that Jimmy is a little religious and a little bit paranoid about the ancestors, and someone used Bluetooth to screw with him, there's nothing really I can ...'

She trailed off as Tinker's phone beeped again. Tinker opened the email and zoomed in on the image that Casey had just sent.

Holding it up, she turned back to Chow.

'Is this the person who told you?' she said.

Chow looked at the image and nodded.

'That is the informant,' he said.

'Has she ever been in this room?'

'Several times,' he admitted. 'Jimmy would allow her full access. He believed she was his own personal Irish Witch.'

'Why would he believe that?'

'Because she too had Gypsy heritage. She had stolen the item from Flanagan in the first place and was making amends.'

Tinker wanted to scream.

'Look, there's nothing more we can do here,' she said. 'Chow, I can tell you now there is no curse on your boss, because the item that they used isn't real. Now we're starting to work out who exactly is playing this game.'

'Before we leave, though, tell me about the car park,' Davey asked.

Chow turned back to face her.

'What would you like to know?' he asked.

'You sent us footage showing the accident,' Davey said. 'CCTV camera in the car park itself. I was curious how public it was?'

'It's public,' Chow replied. 'But the lower floor is purely for owners of buildings and businesses in the area. So you can't go down there without a pass.'

'Where would you get a pass?'

'You're given one when you buy or rent a location.'

'How did Jimmy get his?'

Chow frowned at the question and Tinker, knowing where Davey was going with this, leant forward.

'Jimmy didn't buy a business, and he doesn't own anything here,' she said. 'Yet his car was downstairs.'

'He used Benny's pass,' Chow replied. 'Both Kenny and Benny had them from when they were here. Kenny's is with him, I suppose. Benny's ... well, it wasn't being used anymore.'

'So realistically, Kenny could have driven down there and attacked his cousin?'

'He could have, but we know where he was that night,' Chow waved the question away. 'He was talking to your thief, remember?'

Davey hadn't finished.

'How many cameras are down there?' she asked.

'Three or four,' Chow replied. 'Not many. Because of the passes, it wasn't classed as such an important thing.'

'The route to the exit goes past one of these?'

'Yes.'

'Do you find it strange, then,' Davey started, 'that Jimmy would have been hit by a car almost in front of one of these cameras?'

'Jimmy always parked near the cameras,' Chow shook his head. 'He said it was a way to know that if somebody did go for his car, he would know who did it.'

'Did everybody know this?'

'I assume he told some people, but it wasn't common knowledge.'

He paused.

'He ran from the car like he saw a ghost. A few feet on he

stopped, though. We heard the faint caw of a crow. It was enough to pause him long enough for the car to hit him.'

Davey nodded.

'So, somebody who hits Jimmy—'

'You mean Zoey Park,' Chow interrupted.

'Whoever hit Jimmy Tsang,' Davey doubled down, 'had to have had a pass to get into that car park; had to know roughly when Jimmy would be leaving; had a Bluetooth speaker like the one up here set in a particular spot, and timed their attack to pause him there. Then hit him just before they passed the camera, knowing they'd be seen. Does that not strike you as strange?'

Davey leant closer to Chow now, as if watching him for a lie.

'If I was going to get into this car park and kill someone, I'd make damn sure I hid my face,' she finished. 'Zoey Park isn't an assassin.'

'No, she's not,' Chow smiled. 'She's a magician who does tricks on the internet and in small theatres. Maybe she's not intelligent enough to understand how this works?'

'But you would?' Davey asked. 'Understand how murder works?'

Chow just stared at her.

'I do not talk about my work for the Tsang Empire,' he snarled. 'So, you would be wise to change your questioning.'

They started towards the door, back into Jimmy Tsang's office. But before they reached it, Tinker looked back at the Chinese bodyguard.

'One more question,' she said. 'You didn't answer us earlier. You worked for Benny and Kenny for years, and you've only been working for Jimmy for months. If Kenny made a play, would you join him?'

Chow smiled; it was a humourless, tight-lipped one, the kind of smile that a serial killer would give before ending another life.

'Who says I haven't already?' he replied.

Tinker didn't know if he was joking or not, so she nodded, shook his hand as a farewell, and left the building with Davey.

'There was something,' Davey said. 'In the back room.'

'What was it?' Tinker asked.

Davey pulled out a clear bag with a torn silver wristband inside.

'I snatched it on the way out. It was on the floor beside the altar. I think it fell out of a pocket.'

Tinker examined the wristband through the bag, nodding.

'That confirms it,' she said. 'At the moment, I think we need to find out what Ellie wants to do next. Because if she's going after this informant, we might have to stop her from killing someone.'

'If Ramsey doesn't kill her first,' Davey replied. 'And he's closer.'

RAMSEY ALLEN WAS INDEED THE CLOSEST TO THE Wunderland theme park on the South Bank, so after leaving the Piccadilly Theatre he'd bypassed the Brasserie Zédel, messaging Casey instead to call them as he headed over to Leicester Square and caught a taxi to Waterloo. This done, he headed towards Jubilee Gardens and, once through the Wunderland entrance, he walked through the park like a man with purpose, storming up to the VIP entrance he'd visited with Ellie the previous day.

One of the guards who had seen him then, now on his own at the gate, held up a hand.

'Sorry, granddad,' he said. 'You know the rules, only people with wristbands can come in.'

He was going to continue, but his voice faded as Ramsey drew closer, his face a mask of fury.

'The bloody place hasn't opened up yet and the bar isn't open,' he hissed. 'I need to speak to the woman behind the bar. Until she starts serving drinks, this VIP place is just a piece of bloody grass with a fence around it and a jobsworth guard in the way. So are you going to let me in or am I going to have to do something worse?'

The guard hadn't expected such a response and paused, eyeing Ramsey up and down.

'What is your connection to that woman?' he said. 'We saw you chatting with her yesterday.'

Ramsey slumped now, his anger seeping away as he wiped a tear from his cheek.

'It's personal,' he said. 'I'm sorry, I didn't mean to snap. But it's a family matter.'

'What sort of matter?' The guard, realising there was more to this was leaning closer now, caught in the story.

'It's personal between me and my estranged daughter,' Ramsey said, looking through to check the bar, the glance now a pointed end to the sentence, and one the guard now noted. 'I only have a few months, and time, well ...'

The guard, guessing what Ramsey was alluding to, paused, then nodded.

'I can give you two minutes with your daughter,' he said,

checking his watch. 'But the place opens in ten and you need to be out.'

'That's all I need,' Ramsey replied with a smile, grabbing the guard's hand and pumping it wildly. 'Thank you.'

Bypassing the guard, he walked up to the bar where Veronica Carter was preparing for the day's events, another barman further down the bar.

When she looked up and saw him her face darkened.

'Hello, Mister Allen,' she said, and Ramsey noted the use of his name. When they'd come by the previous day, only Ellie had given her name.

'Hello, Veronica,' he replied. 'Or should I say Mary? I think we need to have a little chat somewhere, don't you?'

23

MASKED MAGICIANS

AS FAR AS CASEY WAS CONCERNED, SCRUBBING THROUGH A KEY logger text file wasn't exactly the most exciting of hacking work. But it wasn't the most taxing of hacking work either. So, while his computer put it into some semblance of order, Casey moved on to the next part of his job; finding out what was truly going on in Brasserie Zédel across the street.

Using a voice modulator, he'd called the bar. This AI voice modulator, freely available from most dark web sites, allowed him to convince the manager he was older than he truly was, a patron from two nights earlier who wanted to hire "Joe Kerr," after seeing his close-up table magic. The manager was eager to pass the details along; a mobile number to contact his manager. He also gave a very detailed account of how "Joe Kerr" would come in at eight in the evening and perform magic for an hour, take a break for half an hour, and then continue on until the end of the night, two or three nights every week – depending on his day-job work-load – for a percentage of the takings and any tips he received.

It was pretty much what they'd been told – this wasn't Joseph's job; it was more a fun hobby he enjoyed, but even so, Casey played a hunch.

'Hang on a second,' he said, his voice sounding far deeper and older than he was. 'You're saying he was there from nine onwards? He was gone for a good half an hour when we were there two nights ago. We watched him leave. Does he do this a lot? Should we be worried if we do hire him?'

'Oh no,' the manager replied. 'I mean yes he left, but no, you shouldn't worry. His usual hours are what I said. But two nights ago, there was an urgent call from his mother around nine forty-five, and he had to disappear for half an hour. He did tell me about the call, though, and he was back once his personal issue was sorted. If you were there until the end, you'd have seen he did finish the evening.'

Casey thanked the manager and looked back at his notes once he disconnected the call. Joseph Kerrigan had walked out of Brasserie Zédel about ten minutes before Zoey Park started her finale. From the looks of things, he'd returned about ten minutes after everything went wrong there. Plenty of time to run across the road, climb up into that seat on the gallery and film the scene.

His next call was to Lenny Clarence.

'Who's this?' Lenny asked, sounding suspicious at the "Caller ID Withheld" he'd likely have seen appeared on his phone.

'Lenny, I was given your details by Nicky Simpson,' Casey replied, using the AI modulator now to give him an older, gruffer voice, with the slightest Irish lilt in the tone.

Lenny's voice suddenly changed, the suspicion now gone, replaced by a curiosity whether this was an offer of more work.

'Oh yes?'

'Yeah, I'm looking for somebody who can work on videos,' Casey said. 'Nicky told me that you did an awesome job on the Zoey Park video that came up yesterday. What in the world—'

'You mean "where" in the world?' Lenny corrected.

Casey grinned, playing along. He knew once he had Lenny feeling he was superior in the call, his suspicion as to this stranger on the other end would lower.

Well, for the moment, at least.

'Yeah, that's the one. Nicky showed me how you'd done some filters on it.'

'How would Nicky know this?'

Casey sounded wistful.

'You didn't know? The two of them were shacking up last night,' he chuckled. 'We were really impressed by how you were able to take the footage, zoom in, and make it look grainy. We're guessing you used a long lens and a high-definition 4K camera to get the shots. But how did you manage to get it from such an angle? I was told by Nicky you're acrophobic.'

Lenny's voice changed, sounding wary.

'Who are you?'

'All you need to know is I represent a certain Irish family who's very unhappy with what you've been doing,' Casey replied, trying to be assertive.

There was a pause before Lenny finally said, 'You're a Flanagan.'

Casey waited, allowing the moment to fall out. As long as he didn't speak, Lenny's own imagination would fill in the blanks.

'I didn't do anything wrong, I swear,' he eventually said.

'I didn't say you had,' Casey replied, the AI modulator still making his voice sound like a gruff Irishman. 'Although I'd like to know a little more—'

'Look, I think you should really speak to him.'

For the first time, Casey felt thrown. He didn't know who the "him" was here.

'Why would I speak to him?' he asked, as he mentally shuffled through his list of male suspects. If Joseph Kerrigan had taken the video, there was every chance that it was Kerrigan who'd sent it to Lenny. Was this the "him" he spoke about?'

'I was just given the card,' Lenny continued, still nervous.

'Okay, so you weren't part of the plan to focus on certain people on the stage and leave others out?'

'No, no, God, no,' Lenny replied. 'I was just told to follow the notes.'

Casey considered this. He didn't know how to play the next line.

Because if he said the wrong name, he knew everything would go wrong.

'How did he get you the video?' he said. 'I mean, it was filmed by Joe Kerrigan, right?'

'Yeah, I'm aware it was filmed by Joe,' Lenny said dismissively, now back on familiar ground. 'The guy can't hold a camera to save his life. I didn't have to do much on the change-arounds with the shuddering effect as he bounced it all over the bloody place, but God, I had to really focus on some of the scenes he'd missed out on.'

Casey kept quiet, and Lenny naturally carried on.

'But when he sent it to me, he had a list of things that needed to be seen, and gave me everything I needed. He told me where to upload it, too.'

'You shouldn't put your tones at the start of it,' Casey said angrily, hoping to scare a little more out of the man. 'The police have worked out that you made the video.'

'Yeah, but they can't prove anything,' Lenny said. 'All I'll say is I was told to do it. You know, Jacob is Zoey's partner, and it was just a bit of press and PR.'

Casey did an invisible fist pump.

Jacob.

But that didn't fit with what Ramsey had just sent back from his conversation that morning with the man – he'd claimed he knew nothing.

Why was Jacob lying?

'You did well,' he said, desperately trying to keep the eagerness out of his voice. 'Keep quiet until one of us calls you.'

'How will I know if it's one of—'

'You will know,' Casey said mysteriously, 'when we turn up on your doorstep.'

He disconnected the call, leaning back in his chair.

Joe Kerrigan had filmed the scene – that he was now sure of. He had snuck out of Brasserie Zédel in the middle of his show, hurried across the road, sat in that seat and filmed the final trick before leaving, returning to his show as if nothing had happened. At some point, he had passed the SD card over to Jacob, who would then send it on with important notes to Lenny Clarence.

The question was, were the two of them working together? Or had this been some kind of scam on Joe – or on Jacob? And how was Zoey involved in this, if at all?

There was movement to the side, and Casey looked up to see Robert standing in the doorway. He seemed a little better than he had been the previous time he'd been out of his office, a little more relaxed, but more resigned to the situation.

'Ellie just called,' he said. 'We're meeting down in the diner.'

'Good,' Casey said. 'I've got something. Have we heard back from Tinker and Davey?'

Robert nodded, but it was a tight-lipped, narrow-eyed one.

'Davey reckons she's got a clue about something to do with these Zoey appearances,' he said. 'What it is, I don't know. I'm sure she'll dazzle us with her intelligence later on.'

'I'm starting to think you're not enjoying this,' Casey said.

'This?' At the line, Robert actually laughed. 'How could one not enjoy this up and down life we have?'

His smile faded though, as he looked out into the corridor. Casey glanced after him, but couldn't see anything out there worth staring at, and realised Robert was miles away right now.

After a moment, Robert shook his head and forced another smile.

'Don't worry about me,' he smiled, but it was a fake one for the crowd. 'I'll be fine when it comes up. Time for my close-up. Let's just get this fixed, finished, and move on. Any news on the key logger Nicky Simpson gave us?'

Casey shook his head.

'The problem with key loggers,' he explained, 'is that they only record the keys. If you're using a mouse, or a stream deck or anything else, like shortcut key commands that set macro commands off, we don't see it.'

At this, Robert nodded knowledgeably, and Casey wondered whether he was just making the motions, without a clue of what the young man was talking about.

'Does it at least give us an idea of why she was on the laptop at three in the morning?'

'So, she gets up in the middle of the night,' Casey explained, opening up the key logger text file and checking it. 'She opens up Nicky Simpson's laptop. She checks her emails.'

'You see the keys for this?'

Casey nodded, pointing at a line of text.

'Right there, it tells us she has a Gmail account, with a password address, but I'm not really happy about going into it,' he replied, almost sheepishly.

'Am I sensing morals from you, young Casey?' Robert faked a shocked expression.

Casey shrugged.

'If it's a criminal or some kind of dodgy Corporation, I don't mind doing it,' he said. 'But Zoey was nice to me, and she's in trouble. I feel a little off checking her emails.'

'But you're happy to look at every keystroke she made?'

'That was given to me by someone else. That wasn't an act on my behalf,' Casey looked back at the screen. 'You're a lawyer. Surely you understand this.'

'So, tell me what she did,' Robert decided to change the subject.

'She checked her emails. She didn't reply to anything, so she was obviously just having a look. Then she typed in the web address of a magic forum, she typed in her password and user ID—'

'Did she go on a particular thread?'

'I don't know.' Casey rubbed at his chin as he stared harder at the lines of text, as if hoping they'd give him more. 'That's the problem with key loggers. As I said, if she clicked on a thread, or clicked on a button that started a new thread, it's blank to me. Unless she actively searched, which she didn't, I can't see it. All I know is she typed in a message on this forum, but it was just about magic tricks.'

'Well it is a magic forum.'

'Exactly. She was asking about a large trick she's looking to do on tour involving flash paper,' Casey continued. 'She wasn't too sure what accelerants to play with to get the best result for a long-term burn. It was completely irrelevant to what was happening in her life right then. About five minutes later, she typed one word, "thanks," and then probably deleted all of her browser history, because the only other button she presses is the power one.'

'That's it? I was expecting more.'

'No,' Casey said. 'Sorry. She literally asked about a magic trick then left it. I searched the site for any of the words she used, but no threads came up, so she probably deleted it as soon as she got an answer. It's an LA based site connected to the Magic Castle in Los Angeles, so maybe she was doing it then to catch someone on Pacific time.'

'So, she deleted the thread because ...'

'Maybe she didn't want to draw attention, maybe she didn't want someone to steal the trick ...'

Casey shrugged as he closed the laptop, sticking it in his backpack.

'All I can guess is that she couldn't sleep and had been discussing this new trick before the show that went wrong, so decided to get it out of the way.'

'It was worth a try,' Robert sighed. 'Come on, let's get to the diner.'

ELLIE WAS IN THE DINER WHEN THEY ARRIVED, SITTING AT HER favourite booth with a sense of triumph on her face. Casey wondered if she'd waited for the booth, or simply strong-armed someone out. But either way, Ellie was relaxed.

Scarily relaxed, in fact.

Tinker was sitting beside her.

'I thought you were off with Davey doing something?' he asked.

'Davey's gone back to the office,' Tinker said. 'She realised a couple of things while we were at Jimmy Tsang's office, and she wanted to check some things.'

Robert frowned.

'I didn't see her in her office,' he said. 'We've literally just walked past it.'

'Not the office you gave her,' Tinker smiled. 'She requisi-tioned a storeroom.'

'Why would she requisition a storeroom?'

Tinker looked to Ellie, who patiently placed her hands on the table and looked up at Robert.

'Because if you have somebody examining a life-size doll of somebody, to the point where they're slicing into it – perhaps with scalpels – the last thing you want is glass windows,' she said.

Robert reddened.

'Fair point,' he said. 'I hadn't considered that. So will she be down?'

'She said she wanted to prove a point,' Tinker said. 'I presume she'll be back any second now.'

Casey settled into his seat, pulling his laptop out.

'What do we have?' he asked. 'I'm guessing by you calling us in, you know something more?'

'We know that Zoey Park's mum is alive,' Ellie nodded. 'We spoke to her yesterday. Ramsey's bringing her in now.'

'You and Ramsey spoke to ...' Casey trailed off as he realised what she was saying. 'Oh, well, that changes everything.'

'Yes and no,' Ellie replied. 'But it makes us wonder who's playing who here, because we're getting to the point where we need to know whose side *we're* playing on.'

She looked up at the main entrance and her eyes widened.

Casey couldn't help himself; he glanced around to see what she was looking at, and was surprised to see Zoey Park walking through the door to the diner.

She wore a black hoodie, hiding most of her hair and face, but it was obviously her.

However, as she arrived, there was something slightly wrong with the image, something that became more obvious when Zoey Park walked up to the table, pulled off her hood, and then tore off her own face to reveal the smiling redheaded features of Joanne Davey.

'All right, guys?' Davey said as she tossed the silicone face-mask of Zoey Park onto the table. 'So, I've been having a little play around, and I think I know what happened.'

24

THE TRUTH

ELLIE STARED DOWN AT THE FACE MASK OF ZOEY PARK.

'I'm guessing this is from the doll?' she asked.

'It's why I had to have a check,' Davey nodded. 'I thought it might have been this when I started looking at the CCTV again.'

'What about the CCTV made you think this?' Casey asked, staring in horror at it.

Davey replied by tapping the side of the face.

'See here?' she asked, finally sitting down at the booth and waving to Sandra to come over. 'There's no graze, no scratch, no plaster with the bumblebee on it. Look at the CCTV that we were sent of the accident with Jimmy Tsang.'

Casey brought it up on his laptop.

'It's grainy because they zoomed in on it to show that Zoey Park was driving,' Davey explained to everyone. 'But what it also shows is that this Zoey didn't have a plaster on—'

'A plaster that she got earlier that day, and was wearing in the morning that I came to pick her up,' Tinker said, realising where Davey was going with this.

Davey smiled as she nodded, grateful that someone got this.

'Ramsey reckons he saw Zoey in the gantries above him,' Ellie said. 'We'll hear from him when he arrives, on whether the "Zoey" he saw had a mark or not.'

'I had a look at the CCTV camera footage that Casey found in Joe's house, too', Davey added. 'The masked and hooded Zoey we see there didn't have the grazes or plaster either—'

'That was before the accident she had in Covent Garden,' Tinker said.

'Yeah, but there was still something off, especially when she looked up at the camera,' Davey replied. 'It was a deliberate close up, like she wanted to be recognised. If you know what you're looking for, you can see there's a slight double image around the eyes where the real eyes are looking through eye holes.'

'They were wearing this mask,' Ellie picked up the face, staring at it. It felt surreal. The image was absolutely lifelike. 'Well, the other one, anyway. Somebody put Zoey Park's mask on to place the fake Zoey Park's body down.'

'Yes,' Davey replied. 'Chronologically, somebody broke into her lockup and stole the duplicate, which was probably dumped in a corner and forgotten, took the face off in the same way that I have – it's quite easy, it's fixed over a mannequin body – wore it with some kind of mask or hoodie on to hide the seams, went into Zoey and Joe's house, and set the scene.'

'It wouldn't be Joe, he's too large.'

'Likewise Jacob,' Tinker mused. 'Flanagan's built like a brick shithouse, I don't think it would have been her.'

'Still leaves us a list we need to narrow down,' Ellie said, looking around the table at the others. 'Casey, what did you find out?'

'Joe Kerrigan was performing at Brasserie Zédel the night of the accident finale,' Casey replied. 'We all know that. What we didn't know until today is that he disappeared for half an hour at roughly the same time that the accident happened. I checked with the staff at the Piccadilly; there's still a few working today, and they said Joe has an open invite whenever the two seats in the royal circle are empty to come and watch the show. When I spoke to Lenny Clarence, he said he'd been given the files by Jacob, but that Joe was the one who had filmed it. He even mocked his technique, before he said Jacob had told him exactly how they wanted it made.'

'They probably gave the poor bastard the impression it was some kind of promotional video,' Robert muttered darkly.

'Exactly. That's what he said, and at no point did he think he was helping any kind of criminal act. I spoke to Ramsey after he spoke to Jacob, and he said Jacob claimed to not know anything, which, if Lenny's telling the truth, shows Jacob to be a liar.'

Ellie nodded at the new information.

'So now we know Joe and Jacob are working together,' she said. 'What else do we know—'

She stopped as the door to the diner opened once more, and Ramsey walked in with Veronica Carter.

No, not Veronica Carter.

He was now walking in with *Mary Park.*

She looked like she didn't want to be there, and Ellie understood exactly why. They walked over to the booth, and everybody shuffled over so the two could sit down.

'I want you to know I'm here willingly,' Mary said. 'He didn't have to bring me.'

Ellie glanced quickly at Ramsey, who gave her a "whatever" kind of shrug.

'So, do you want to tell me what was going on?' she asked, looking back at Mary, who was observing her.

'First, tell me how you knew who I was,' Mary asked. 'I've been so careful.'

'Mama Lumetta says hi,' Ellie said as an answer, and Mary slumped back into the chair.

'The bitch,' she sighed.

Ellie nodded.

'I'll be honest, though, all we know is that Mama Lumetta helped you change your identity,' she said. 'I have no idea what else you've been doing.'

'Can I at least get a coffee?'

'Order yourself anything off the menu,' Ramsey smiled as Sandra approached. 'I'm having a twenty-seven with a tea.'

Sandra nodded, but as she turned to go away, Davey raised her hand.

'I'd like to have a twenty-seven as well, please,' she said.

'You don't even know what a twenty-seven is,' Ramsey quipped.

'True, but if you can eat it with your fragile old man stomach, I'm sure I'll be fine.'

Sandra took the rest of the food and drinks orders, mainly a couple of slices of toast and a bowl of fries for Casey, and then walked off.

'What do you want to know?' Mary asked.

'How's your relationship with your daughter right now?'

Mary looked as if she wanted to spit on the floor. She didn't, but the expression was one of disgust.

'My daughter,' she said, 'thinks I'm dead. So as far as I'm concerned, I don't have one.'

'Yet you were on stage with her two nights ago,' Ellie replied calmly. 'How did that come about?'

'Anna Lever called,' Mary explained. 'She needed me to be there. She knew I was a good pair of hands and could provide cover if there was a problem.'

'Why two nights ago in particular?'

Mary leant back in the booth.

'Before I tell you that, let me explain what happened before that,' she said. 'Because otherwise you don't have context.'

She steepled her fingers in front of her, elbows on the table, and she rested them against her face for a moment, working out how to explain this.

'I used to work for Luana Flanagan,' she said. 'I was everywhere. I performed escapology, sleight of hand, anything I could learn. I performed, and I was good. I was really good. Then Flanagan took the credit for every trick I created, including the one with the chains.'

'Chains?' Ellie asked.

'Cú Chulainn's chains. Flanagan claimed her family had had them for generations, most likely since the poor bugger chained himself to a stone, probably. There was likely a Flanagan back then, sneaking up behind him, ready to nick them from the corpse before anybody else turned up.'

'Did everyone know about these?'

'Christ, yeah. Part of Flanagan's act as the "Queen of Conjuring" was to have these chains tied around her in an escapology act. We were travelling around Ireland at the time, and the mythology of the story made it into a fantastic trick. She even performed the story chained to a stone on the stage. As people prepared to attack her – but this time with rifles rather than spears – a cloth would come down over her as the guns would fire. She was reenacting the scene, you see, where Cú Chulainn was tied to the stone, and one by one, people would try to kill him until he eventually died.'

She looked up at the ceiling, watching the fan slowly turn in circles.

'It wasn't really stone; it was wood made to look like marble, but that's show business for you. You'd see the bullets go through the cloth, and then it'd be brought down, and she'd be gone. She had escaped.'

'Let me guess, there was a pathway out the back?'

'Oh no,' Mary replied. 'She was still hiding in the bloody stone. As I said, it wasn't real, just made to look real. She took the chains off, slipped inside, the gunshots went off.'

'She wasn't scared about being shot through the wood?'

'Flanagan wasn't afraid of being shot, she'd had it happen in real life enough times,' Mary chuckled. 'She'd covered the inside with metal around the areas the bullets would hit, and used very small calibre bullets. It was all about the visual side of it, you know. But I created the trick; I was small enough, I could do it quickly. But as it built up in popularity, Flanagan wanted it for herself. So she took it.'

'What about the chains?'

'Picked them up from some scrap yard in Shannon,' Mary spat. 'Cú Chulainn was never chained; he was tied. But why let the truth get in the way of a good story?'

She gratefully accepted a coffee that was passed over by Sandra, sipping at it as she considered her next words.

'I'd had enough, and I'd met a guy. He worked with the animals that often came along with the shows. We decided to leave, get away, as I was pregnant at the time. I went public about the trick, pointed out the chains weren't real. I spoke out against Flanagan and she didn't like it because people started asking questions. The Flanagans have been talking about this priceless artefact for hundreds of years, and here was this girl saying they'd been found in a scrapyard? It didn't go down well.'

'I bet it didn't. What did you do?'

'Ran like hell to Birmingham,' Mary laughed. 'We were young. We were immortal. But then a few years after Zoey was born, when she was maybe ten I think, Michael, that's her father, he left and found a job on a farm or something. I can't even remember. All I remember is he disappeared from our lives, and even before that, it hadn't been easy. We were doing whatever we could to make ends meet, and I was finding it tough.'

'So when did you return to Flanagan?'

'Around then,' Mary replied. 'I had a message from her telling me she had a job for me. I thought I'd hidden myself, but it wasn't good enough. She wanted to start the trick again. She felt enough time had gone past, and people had forgotten the lies that I had told.'

She chuckled at this.

'I had nothing, but she promised bygones were bygones, and came up with a large cash offer. So, I turned up.'

'What about Zoey?' Ramsey asked.

At this, Mary looked down at the floor.

'I'm not a good person,' she said. 'I grew up under the influence of Flanagan, and I was selfish. I was *so* selfish. I wanted to believe this was an opportunity to be great again. Once more, I could be in the spotlight. I could make enough money to bring Zoey back because she was in London at the time with me, so I just left, packed my bags, told Zoey I'd be back shortly.'

'You left her alone?' Davey asked, horrified.

'I'm not that much of a monster,' Mary snapped back. 'I had a plan. When I was gone, she was being looked after by a friend of the family. But I didn't know that the friend would die within a year, and Zoey would be left alone and thrown into the system. But by then, I was too far gone.'

'What do you mean?' Ellie asked.

'Flanagan lied to me,' Mary replied. 'She deliberately set me up. She hadn't forgotten what I'd done, and now she had American Irish wanting to buy the chains for good money, a quarter of a million dollars.'

'But she couldn't sell them because they weren't real.'

'No,' she continued. 'But she could *insure* them. Not with official insurers; they'd need provenance and things like that, but there was enough story behind it to claim they were real, and, as far as she was concerned, she could make her money from these people. Powerful moneylenders who worked with the people she worked for. So, she brought me in to do the trick. But one day I turned up, and there was Gardai everywhere. The police were looking around and, when I asked what was going on, I was told that the night before I'd stolen the chains.'

She sniffed, picking up a napkin and wiping her nose, dabbing at her eyes as tears appeared.

'I was so full of drugs that night,' she said. 'I don't know what I was on when I blacked out – I couldn't remember a thing – and now I'm being told that I'd stolen the chains. I didn't have them; the police couldn't find them, and although they couldn't prove I'd taken them, I couldn't prove I *hadn't*.

But everybody who worked for Flanagan said they'd seen me do it.'

'But they had no proof,' Ramsey finished the line.

'No. I couldn't be arrested or charged. Flanagan fired me the same day, left me with nothing. My reputation, all I'd built, that was gone. I was thrown onto the streets of Dublin.'

'So, with this investigated, Flanagan could claim it was theft?'

'Fairly simply if I'm being honest. They gave her money, but not the full amount, because again, there was nothing to prove. She was angry. She thought she was going to get a bumper payout, and all she got was a pittance, not much more than she would have made doing the tricks, anyway.'

Mary shuddered, sipping at the drink again.

'She found me, and she told me she was going to take it out of my hide. I owed her a debt now, almost two-hundred grand of lost sale profits, and if I didn't pay it off, she'd kill Zoey, make me watch her as she did it. I realised my only way to save my daughter was to fake my death.'

'Flanagan sounds like a fun person to be near,' Ramsey muttered. 'Must be fun at parties.'

'I had made friends with people in Dublin before this, and one of them, Matteo Lumetta, introduced me to his mother and explained my problem. They spoke to a contact they had in London.'

'What was the contact's name?' Ramsey asked.

'Annabelle Lever,' Mary replied.

'So, Lever was your contact in England?' Ramsey added.

'Lever arranged for me to have a new life, a new identity, but first, I had to fake my death,' Mary nodded. 'So I was publicly seen at *Durty Nellies*, the pub beside Bunratty Castle, loudly proclaiming how I hated everyone, wanted to end it all, things like that. The following day, I was found dead of an overdose.'

She blew her nose on a napkin.

'I say I was found; there was no body, and the coroner was paid to say it happened,' she continued. 'But at that point, "Mary Park" died, and "Veronica Llewellyn" came to life. I moved to London, but I knew I could never see my daughter again.'

'Why?' Ellie asked.

'Because I was dead, and if I appeared again, Flanagan would find her and kill her,' Mary snapped. 'It was better that she was left alone. Then, a few years after that, I got married. Jerome Carter, my husband's a lovely guy; he doesn't know any of this.'

Mary reached across and stole one of Casey's fries – he didn't stop her.

'But then I saw Zoey on TV. She was a spitting image of me when I was her age, doing these tricks with such skill. I cried; I was so proud. But I couldn't tell anybody she was my daughter.'

'Did you try to find her?' Casey now asked.

Mary nodded.

'I found out where she was, and I decided I should meet her. Anna had promised to find a way of getting through to her. Zoey had worked as a street performer for a while, and Anna had kept an eye on her over the years. But Anna told me it'd be a bad idea. If she realised I was alive, Zoey wouldn't be able to stop herself from going for Flanagan ...'

She looked away, her face darkening.

'Worse than that, she might tell me she never wanted to see me, and I didn't know if I could take that. Zoey believed I'd left her for dead, which I had. She didn't understand that

Flanagan's threats had forced me to try to save her life. As far as she was concerned, I was self-centred and gone, and it was best I left it that way.'

Before Ellie could add anything, Sandra wandered over, passing across some cups of tea and a Coke for Casey.

'I see your friend's on TV,' she said, nodding at a small flat-screen television on the wall by the "kitchen" area. The sound was off, and it was set to *"Peter Morris in the Afternoon,"* the chat show Ellie had been on recently herself.

She grimaced at the memory, but could see on the screen that Peter was talking; behind him was an image of Zoey Park.

'That can't be good,' she said as she rose. 'That can't be good at all.'

25

PM IN THE PM

RISING, ELLIE WALKED OVER TO THE TELEVISION.

'Ali, do you mind if I ...' she asked, nodding at the TV.

Ali, the owner of the restaurant and working at the hot plate, nodded, waving at the remote beside the television as she turned it up.

'Joined today by Zoey Park's manager, Claudette Storm,' Peter was smiling into the camera, pulled back to show Claudette sitting beside Jacob Morrison and Luana Flanagan, the three of them relaxed as if nothing was wrong in their lives.

'So tell me more,' Peter said as he looked back at them. 'Where in the World is Zoey Park?'

There was a smattering of laughter from the audience, and Ellie knew from experience this was a man with a card telling them to clap, laugh or cheer.

'We don't know,' Claudette smiled. 'After her last magical trick, she simply disappeared.' There was more laughter from the audience, and Claudette raised her hand to wave it back down.

'That's not a joke or a glib comment either,' she added, leaning closer. 'We genuinely don't know where she is. The police are looking for her, too. We're worried about her mental health. She believed that she was being targeted, and we hope she's going to find a safe place to get better.'

'I presume this is affecting the West End show?'

'Of course, it's affecting the show, Peter,' Flanagan replied, only just holding back her anger at the question. 'We don't have the main act. How can a show happen without it?'

She looked directly at the camera.

'Zoey, if you're out there watching, know that we're keeping this going for you, my love. Take as long as you need, and when you're ready, we'll be here for you.'

The camera turned back to Peter, who did his best to look interested and sympathetic to the statement.

'Strong words indeed,' he said. 'But how will you keep this open? I understand that with the West End show, people are already asking for their money back.'

'They are,' Claudette nodded. 'Rightly so. We're looking to finish the run with a different show, but tonight, we have a different style of performance. A one-off spectacular to honour Zoey, doing her favourite tricks, with all proceeds going to a variety of mental health charities. Anyone who attends, who had a ticket already, will gain a ticket for the first of Zoey's shows when she returns.'

'But they'll also get a tribute show, right? Something exciting?'

'Exactly,' Claudette looked at Jacob, who now leant closer.

'I met Zoey when we were auditioning for a TV talent show years ago,' he said. 'But while I've been the guy creating the tricks, standing behind the curtain making sure Zoey looks a million dollars, I'm a magician in my own right.'

'He creates most of the tricks that Zoey uses,' Claudette beamed at Peter. 'For the first time, he'll be performing on the Piccadilly Theatre stage and Zoey's partner, Joe Kerr – again, another ex-Covent Garden street magician – is coming on board as well, and he will perform some close-up magic for us. And Luana Flanagan herself—'

The camera panned across to Flanagan, who made an "oh, please" shushing kind of gesture as Claudette continued.

'Luana Flanagan is known across Ireland as the onetime "Queen of Conjuring," a name she bestowed personally upon Zoey when she retired. But, she'll be coming out of retirement, and performing as well, including her famous Cú Chulainn escape trick, something that has been seen across generations in Ireland, and with the very chain that held the Irish hero to the stone where he died.'

'It's been lost for decades, but we recently regained it,' Luana stated simply.

'Well, this sounds like a great show,' Peter smarmed at the camera. 'Tell me where this is exactly?'

'Piccadilly Theatre in the West End, tonight only,' Claudette beamed at the camera as she spoke. 'If you've got a ticket for Zoey and you don't want to see it, we totally understand, and we will refund you. But if you want to come to this instead, we will provide you a ticket down the line at no extra charge. So you get two shows for the price of one. If you're in the mood for a magic trick and haven't already booked? Tickets for this limited, incredible, never to be seen again show are on sale at the box office and on Ticketmaster—'

Ellie turned the television off, walking back to the others.

'Did you hear that?' she said.

'You played it so loud that people across the street could

hear it,' Ramsey muttered. 'I can't believe I fell for that lying toe rag's bollocks about not being involved in anything.'

'I'd say you trained him well, but it's a bit of a rubbish joke,' Davey muttered.

'I reckon they'll cancel the show from tomorrow, claim it on the insurance,' Ramsey continued. 'They were running the props out when I was there. This is a cash grab, one night only. Bastards.'

Ellie sat down, staring at her mug.

'I get it,' she said. 'Well, that is, I'm starting to get it. We thought this was a missing person, being hunted by Luana Flanagan for a debt. We then thought that people were trying to frame Luana Flanagan with the Tsangs, and get her out of the way. Now I think we're being aimed in a particular direction while something else is happening.'

'Classic misdirection,' Mary replied. 'It's what they're all good at.'

'I didn't hear Anna being mentioned,' Ramsey said, his voice soft, barely more than a whisper.

'What?'

'They named all the acts, but they didn't mention Anna Lever,' Ramsey repeated. 'She's a solid close up card artist, has been a consultant to Zoey on the show, and they're not using her. I wondered why.'

'Maybe because she's not part of the team?' Tinker asked as her phone beeped, and Ramsey mouth-shrugged at this, accepting the suggestion.

'Hey,' Tinker said as she checked a text she'd just received. 'Jimmy Tsang has just checked out of hospital.'

'He'll be on the warpath right now,' Davey replied. 'Especially if he thinks it was Zoey who tried to kill him.'

'What did you tell Jimmy?' Ellie stared hard at Mary.

'I don't know what you mean—'

'Don't tell us you weren't there,' she said. 'We found your wristband on the floor in his office.'

'I wasn't going to,' Mary replied. 'I was there. I visited him several times.'

'Why?' Ramsey asked.

'Because Anna asked for my help,' Mary said, looking around the booth. 'Zoey was in trouble. Flanagan was being pressured for the non-existent money owed, and so was gunning for her, using her to distract away from her own shortcomings, and we needed to get her out of there.'

'Why don't you tell us what happened?' Ellie asked, leaning forward. 'You weren't involved in Zoey's life. Yet here you are, speaking to gangsters on her behalf.'

'It wasn't like that,' Mary shook her head vigorously. 'Flanagan had got Zoey caught up in a contract. Anna had tried to stop it, but she hadn't realised Flanagan used surrogates, and Claudette had helped. Once Zoey was tied down, there were problems, but Anna had a plan to stop this.'

'What sort of plan was that?' Ramsey smiled darkly. 'Knowing Anna of old, usually her plans turn into shit. So far, all we're seeing is chaos and disorganisation.'

'With the power of hindsight, I can see what you're saying,' Mary nodded. 'Look, I'd made my peace. I'd never see Zoey again. I love Jerome, and we were making a life for ourselves. Then one day, a few weeks back, Anna turned up at my house and reminded me I owed her for what she had done when I escaped Ireland. She explained Flanagan had found a way to find something on Zoey, a way to lock her down and get her money back.'

'Do you know how?' Ellie asked.

'This,' Mary indicated to the television. 'That bitch on the screen, Claudette. She used to work for Flanagan. She also knew Anna, and went to her, convincing her she had a great idea for Zoey's next show. Got her a West End engagement. Limited run, two months only. Warm-up shows around Europe to get used to it, all of which was secretly funded by Flanagan as she tried to find a way in.'

She looked around the table.

'Did you know her stepson is Joe Kerrigan? He reckoned he was sick of his stepmother and was trying to get out from underneath,' Mary laughed bitterly at this. 'Maybe he was, but not when I saw him.'

'So, was Joe basically Flanagan's way in?'

'Zoey had managed to piss off a lot of people in her time,' Mary sipped at her coffee. 'She was good at what she did – too good – but she wasn't clever enough to stop gloating. Jacob couldn't hold a candle to her, but he was clever. He could make amazing tricks, and she would be the one that performed them. That made people go "wow" when they saw them, while he watched from the wings.'

A shadow crossed her face.

'Trust me when I say that's not an easy thing to do.'

'So Flanagan started turning people against her?'

'Luana Flanagan promised Joe the keys to her kingdom if he helped her, offered to wipe a debt he had,' Mary nodded. 'She promised Jacob his own show down the line. She promised Claudette a percentage of the profits. The devil in the ear, whispering honey and lies.'

'Were you and Anna the only two who tried to stop this?'

'No, at the start, nobody was listening, including Joe, so

we were all in on this. Zoey too, although I don't think she realised I was part of the team,' Mary said. 'The plan was simple. Luana was still going on about these chains, claiming that I'd stolen them back in the day, and Zoey now owed the debt of the insurance that was never paid. When Zoey tried to get out of the deal, Flanagan explained there was nothing Zoey could do. The contract she'd signed, the one Claudette had helped set up, whether it was unknowing, was cast iron, and she had to earn her way out.'

She leant back on the booth seat, and Ellie could see she was getting irritated.

Mary went to continue, but paused.

'Is that a dog under the table?'

'Her name's Millie,' Ellie replied calmly, allowing Mary to have a moment. 'She likes sausages and belly rubs.'

Eventually, after ruffling Millie's head, the woman looked back up.

'Flanagan wanted more than just the West End, though,' she continued. 'She wanted power. She's been a middle management bitch in Ireland for decades and wanted out. Last year there was a big shift in the power struggle of London, and Flanagan thought she had a chance of getting in there, but by the time she got ready, Jimmy Tsang had become the latest player on the board. But Jimmy was very superstitious, so Luana started working with his cousin Kenny to find a way to get him out, name dropping her bosses to make him think she was part of a bigger network.'

'So the suggestion of a curse was made?'

'Flanagan wanted Zoey to be involved in it, as part of the "paying back," but we saw this as an opportunity.'

'So, then what happened?' Ellie asked.

'Anna didn't want Zoey getting involved in this gangland shit, but knew she had to do what Flanagan wanted – to curse Jimmy. She couldn't bring Joe or Jacob in, as they were too well known. I, however, was dead. So, she asked for my help,' Mary said. 'She used suggestion and her mentalism tricks to convince Jimmy the curse was real, while Kenny and the bodyguard—'

'Chow?'

'Miserable bugger, built like a tree? Anyway, they started priming him for the big finale, and I turned up, found by – Chow, you say? – and offered my services to remove the curse from Jimmy. Then I aimed him at both Flanagan, as the cause, and you as the solution.'

'Why me?' Ellie asked.

'We knew you had history with him, and also that Jacob had a history with Mister Allen there. I knew this would distract him.'

'By him, you mean Jacob?' Ellie questioned.

Mary nodded.

'He was starting to listen to Flanagan a little too much, the whisperings that he was the genuine star of the show, and if Zoey wasn't around ...'

Mary didn't continue, simply shrugging, as Tinker straightened in her chair.

'So Flanagan wants Jimmy out, uses Zoey to scare him, knowing she can throw her to the wolves if needed,' she said. 'You and Anna leap in, trying to keep Zoey out of this. So why did she disappear?'

'We'd talked to Zoey – that is, Anna talked to Zoey – about the whole situation, and it was decided that the only way to fix this was to screw over Flanagan, get her into serious issues with her bosses. Jimmy and the police needed to hunt her, but we also needed everyone else tied into this too.'

'So you got a hold of a double of Zoey, some weird sex toy thing you could use the face from, to fool cameras?'

'Anna placed the face on, went to Zoey's house, and set up a body to be stabbed,' Mary nodded. 'She'd also grabbed a fingerprint from Flanagan that they could stick onto the knife. She deleted the footage but badly enough so either you or the police could find it.'

'So, setting up Flanagan was going quite well?'

'Joe was conflicted, but by this point, he had realised he was on the wrong team. Or, more likely, he realised he wasn't getting out of the debt he owed.'

'What happened next?'

'So, we had planned this elaborate scheme out where Luana Flanagan would be blamed for everything. The body with the blade was a nice touch and enough to start an inquiry once the police got involved, and we were hoping the recently transferred Delgado would do that, just to piss you off. At the same time, the whole thing was set up to show Flanagan was the one who had cursed Jimmy Tsang, and that would set him against her. We would just sit back, hide out for a few days, and then return when the blood had been washed away.'

'But it didn't happen like that, did it?' Robert spoke now.

'No. Flanagan was clever and immediately started to work out what was going on.'

'How many sides is Anna playing?' Ramsey asked. 'Why did she run over Jimmy Tsang with Zoey's mask on?'

Mary chuckled.

'That was last minute,' she said. 'We heard about Zoey's fall from Sean and Liam – we'd sent them to pretend to be working for Flanagan, loudly state it all over Covent Garden, do more to screw up her rep, and then we realised that if we used it again after her accident, it could be proven as an obvious mask, right before we placed the fake face in Flanagan's hotel room at the Kensington.'

Mary rubbed at her mouth, and there was a hint of triumph in her eyes.

'When the police eventually search the room, or if Jimmy sends his goons in, whoever gets there first, they'll find her. As far as they'll be concerned, Flanagan will have worn the face to try to kill Jimmy Tsang and frame poor Zoey Park.'

'So what went wrong?'

'Me,' Mary admitted. 'I was on stage, I checked the straitjacket, and I had a moment, alone with her. I'm a mum. I couldn't help it.'

She sighed, looking away.

'I told her Joe was lying, was Flanagan's stepson. She knew Anna had a plan to get her away that night, but, concerned she was being set up for a bad accident, before I could mention the missing key, she ran.'

'Do we know where Zoey is?' Ellie asked. 'Ramsey, is your tracker still there?'

'You have Zoey being tracked?' Mary was shocked at this.

'Seemed the safest thing to do,' Ellie shrugged.

Ramsey looked at Casey, who quickly tapped on the screen.

'The tracker's in Piccadilly,' he said. 'The Queen's Head pub.'

'Which is next to the Piccadilly Theatre,' Ramsey replied. 'Zoey's going there. She must know she got screwed over. She'll want revenge.'

'But how would you gain revenge on everybody in one go, without burning down the theatre?' Robert asked.

At that, Tinker paled.

'*It's very volatile. I never have more than a sheet with me, as if it went up, it could really burn something down,*' she said. 'That's what Zoey told me when we first went to Nicky Simpson. He asked about the flash paper Zoey used in her tricks, and she said there was flash paper held under the stage where it was safe and cool, so it wouldn't overheat and explode.'

'Is there a major problem if it explodes?' Casey asked.

'Oh hell yes,' Davey nodded. 'Fire is bad, little boy. Especially that much fire.'

'Zoey was under the assumption that if the flash paper went up in flames, it would create a fireball that was quick enough to destroy the entire theatre,' Tinker shuddered. 'If she thinks she's got nothing to lose, and that all of her enemies are above her on a stage? There's a very strong chance that's what she's intending to do tonight.'

'Surely she wouldn't …' Ellie started, but paused as she looked at Casey. 'You okay? You look as if you're about to throw up.'

Casey looked over at Robert, and the lawyer's face changed as he understood.

'The key logger,' he said. 'Casey, open the app that holds the text and read it out to us.'

Casey opened the app, looking around the table.

'Zoey wrote this in a thread on a magic forum,' he said. 'We thought she was just asking about a trick, but …'

He swallowed and then started reading the text on the screen.

'Hey there,' he said. 'I've got an excess amount of flash paper and I need to help work out how to do an explosion in a large trick soon. I want something exciting, and which goes off with a bang. But I'm not sure how to get the flash paper to *not* go up at once, so instead of having it burst away in a second-long fireball, I want to give it some kind of delayed explosion. Something big and bombastic. Can you suggest accelerants that could help?'

He looked at the others and saw from their expressions they were understanding the meaning, too.

'I checked the site,' he said. 'There was no thread that asked this question. The chances are Zoey deleted it and moved on. After saying thanks, which means she had a reply. Someone told her how to do this – how to create an explosion with flash paper and accelerants that stays burning.'

Ellie shifted in her chair, glancing at Millie, asleep on the floor under her.

'I've got a lot of excess flash paper and I need to help work out how to do an explosion,' she said. 'Zoey Park knew about this and typed it last night. She had a plan on how to end it before we even guessed what it was.'

'The question is,' Ramsey replied, 'how far along is she?'

Casey was watching the AirTag.

'Oh shit,' he muttered, before looking up at the others. 'The tag's moving, and not in a way it should.'

'How do you mean?' Tinker looked at the screen, and could see the AirTag had now moved onto the theatre.

'She can't just move through walls,' Casey explained. 'For her to move like that—'

'She wasn't in the pub,' Ellie nodded, understanding. 'She was on top of it. The roof. She's using the route she escaped to get back in.'

Ellie leant back, considering this.

'Flanagan will be in there, so will Jimmy as soon as he

gets his army together, Kenny too, maybe. We need to get them all out in case she blows the whole thing up.'

'How are you going to do that?' Mary asked.

'I have a plan,' Ellie smiled. 'How's your pick-pocketing skills?'

———

26

FIND THE LADIES

Lɪú Yǔɴ ᴡᴀs ᴀʙᴏᴜᴛ ᴛᴏ ᴄᴀʟʟ ɪᴛ ᴀ ᴅᴀʏ ᴀɴᴅ ᴄʟᴏsᴇ ᴜᴘ ᴡʜᴇɴ sʜᴇ saw the SUVs.

It had been quiet all day, and she'd even sent Sonia off to do some chores they'd been putting off for ages, purely because they had the time now. Standing outside the shop, smoking a roll up, something she couldn't do when Sonia was around, she nodded at old Mister Yifan. In actual fact, Chen Yifan was probably only five or six years older than her, but he carried himself in the way of a far older man.

He walked over, nodding for a puff of her roll up.

'You hear about Kenny Tsang?' he asked softly, looking around to make sure nobody else was listening. 'My son works for him, says he's making his move today.'

'Against Jimmy?' Liú Yǔn frowned. 'That's going to leave bodies. I think I might close up and get—'

There was a revving of cars, and they both looked over to the car park on Newport Place, where three black SUVs, all filled with men drove out, heading towards Shaftesbury Avenue.

'Yeah,' she said, stubbing out the roll up and nodding a thanks to old Mister Yifan. 'I think I'll be doing that right now.'

As old Mister Yifan walked off, however, another walked to her shop; Tinker Jones moved close, passing her a plastic card, the size of a credit card.

'Thanks for the loan,' she said with a smile.

Liú Yŭn took the card, placing it in a pocket.

'Did you get what you needed?' she asked, and Tinker nodded.

'It's amazing what people leave in their cars,' she replied, as she looked at the SUVs, now turning left onto Shaftesbury Avenue. 'Give Sonia my love. I'll drop the dress back later.'

As Liú Yŭn returned to the store, Tinker headed after the SUVs on foot. It wasn't far to the Piccadilly Theatre from here, and Robert would be waiting for her on Greek Street. They had to hurry though, as there was no way on earth Tinker wanted to miss *this* show.

RAMSEY HADN'T BEEN SURPRISED TO FIND ANNA LEVER IN THE upstairs bar of the Punch & Judy pub in Covent Garden. It was a known performers' bar, with many of the others long gone now.

Anna was nursing a wine, sipping gently as he walked over to her.

'Sour grapes?' he asked. 'Not like you, Anna.'

'Actually, the grapes are quite fine,' Anna looked up with a slight smile, holding up the glass. 'I intend to test quite a few of them tonight.'

'Not going to watch the show?' Ramsey asked.

Anna glared at him.

'She won,' she replied. 'Bloody Flanagan won, no matter what we did. She's controlling the narrative, and Jacob, sodding *Jacob*, turned out to be the traitor.'

Ramsey shrugged, sitting opposite her.

'Takes after the people who raised him then,' he said. 'You can take equal responsibility here, Anna. You showed him what he could be. I showed him what *not* to be. Unfortunately, the two don't really help.'

'So, why are you here?' Anna placed the glass down, leaning back and folding her arms. 'And how the bloody hell did you find me?'

Ramsey leant forward with a smile.

'I asked about and they aimed me here,' he said. 'As for why I'm here, I've got a trick for you to do, if you're up for it.'

LUANA FLANAGAN STOOD ON THE STAGE OF THE PICCADILLY Theatre and smiled to herself.

I own you, she thought as she looked out at the seats. *I own you all.*

There was a polite cough from behind her, and she turned around, the phantom audience forgotten.

'Yes, son?' she asked.

'We're getting ready for the technical rehearsal,' Jacob said as he stood to the side of the stage. 'Joe hasn't turned up yet though, and Anna's still out there doing God knows what.'

'Anna is a snake who needs to be put down,' Flanagan muttered, her lips thinning in anger. 'Also, Joe can stay away as far as I'm concerned. He was never the son to me you've become, Jacob.'

Jacob reddened at this.

'I appreciate your trust,' he said. 'I just worry—'

'You just worry,' Flanagan smiled warmly. 'Don't stress it. Go get everything ready. Tonight we start to build a new family. We'll go back and show those bastards they should have raised me higher, as I cut them all down.'

Jacob nodded hesitantly.

'I still need the chains for tonight,' he said. 'I need to go over them for the trick.'

'Don't you worry about those,' Flanagan shook her head. 'I've got that covered.'

And she did have that covered; right now, one of her men was scouring the East End scrapyards, looking for something she could claim as the historical chains of old. She would have preferred the ones she used to use, but they were in the River Liffey, and had been since she blamed Mary Park for the theft.

Jacob nodded, smiled and then hurried off, leaving Luana Flanagan alone on the stage once more. She took this opportunity to pull out the letter she'd had left for her in the Kensington Hotel. The receptionist had said it was a woman, someone who'd been seen talking to Claudette Storm. She'd left this note on old headed paper for her, and Flanagan had read it and re-read it since she received it.

You're playing with fire and you'll get burnt. Back away.

She didn't know if this was a warning or a threat; she'd confronted Claudette, but the bloody woman had played innocent, claiming the receptionist was wrong. Someone else had spoken to the woman, and it wasn't her, even though she was in the same hotel.

Was this a note from Zoey? From the Tsangs? Or from that bloody private detective?

Flanagan read the note once more and, wanting more than anything to crumple it into a ball and toss it, she once more folded it up, and placed it into her jacket.

Her phone started buzzing, and Flanagan saw it was a FaceTime call from Tommy, one of her men, someone she'd sent back to the hotel. There was something off, and Flanagan didn't trust Storm to not screw her over, so she'd sent Tommy to check for cameras or bugs. He'd been happy to do it, probably caught up in the exciting world of spies, and although she thought this was going to be a pointless task, there was a moment of fear when he called.

If he was calling, there was a problem.

'What?' she said as she connected, and the face of Tommy appeared on her screen. He was still in her room, and he was nervous. This wasn't a good sign.

'I found something,' he said.

'Bug?'

'No, not really,' he replied, holding up something in his free hand. It looked like a Halloween mask.

'What the hell is it?' Flanagan frowned. Tommy, to explain, took it upon himself to put it on, and now a masked Tommy stared at her down the phone.

The mask was obviously Zoey Park.

'Take it off,' she hissed. 'Get rid of it. Where did you find the bloody thing?'

'It was hidden under the bed,' Tommy pulled the mask off now, tossing it to the side. 'But not that well.'

'They wanted it to be found,' Flanagan growled. She knew that "Zoey" had been seen attacking Jimmy Tsang – this mask was obviously what was worn. She didn't know what else it'd been used for, but she could guess it wasn't good, and likely to have her facing Jimmy down the barrel of a gun.

Or had this been Kenny? She'd wondered how the driver had got into the car park – was Kenny reneging on their contract and setting her up for a fall?

She remembered the words on the paper again. Had that been left as a warning before they placed the mask in her room, most likely during room service this morning?

'Boss?' Tommy, still on the line, spoke now, bringing her back to the present. 'What do you want me to do?'

Flanagan considered this.

'Bring it here, with as many men as you can find,' she said. 'I think I'm about to be double-crossed.'

She disconnected the call, and turned to walk back to the wings, but one of the stagehands, a woman with short black hair, unable to move out of the way fast enough, knocked into her.

'Sorry,' she said, running off. Flanagan watched after her, frowning.

You should be more scared of me, she thought as, the woman now gone from her head, she walked off the stage and towards the wings.

'It's time,' she said. 'Let's try my trick.'

'You sure?' Jacob asked, glancing around. 'We don't have the chains—'

'The chains are just chains,' Flanagan hissed, looking back across the stage at the woman who'd knocked into her. 'Sort it out. I'll be a moment.'

She walked over to the woman who, immediately upon seeing her approach, started to turn and leave.

'Oh no, don't go on my account, stay a while,' Flanagan

said, grabbing the woman's arm and turning her around. 'I thought as much. You were on the stage the night Zoey disappeared, weren't you?'

'Yes,' the woman nodded. 'I was set up as a stooge.'

'Good, you can stooge tonight,' Flanagan said with a smile. 'Stay beside me. *Right* beside me.'

She started towards the centre of the stage where a large fake rock was being placed. It looked like a menhir, the style of rock that Obelix in the Asterix books would hold, and was an exact copy of the Clochafarmore Stone, used in many statues and paintings over the centuries.

'I didn't ask your name, did I?' she asked, looking back.

'It's Veronica.'

At this, Luana Flanagan shook her head.

'Oh, I don't like that,' she said. 'You're not a "Veronica" type of woman.'

She leant closer.

'I think I'll call you "Mary."'

THE STAGE DOOR WAS AT THE END OF A PASSAGEWAY THREE shops from the theatre itself, a usually locked wall of metal that opened for large stage props and then led to the door itself, which then took you into the back corridors of the theatre.

Arthur had been there for a few years now, one of many stage door managers the theatre had, and over the years he'd built up a good autograph book of names, and felt he knew many of them on a first name basis. He didn't understand what had happened with Zoey Park, but he felt he knew her better than most here; she'd entered and exited through his door every day, and had always given him the time of day, something that some of the other actors appearing in shows hadn't done.

Today, however, was different.

Zoey walked in, head down, and hood up. She didn't look at Arthur, simply passing through. Knowing the show this evening was a tribute, Arthur had asked her whether she was performing, or just gathering some items – Zoey ignored him.

Which actually stung a little if he was being honest about it.

But a moment later there was a knock on the metal door, and Arthur walked out of his little room, over to it. The chances were something bigger for the show had arrived, and he'd have to open the whole bloody thing again—

He stopped as the gun on the other side of the entrance was aimed at his face.

'I'd like to come in,' Jimmy Tsang said. 'And my men would like to accompany me. Will that be a problem?'

'Not at all,' Arthur shook his head quickly, backing away to the side as Jimmy Tsang and his men passed by. 'Welcome to the Piccadilly Theatre.'

Zoey was under the stage when Joe Kerrigan arrived.

He'd come through the stage door earlier, but had been sitting in the back of the audience, wondering what to say or do for a good hour, before making his way to the bowels of the theatre. He'd gone to see if there was anything still there of the show; what he hadn't expected was to see Zoey standing there, staring at a metal box, as if working out how to open it.

She started as she saw him, backing away from it, heading back into the shadows.

'No,' he held a hand up to stop her. 'Please don't go. Let me explain.'

Zoey stopped, watching him, her face in the darkness.

'I know, you were told who I am,' he started. 'But that's not who I am. I shouldn't be judged on who my father marries.'

'You owed her,' Zoey whispered, the voice barely audible.

'Yeah, I did,' Joe nodded. 'I fell into debt, I was living above my means. The apartment needed work, I could find a dozen excuses. All you need to know is I was terrible at money, and I borrowed from my dad – who didn't tell me he'd borrowed from her before he had the heart attack. I assumed it was a debt I didn't need to pay until she found me last year, and told me I needed to pay it back.'

He scuffed his foot against the floor.

'She told me to contact you, get to know you,' he said. 'So yeah, I did it. You weren't anything to me. But don't make out I was anything to you, either. I know now you were already planning to take Flanagan down, and you didn't keep me in the loop.'

'Why should I?' Zoey whispered again, still staying in the shadows.

'Yeah, that's fair,' Joe nodded. 'But I wasn't the one who screwed you over, was I? That was Jacob.'

He looked around the space.

'I don't want to do this show tonight. I'm being forced,' he said. 'I wanted to help Anna, but I couldn't. She didn't trust me, either. All I could do was let her into the house to plant the body, and then remove the footage so the police would be led to Luana. I did that for you. Me.'

Zoey said nothing, watching him from the shadows.

'I also did the filming for Anna, sorted out a distraction for Jacob—'

'Did you bring my mum in?' Zoey asked, her voice a little stronger, a little huskier, but still keeping it down, maybe in case someone on the stage heard.

'Your mum?'

'Veronica Carter.'

At this, Joe looked horrified.

'Oh, God,' he said. 'No, sorry, Anna arranged it. She convinced Claudette it was her idea. I didn't know, I swear.'

'So, what now?'

Joe looked up at the stage.

'There was something going on at the stage door when I came down,' he said. 'Chinese men with guns. I think they're pissed at my step-mum. Or you for cursing them.'

He held a hand up.

'I know it wasn't you,' he added. 'Just as much as I know the chains she has upstairs probably came from Hackney, not Dundalk.'

There was a commotion on the stage.

'You should get out of here, in case they're after you,' he said.

'You ...' Zoey asked, her face expressionless.

'I'll make sure they don't come after you,' Joe replied. 'It's the least I can do. Who knows, if things settle down, maybe we could meet up for a drink? Start again?'

'Do you really want that, Joe?' Zoey asked, her voice strangely different now. Joe frowned, unsure of what had just happened.

'It doesn't matter what I want, it's about what you want,' he said.

'How about you, Zoey?' Zoey asked, looking behind him, and Joe turned to find another Zoey Park staring at him from the stairs.

'What the hell's going on?' he asked, looking back at the shadowed Zoey, who now reached up and pulled her face off to reveal Ellie Reckless.

'I needed a way to get in, and have you speak honestly for a change,' she said. 'Don't worry, your words weren't wasted. Zoey's been there all the time, listening to you. Haven't you?'

Zoey stared in anger at Ellie.

'What were you doing down here?' she asked.

'Making sure you weren't setting fire to the theatre.'

'Why would I do that?' Zoey cocked her head, confused.

'Because you asked about ways to use accelerants to delay flash paper explosions, and we know you have a ton down here?' Ellie felt like she was losing control of the situation slightly, so narrowed her eyes as she continued. 'That's what's under here, right?'

'Ah,' Zoey smiled now, but it was a dark smile. 'Yeah, there was a crap ton of it down here in those secure boxes. But I moved it.'

'Where?'

Zoey pointed a thumb up at the stage above them.

'Into Luana Flanagan's fake rock,' she said. 'When she hides in it, she's going to go up like a candle. I worked the door, setting it up to ignite a spark from a flint when it closes.'

Ellie started for the door.

'We need to stop that!' she exclaimed.

'No we don't,' Joe held a hand out to pause her. 'She deserves everything she gets.'

'It'll get revenge for my mum's death,' Zoey added.

'Your mum's not dead!' Ellie snapped now as she pushed past Joe, running for the stairs. 'Right now she's probably standing on the stage right beside Flanagan, just as the whole bloody thing goes off!'

27

FIRE SAFETY

ELLIE NEEDN'T HAVE WORRIED, AS WHILE SHE RAN FOR THE stairs to get to the stage, Luana Flanagan had found herself stopped by a group of men arriving, led by a furious Jimmy Tsang.

'You bitch!' he cried out. 'Your witch tried to kill me!'

'I did no such thing!' Flanagan shook her head. 'If Zoey Park tried to curse you—'

'I don't mean the *curse*, woman!' Jimmy was still focused on her, ignoring the others in the auditorium. 'I mean she tried to run me over!'

'I heard,' Flanagan replied calmly. 'I can tell you, I had nothing to do with it ...'

She trailed off as she realised Jimmy Tsang was no longer staring at her anymore. Instead, he was staring at the woman beside her.

'You?' he exclaimed in surprise. 'You work with her?'

'No,' Mary Park stepped away defiantly. 'I want her dead as much as you do.'

'She also wants you dead too, though,' another voice spoke now, as Kenny Tsang walked onto the stage from the auditorium, having entered from the front of the theatre, a couple of his men behind him. 'Hello Jimmy. Is it chess time yet?'

'I know you're working with that Irish bitch,' Jimmy waved his gun at Flanagan. 'What, you let her keep the theatres and you take everything else? Is she your new Benny?'

At this, Kenny straightened, and his own gun appeared.

'Nobody replaces Benny,' he snarled. 'Not even you, cousin. I intended to cut her loose the moment she was no more use to me.'

'Funny enough, she intended to do the same to you,' an even newer voice spoke as Ellie walked onto the stage now, Zoey and Joe following her. 'Hey Kenny. Hey Jimmy.'

Jimmy saw Zoey behind Ellie, and his eyes widened in anger.

'I didn't do it,' Zoey said loudly, not backing down before he could say anything. 'I was as much a pawn in this as anyone else.'

She looked across at Mary, and her face softened.

'You should have told me,' she said.

'Why?' Mary replied coldly. 'I warned you about Joe, and he's right beside you.'

'Not by choice,' Zoey gave the smallest of smiles, before looking back at Flanagan. 'She's the one who "cursed" you, with chains that don't exist.'

'Then someone better give me a reason why I shouldn't kill this bitch,' Jimmy said, staring coldly at Flanagan.

'The favour,' Ellie replied. 'I could call it in. Stop you.'

'I don't give a shit about my cousin's favour,' Jimmy

replied. 'Do you think Kenny owing you anything means a single thing to me?'

'I didn't mean Kenny's favour,' Ellie stepped forward. 'I'm on about *your* favour. You said you owed me once we sorted this curse out.'

She waved at Luana Flanagan.

'I think we can agree Flanagan's curse isn't worth the paper it's printed on. The chain isn't real, she only kept the story going so Mary there and her daughter Zoey were kept in debt, and from what I hear, it's in the bottom of the River Liffey. Therefore, there is no curse, and therefore, you are not cursed.'

Her voice hardened.

'Therefore, *you owe me a favour.*'

Jimmy considered this and then laughed.

'If there was no curse, then there was no curse for you to find.'

'That's irrelevant. You told my colleague if I removed the curse, you owed me a favour,' Ellie said as she looked around the stage. 'I'll be honest, I'd rather not use it. I'd rather you came to your senses and realised that attacking someone on the middle of a West End stage was a bloody stupid thing to do, and was likely to get you not only deported back to Shanghai, but probably put in prison.'

Jimmy now looked at Zoey Park, standing at the back of the stage.

'No matter what she claims, she tried to kill me,' he said. 'I want her dead.'

'You know damn well it wasn't her,' Ellie replied. 'But you're right, someone needs to pay for it. But the question is who?'

She looked around the stage, and then she pulled out the fake Zoey mask.

'You did it?' Jimmy asked in surprise.

'No, this is one of two,' Ellie smiled, tossing it to the floor in front of Flanagan. 'Found by one of my team today. Flanagan has the other one, though. Maybe you should check her hotel room.'

'It's not there anymore,' Flanagan smiled darkly.

'Oh, so you admit you moved it?' Ellie asked.

Flanagan, realising she'd spoken too soon, went to speak, but then stopped herself.

'This is the problem with what we have,' Ellie took control of the stage now. 'Flanagan here? She wants your buildings. Your businesses. Your money. She thought she could align with your cousin, and stiff the pair of you over, but she's simply not that bright. More of a monopoly player than a chess one, and even then she steals from the bank when she can – although from what I hear the bank is catching up *real* fast.'

'Then she needs to die,' Kenny now agreed with his cousin.

'Yeah, about that,' Ellie smiled. 'I haven't finished yet.'

———

STAGE DOOR ARTHUR STOOD AGAINST THE WALL, CHINESE henchmen on either side of him. He hadn't been allowed to return to his little room at the side of the stage door after they'd entered, and now the two men effectively held him hostage, guarding the door from anybody else entering through the metal gates and into the stage door area.

'Look,' he said. 'The show's happening soon. There's a rehearsal. I could get the stage door book—'

'Shut up,' the first of the two muscles said. 'We're busy. Or I'll take your stage door book and shove it up your—'

He stopped as another figure walked through the door. It was Chow, Jimmy Tsang's right-hand man.

'You're late,' he muttered. 'Jimmy is absolutely furious.'

'Stand down,' Chow interrupted.

'You don't understand—'

'I said, *stand down*.' Chow loomed over the henchmen. 'This fight ends tonight, and we will not be involved.'

'Jimmy said—'

'We serve the Tsang Empire,' Chow replied. 'Not Jimmy. Not Kenny. We serve the Empire. Whoever stands at the end we serve, and we do not take sides.'

The two henchmen looked at each other and then nodded. Regardless of who they'd worked for, they'd stood beside Chow for many years now.

This done, Chow turned to the main metal door and whistled.

'You can come in now,' he said. 'There won't be a problem.'

At this, Tinker and Robert walked through the door, passing the two guards.

'I didn't need that,' Tinker smiled. 'I could have sorted it out myself.'

'Yes,' Chow replied. 'I'm sure you could. But I'd have preferred my men to not be losing their livelihood anytime soon. Your penchant for breaking limbs would have left them on the shelf at a time when I think I will be needing them.'

'Why do you think you'll need them?' Tinker asked.

'Surely you'll be siding with Kenny or staying with Jimmy if he wins.'

'Jimmy won't take me anymore,' Chow replied, almost sadly. 'He'll know by now that the woman I brought to him, the Irish witch to break his curse was connected to the very woman who cursed him in the first place. He'll know that I dealt with Kenny, that I placed red thread in the car and that the woman I brought to speak to him was there purely to give him more superstitions.'

'So it's Team Kenny now, then?' Tinker nodded at this.

'Yes,' Chow shrugged. 'However, who knows? If they kill each other, maybe I'll take the job myself.'

At this, Tinker patted him on the arm and gave him a smile.

'You know what they say? I'd take those odds.'

And with that, Robert and Tinker entered the theatre, heading towards the lower levels.

Chow looked back at Arthur.

'Don't you have a stage door to sit at?' he asked, with the slightest of smiles.

———

ELLIE STOOD IN THE MIDDLE OF THE STAGE NOW AND SMILED.

'The way I see it, it's quite simple,' she explained. 'Kenny wants his empire back, Jimmy doesn't want to share. Flanagan wants both to go away so she can take it on herself.'

She looked over at Zoey.

'You never had a part in this,' she said. 'It was all set before you started performing and arranged before you were even born.'

'I know,' Zoey pointed at Flanagan. 'You screwed my mum

over, and made sure I never saw her again. All for a bit of chain that wasn't worth the legend.'

'I'll have you know that chain—'

'Just stop!' Mary shouted, frustrated. 'It was never real. Never has been. Never will be. You only claimed it so you could get money! I stole nothing from you because it never existed!'

Mary looked around the stage pleadingly.

'She's been claiming a debt for nothing for over twenty years now. Now it's led us here, where this man and his mates want to kill everybody here, his cousin wants to kill him, and my daughter wants to blow the whole damn place sky high for what you've caused here!'

She glared at Flanagan now.

'Can't you see this is all your work? You and your stupid, elegant ambitions to be more than some Gypsy Queen?'

Flanagan stared daggers back at Mary Park then she turned and looked at Jimmy.

'I didn't drive the car,' she said. 'Also, I found the mask before they were able to set me up. Yeah, I knew. My son told me.'

Everybody looked at Joe at this point.

Joe, however, shook his head.

'I knew nothing,' he said.

'I said I didn't mean you,' Flanagan replied. 'Sons aren't just by blood. Sons are love, loyalty, affection.'

She turned to Jacob, standing at the far side of the stage, watching the scene.

'Jacob told me what was going on,' she said. 'He kept me in the loop. I promised him his own show, and it seems the ambition you just complained about runs strong in many families.'

'So you and Jacob, is it?' Ellie asked Flanagan, stepping forward, looking at Jacob. 'You're happy with this?'

'You don't get to talk to me like you're my mother,' Jacob replied. 'In the same way Ramsey doesn't get to talk to me like a father. I don't have either. Luana here has been the closest I've had in years. She's looked after me.'

He glanced back at Zoey.

'For five years, I've helped you with your tricks. Not once have you given me a chance to show my own. Not even a warm-up act for you. I'm just a guy who makes your tricks.'

'I thought you were happy with that,' Zoey replied, shaking her head. 'If I'd have known—'

'If you'd known, you would probably have fired me,' Jacob laughed. 'Luana showed me what you've done with your previous friends, your previous helpers.'

He looked over at Kenny and his men.

'Mister Tsang here? He's happy to make an agreement with us,' he said. 'He'll give us the muscle and working tandem with Luana Flanagan, I'll have my own West End residency.'

'Over my dead body,' a woman's voice snapped from the back of the auditorium, and everyone looked to see Ramsey and Anna walking towards them, Anna dressed in the fineries of a Chinese Magician, the gold thread shimmering in the light as they walked onto the stage.

'If you're going to attend a magic show, you should at least see a magic trick,' she said, walking up to the fake stone.

'I wouldn't stand too close to that,' Ellie suggested. 'One light and the whole thing goes up.'

Anna nodded, looking back at Jimmy.

'You're the superstitious one here, so how about we see what the ancestors think of what you're doing?' she asked, pulling out a pack of gold-plated playing cards. 'Ready to see your future?'

'This is stupid!' Flanagan shouted. 'She's playing for time!'

'Shut up!' Jimmy snapped. 'Show me my cards, woman.'

Anna shuffled the cards and pulled off the top one.

'Five of Hearts, someone in your life is jealous,' she said, nodding at Kenny. 'I think we know that one. Next the Two of Spades – deceit, lies and double crossing. Are you double crossing us, Jimmy?'

Jimmy looked around, chuckling.

'Everyone's double crossing,' he said.

'Yes, but only two of you are talking to the police,' Ramsey muttered. 'Or haven't we reached that part yet?'

At this, Jimmy turned his gun on Ramsey.

'You saying I'm a snitch?'

'I have a contact that says you called the police before you left Chinatown,' Ellie now said, watching Jimmy carefully. 'If this is a lie, you can prove it by showing us your phone.'

'Now listen here—'

'Jimmy, show us your phone,' Kenny replied, his men moving closer. As he did so, Jimmy saw Chow and his men enter from the side, guns aimed at him as well.

'Fine,' Jimmy pulled his phone out.

'Now dial the last number called.'

'I haven't called anyone—'

'I'd do it,' Ellie replied. 'It'll likely be Kate Delgado. That's who you've been informing to, right? That's why you brought her to Soho?'

Jimmy, angry and ready to prove a point, went to the last number dialled and, without even looking at it pressed redial, turning it onto speaker.

After two rings, it was answered.

'DI Delgado,' the woman's voice answered. 'Jimmy? Is that you? We've been waiting for your call. Is it time?'

There was a change in the atmosphere for a second time.

'Who is this?' Jimmy whispered in horror.

'Jimmy, are they in position?' Delgado continued. 'We can come in once you and Flanagan are out. She's just texted me the time and location.'

At this, everyone now turned to Luana Flanagan, who paled.

'Lies,' she said.

'We're on our way,' Delgado continued. 'We'll fake arrest the two of you, keep your covers.'

This said, Delgado disconnected the call.

Now, Jimmy turned his guns onto Flanagan.

'You set us up! You've been working with the police all this time!'

'I don't know if you were listening, but it was your phone that outed you first!' Flanagan snapped. 'This is all bullshit! I didn't send anything! Look!'

She pulled her own phone out, showing it, but then stopped as she saw the last sent text messages.

TO: DI DELGADO

> We're almost ready. Main stage. Bring backup, they're armed. Honour our deal.

> What about your allies?

> Screw them. I can make new friends. Make sure you arrest Jacob too, the needy prick.

> Will do.

'No, that's not right,' she said, looking around.

'Show me,' Jimmy snatched the phone, reading it, looking up as Ellie took it from him, showing it to Kenny and then Jacob, before passing it back to Flanagan.

'There,' she said. 'Don't want to lose that, do you?'

Jacob stared at Flanagan now, horrified.

'How could you do this?' he whispered.

Flanagan looked around.

'She did this!' she snapped, glaring at Mary. 'I don't know how, but she did it!'

'You've got a bit of a conundrum now,' Ellie said, looking back at Jimmy. 'If you kill Luana Flanagan, the police will have you done for murder. If you walk away, you're wondering if Kenny there will be taking over the area.'

At this point, she looked back at Kenny.

'But now you *also* know she's been lying to you, and she was the one claiming to have an alliance *against* Jimmy. So, you also have the option to kill her and do the same things as Jimmy was going to do and take the same punishment once their buddy Delgado arrives.'

'If you know anything about our family,' Kenny said, 'you know we can't just turn around and walk away. Honour provides honour.'

Ellie held a hand up to stop him.

'I've seen your honour repeatedly, Kenny. I've seen your cousin's as well. As for you—' She looked at Jimmy as she spoke now. '—I warned you what would happen if you caused issues here. So here's my ruling. You can leave now, you can have your little war, but you can have it somewhere else, or, you decide on how you run Chinatown, but you do it properly, and you give the people who live there, terrified of you, their lives back. If you do that, I'll remove both favours from your ledgers. Kenny, you won't owe me anything, and Jimmy, you won't either.'

Jimmy went to speak once more, to point out he technically didn't need to, as he didn't technically owe her anything, but Ellie just shook her head, stopping him.

'Don't. Take the loss.'

'What if I don't?' Kenny asked.

'Then I will use every other favour to destroy your precious Tsang Empire,' Ellie said coldly. 'Mama Lumetta has even offered to give *me* the West End, and would go to war beside me, providing me my own army.'

Kenny paused, and Ellie could see that not only had this surprised him, but it was also something he didn't want.

'I'm only doing this because I owe you,' he said, waving to his men to lower their guns. Jimmy did the same. 'Whatever you do now. It's on you. Flanagan, our agreement is over.'

Flanagan was furious at this, and went to reply, but Mary stepped forward.

'Stop,' she said. 'You've caused enough trouble. You wanted Jimmy gone, but he's still here. You wanted power, but that's further away than ever before. You destroyed my life over a debt that was bollocks, and you've tried to do the same to my daughter.'

Zoey also moved forward, walking over to her mother.

'The police don't need to get involved,' she said. 'Jimmy had an accident, Kenny and Jimmy have issues they need to fix in therapy. I had a bad show, and you tried to benefit from it. We walk away right now and restart our lives.'

'I don't want to restart my life!' Flanagan hissed. 'I want revenge!'

She grabbed a gun from one of Kenny's unsuspecting guards, aiming it at Anna Lever.

'This is all your fault, you bitch!' she said, firing, but a moment before she did, Anna flung the gold plated cards at her, the edges slicing at her as she fired wildly. Before Flanagan could react to this, however, Anna, now furious charged at her, the two women stumbling backwards into the fake stone.

'No—' Zoey shouted in horror, as the door closed behind them, but it was too late. The flint inside ignited a spark, and the whole fake rock went up in a fireball of flame.

There was no way anyone inside survived that.

———

ACTUALLY, THERE WAS ONE WAY; A WAY THAT LUANA FLANAGAN and Anna Lever both discovered as they fell through the open trapdoor beneath the stone, landing on a pile of soft crash mats under the stage.

Flanagan, her gun now lost, rose from the mat to find Robert Lewis standing in front of her, a Taser in his hand.

'Like mother, like son,' he said. 'Want me to fire?'

Flanagan sighed, slumping as Tinker walked over, pulling the woman to her feet.

'Just tell me, how did you do it?' Flanagan asked.

'You want us to tell you the trick?' Tinker smiled. 'Sure. We're not bound by any code. I made the call from Jimmy's phone before he left Chinatown. Mary palmed your phone, sent some messages and then replaced it.'

'Were they to Delgado?'

'Hell no,' Robert smiled. 'They were to Joanne Davey, who's back at the office, dog sitting. All she had to do was play the part.'

'So, what now?' Flanagan dusted herself off.

'You leave,' Robert waved the Taser at the door. 'You run all the way back to Dublin, because if you're still here in an hour, I *will* call Delgado and tell her everything. Not to mention the fact both Tsang cousins will be hunting you. I think your West End days are done.'

'I can't go to Dublin,' Flanagan replied. 'I don't have what I owe the families I work for. They'll kill me.'

'I know,' Robert replied. 'You should think up a really good excuse for that. Or, you could stay in London, and when they find you – and they *will* find you – you can explain why you're hiding. I'm sure that'll go better. Or not. Either way, I don't give a shit.'

Flanagan looked up at the stage, now faint with the sounds of fire extinguishers, and then looked back at Robert.

'Sounds like they're about to realise you're not dead,' he said. 'You might want to run, now.'

Flanagan spat angrily at him and turned, running out of the under-stage space.

Tinker looked at Robert.

'You sure this is the right thing?'

'Nobody's going to be pressing charges, and no matter where she goes, the people she owes will be hunting her now the truth is out about the chains, so she'll get justice – just not the type we hoped for.'

'And you're okay with this?'

'Currently yes,' he said. 'Which worries the hell out of me. Anyway, is Anna okay? She's not moved.'

Tinker glanced at Anna, still on the crash mat.

'Oh, shit,' she said. 'She's white as a sheet. Call an ambulance!'

28

LEAVING

THINGS SEEMED TO MOVE QUICK AFTER THE FIREBALL. Flanagan, deciding that survival was the best option, ran before anybody realised she was under the stage, while Tinker called an ambulance for Anna. By the time *that* had arrived, both Jimmy and Kenny had left, Chow still standing between them. Ellie wondered whether the Tsangs would continue as a double act, Kenny and Jimmy finding some way to work together, with Chow as some kind of middle-ground enforcer.

What was sure, was that the war in Chinatown hadn't ended.

Ramsey went with Anna to the hospital. The medics seemed to think she'd suffered a mild stroke when she landed on the crash mat, but it didn't look to be life threatening. However, at her age, it was life-*altering*, and even with therapy, she was unlikely to recover anywhere near the levels she'd once been.

Either way, though, Ramsey went in the ambulance beside his onetime mentor.

Finally, with Flanagan now gone, Jacob realised quickly he'd thrown away his entire career on a woman who would never treat him the way he wanted her to.

Before he left, he had taken off the watch, passing it to Ellie.

'I don't think I deserve this anymore,' he said. 'I don't really know what to do now.'

'You run,' Ellie said coldly. 'Luana Flanagan will throw you under a bus the moment her bosses find her. I'd find a very remote place and hide in a hole before they find you.'

Paling at the comment, Jacob nodded silently before turning and walking away. However, he hesitantly paused beside Zoey.

'I'm sorry,' he added before leaving. Zoey didn't say a word in response.

In fact, Zoey Park didn't really speak to anybody. There were a few quiet words with Joe, probably working out how to pick up her stuff from his apartment, and then, right before he left, Joe spoke briefly with Robert, patching up old wounds, but at the same time, that was another relationship that was never going to be repaired.

So many relationships were killed with one act, Ellie considered sadly.

Ellie had watched Mary too; as soon as it happened, Zoey had moved close to her, but afterwards, she gave no tenderness, or any inclination that she wanted to reunite with her long-estranged mother.

Then it was over.

Delgado and the police didn't arrive because there wasn't technically a crime. Claudette Storm had appeared shortly after and, seeing what happened, she immediately cancelled the show – before being fired unceremoniously by Zoey.

But Ellie didn't know what happened after that, as she and the others had left, their job done, returning to Finders and the diner.

It wasn't the win that Ellie had hoped for. Ramsey had gained and lost a son, and the chances were he was losing an old friend depending on how Anna recovered. Meanwhile, Robert had been through betrayal and loss, and still didn't look as if he had recovered yet.

The job over, they'd all gone their separate ways after the diner debrief, meeting back with Davey and Millie and Ellie wasn't sure which of the two was happier to see them. Davey seemed to have finally got over her distrust of the team.

IN THE WEEKS FOLLOWING THE EVENTS AT THE PICCADILLY Theatre, life fell into a vague sense of normality.

Robert knew that he'd been betrayed, but he was also aware he'd lost it a little too hard when confronting Joe, almost as if a filter he usually had was now gone. It hadn't been just the betrayal; it'd been a constant list of things hitting him at once, and first and foremost was the vision of Mark Whitehouse and a length of pipe.

He'd asked Ellie to meet with him, not at Finders, but at a park nearby.

Charterhouse Square was a short walk from Finders, and a favourite sniffing place for Millie. It was a beautiful, open space and had been involved in most of the significant moments in London's history since 1371. Over the time it'd been a monastery, a grand mansion, a boys' school and an alms-house, although it also had the darker history of being a Black Death plague pit throughout the fourteenth century.

Ellie wondered whether this was what Millie was sniffing, and almost considered not bringing her again, although Millie looked to be more interested in bushes and squirrels than hidden bodies right now. Which was probably a good thing.

Ellie saw Robert sitting on a bench across the square, smiling at her as she walked over.

'What's going on?' she asked suspiciously. 'Why aren't we meeting at the diner or in the office?'

'Because I don't work at either anymore,' he said, simply. 'I thought I was ready to go back, and I'm not, so I've spoken to the partners, and I'm taking an extended leave of absence.'

Ellie stared at him uncomprehendingly.

'You don't need to do this,' she said. 'I'm sure—'

'I had a meltdown.'

'But everybody has a meltdown.'

Robert held his hand up to stop her.

'Ellie, I tried to fire a Taser into someone's face,' he said. 'Purely because they'd lied to me.'

'Tinker has done far worse.'

'Ellie Reckless,' Robert placed a hand on hers, stopping her. 'This is the right call. I need to sort myself out. I don't know how long it will take. I might be back next week. Next month. Next year.'

'No. You can't just disappear from my life.'

At this, however, Robert laughed for the first time since they met.

'Who said I was disappearing from your life?' he asked. 'Ellie, I'm taking a leave of absence. I'm not joining a monastery, flying to the moon or dying.'

Embarrassed a little, Ellie chuckled.

'Sorry, maybe I should have a leave of absence too, for my overreactions?'

'I think you need to have a discussion with the others about what you want to do with me gone,' Robert suggested calmly. 'I know you were treading water, taking jobs while I recovered, but this is a little more long-term. I think it could be time to find a change in the dynamic. After all, I think you've found everything you need to find there.'

'What did *you* find?' Ellie asked. Robert's hand hadn't moved, and now he gripped hers tightly.

'I found you.'

'You're a bloody idiot,' Ellie stared at him. 'We said we'd go on a date and we never did—'

'Things got busy,' Robert leant forward and kissed Ellie lightly on the lips. 'Whatever happens next, you need to decide how to play it.'

Ellie slumped back on the bench, looking out across the park.

'We can still do good,' she said.

'Yes,' Robert replied. 'Also, I know Mama Lumetta said you should take over the centre of London.'

'Are you telling me to become a crime lord?' Ellie raised her eyebrows, surprised at such a comment. 'Maybe your brain injury is worse than I thought.'

Robert shook his head as he leant over to ruffle Millie's head as she sat between them, her attention fixed upon a moving blade of grass.

'Let's see what happens,' he said.

'No, let's work through this.'

'I have.'

'You said you wanted to leave.'

'You said you can still do good,' Robert replied. 'And I think you can, but right now, it isn't with me.'

Realising she couldn't change his mind, Ellie nodded.

'I need to speak to the others,' she said. 'They're waiting at the diner. I was hoping to convince you to come with me, but it sounds like that's not going to happen now.'

'I'm good,' Robert smiled. 'Honestly, I'll just stay here. It's peaceful.'

Ellie nodded, rose from the bench, and motioned for Millie to follow.

And then, on an impulse, she leant back over and kissed Robert Lewis hard on the lips.

'You'd better get better,' she said, walking away, leaving Robert flushed on the bench.

'See you soon, Ellie Reckless, cop for criminals,' he breathed.

RAMSEY ALLEN SAT BY THE HOSPITAL BED OF ANNA LEVER. He'd told the hospital he was her son, and to be frank, the ages probably lined up enough.

She looked frail, and her breathing was now laboured. But after a moment, she opened her eyes and saw him.

'What are you doing here?'

'Checking in on you,' he smiled. 'I thought you were blown up. Seems you had one more escapology trick left in you.'

Anna laughed.

'I'm not dying yet,' she said defiantly. 'Give me a week or two—'

'Anna, you had a stroke,' Ramsey interrupted. 'It wasn't a good one.'

He looked away.

'They said you've lost feeling on the right side of your arm, and your fingers.'

At this, Anna looked down at her hands.

'So, at the moment, your sleight of hand is going to be a little shit,' Ramsey faked a smile, as he began his rehearsed lie. 'But we're going to make it better, you understand? You and me, every day. We'll practise, and we *will* get better. If it's not me there, it'll be someone else.'

'Who?' Anna asked, and then half laughed, half coughed as the door opened, and Mary Park walked into the wardroom.

'I owe you my life,' Mary said. 'The least I can do is give you some lessons on how to do some passable sleight of hand.

'Cheeky bitch,' Anna grinned. 'What about your daughter?'

'We spoke. It was nice. But we're two different worlds,' Mary shrugged sadly. 'Besides, she's already off planning some European tour with Joe; the two of them are going to try to use it as a way to get back to where they were.'

'Which was basically lies and fake love,' Ramsey suggested. 'So possibly not providing anything of note, bar some memorable shagging sessions.'

He winced as Mary slapped his arm. Then he reached into his pocket, and pulled out a deck of cards.

'So how about a game of poker?' he asked with a cheeky grin.

Tinker Jones sat on the steps of the Covent Garden Piazza, watching a performer, some muscled teenager in a hoodie whose street show seemed to be the fact he could handstand over rows of people lined head to foot.

She didn't really classify this as worthy entertainment, but he seemed to gather a crowd, and his patter was good. After a while though, she sighed, stretched her back and stood up.

Looking to her right, she was surprised to see Zoey Park watching her from the edge of the indoor market.

'How did you know I was here?' she asked.

'Nicky Simpson told me.'

'How the bloody hell does Nicky Simpson know?' Tinker looked around now, trying to work out if someone was spying on her. *Did Nicky hire private investigators to follow her?*

'Apparently, you posted on Instagram.'

Tinker reddened at the ease she'd given her location away, but shuddered at the thought Nicky Simpson had found and followed her on Instagram.'

'I hear you're touring again,' she said.

'Yes,' Zoey nodded, although she didn't seem happy about it. 'After the Piccadilly Theatre incident, I seemed to make the news quite a lot. People love to stare at a car crash, after all. As soon as I was free of the contract that Claudette made me sign, my new agent booked me on a cruise ship working through Europe, followed by a quick tour of some of the Czech Republic.'

She looked at the street performer, and Tinker wondered if she was yearning for an easier time.

'After that, I'll return to Scotland for some shows. Do a couple of dates in England and then end in Dublin,' she sniffed. 'I haven't been back in a while. It feels strange to be doing that, but with Luana hiding, and the families knowing I don't owe anything, I think it'll be okay.'

'Are you okay with this?'

'I found everybody I knew had lied to me in some way,' Zoey replied. 'They were either working for Flanagan to take me down, or they were working with Anna to save my life. But no one bothered to ask me what *I* wanted or how *I* wanted to play it. It's strange, it feels odd.'

'I get that,' Tinker replied. 'When do you go?'

'Next week,' Zoey returned her attention to Tinker now. 'Joe and me? We'll probably fizzle out halfway around the tour, but the sex will be great. He'll return to his life as a lawyer and I ...'

She trailed off and grinned at Tinker.

'Maybe I'll check in on a mutual friend or two.'

'I don't want to know any more than that,' Tinker shook her head in disbelief. 'You take care of yourself, okay?'

'Thanks,' Zoey nodded.

'Oh, I forgot, I had something for you,' Tinker reached into her army jacket pocket and pulled out a small plaster statue. 'I got it from a friend of mine.'

'What is it?' she asked, staring down at it.

'It's Oliver Shepard's sculpture of the death of Cú Chulainn,' Tinker explained. 'Tied to the stone. It's a plaster replica, I mean – the real one's in a post office in Dublin. But I thought it might give you luck on the tour.'

Zoey grinned.

'I love it,' she replied as Tinker patted her arm.

'Don't blow up the ship with flash paper,' she said simply before walking off, leaving Zoey, the statue and the street performer and his audience.

Ellie sat in the diner waiting for the others, Joanne Davey and Casey the only two currently beside her.

'So, what's next?' Casey asked. 'I mean, my half-term is about to end, so you'd better not need my amazing computer skills, unless it's like on a weekend basis.'

Ellie looked at him.

'How was your mum dealing with me working with you again?' she asked.

'I think she's fine with it,' Casey shrugged. 'You're paying me. You're not trying to kill me. She's happy with that.'

Ellie turned to Millie, currently on the booth seat sitting beside her, and passed her a treat from a bag, ignoring the glare from Sandra, who probably wanted her to at least purchase a sausage or something to give, rather than giving away her own free treats.

'Robert's – well, he's gone for a while. Possibly a long while,' she said as behind her, Tinker entered the diner. 'Ramsey's keeping an eye on Anna. So that just leaves the four of us.'

'Four?' Casey asked.

'Sounds like you forgot me,' Tinker said as she slid into the booth, catching the end of the comment. 'Ramsey's like a kid with ADHD. As soon as somebody else comes to help Anna, he'll get bored and be with us in a matter of days.'

She gave Millie a scratch on the head as she looked at Ellie.

'Are you okay with what Robert needs?'

'Time?' Ellie smiled. 'I'm willing to give that.'

Tinker glanced around Caesar's Diner.

'So, is this now our office?' she asked. 'I mean, if Robert

isn't running us anymore, are the Finders partners going to want us in the building?'

'He made an arrangement before he left,' Ellie replied. 'We're good publicity for them, weirdly. We'll focus mainly on paid gigs—'

'You know, do what we're supposed to do,' Casey interrupted.

'What the small annoying child said,' Ellie continued, as if Casey hadn't spoken. 'We'll see how that goes.'

'What if it doesn't work?' Davey now asked. 'I don't really relish the idea of begging for my old job back.'

'Nicky Simpson's offered us business space, above one of his gyms,' Ellie waved for a menu, noting Tinker flinching at the thought. 'If that doesn't work, we still have Mama Lumetta, who said if we get bored, she's happy to back us taking over the West End of London as a crime family. So I think we've got our options open.'

With the others silent, processing the idea of Ellie running her own crime organisation, Ellie smiled and leant forward, her arms resting on the surface as she looked around the table.

'So, what's next?' she asked.

Ellie Reckless and her team
will return in their next thriller

Released Mid 2024

Gain up-to-the-moment information on the release by
signing up to the Jack Gatland VIP Reader's Club!

Join at www.subscribepage.com/jackgatland

ACKNOWLEDGEMENTS

When you write a series of books, you find that there are a ton of people out there who help you, sometimes without even realising, and so I wanted to say thanks.

There are people I need to thank, and they know who they are, including my brother Chris Lee, who I truly believe could make a fortune as a post-retirement copy editor, if not a solid writing career of his own, Jacqueline Beard MBE, who has copyedited all my books since the very beginning, and editor Sian Phillips, all of whom have made my books way better than they have every right to be.

Also, I couldn't have done this without my growing army of ARC and beta readers, who not only show me where I falter, but also raise awareness of me in the social media world, ensuring that other people learn of my books.

But mainly, I tip my hat and thank you. *The reader.* Who once took a chance on an unknown author in a pile of Kindle books, thought you'd give them a go, and who has carried on this far with them, as well as the spin off books I now release.

I write these books for you. And with luck, I'll keep on writing them for a very long time.

Jack Gatland / Tony Lee,
London, November 2023

ABOUT THE AUTHOR

Jack Gatland is the pen name of *#1 New York Times Bestselling Author* Tony Lee, who has been writing in all media for thirty-five years, including comics, graphic novels, middle grade books, audio drama, TV and film for *DC Comics, Marvel, BBC, ITV, Random House, Penguin USA, Hachette* and a ton of other publishers and broadcasters.

These have included licenses such as *Doctor Who, Spider Man, X-Men, Star Trek, Battlestar Galactica, MacGyver,* BBC's *Doctors, Wallace and Gromit* and *Shrek*, as well as work created with musicians such as *Ozzy Osbourne, Joe Satriani, Beartooth, Megadeth, Iron Maiden* and *Bruce Dickinson.*

As Tony, he's toured the world talking to reluctant readers with his 'Change The Channel' school tours, and lectures on screenwriting and comic scripting for *Raindance* in London.

As Jack, he's written several book series now - a police procedural featuring *DI Declan Walsh and the officers of the Temple Inn Crime Unit*, a spinoff featuring "cop for criminals" *Ellie Reckless and her team,* and a second espionage spinoff series featuring burnt MI5 agent *Tom Marlowe*, an action adventure series featuring conman-turned-treasure hunter *Damian Lucas*, and a standalone novel set in a New York boardroom.

An introvert West Londoner by heart, he lives with his wife Tracy and dog Fosco, just outside London.

—————

Feel free to follow Jack on all his social media by clicking on the links below. Over time these can be places where we can engage, discuss Declan, Ellie, Tom and others, and put the world to rights.

Want more books by Jack Gatland?

Turn the page...

LETTER FROM THE DEAD

"BY THE TIME YOU READ THIS, I WILL BE DEAD..."

A TWENTY YEAR OLD MURDER...
A PRIME MINISTER LEADERSHIP BATTLE...
A PARANOID, HOMELESS EX-MINISTER...
AN EVANGELICAL PREACHER WITH A SECRET...

DI DECLAN WALSH HAS HAD BETTER FIRST DAYS...

AVAILABLE ON AMAZON / KINDLEUNLIMITED

THEY TRIED TO KILL HIM...
NOW HE'S OUT FOR **REVENGE.**

NEW YORK TIMES #1 BESTSELLER **TONY LEE** WRITING AS

JACK GATLAND

THE MURDER OF AN **MI5 AGENT**...
A BURNED SPY **ON THE RUN** FROM HIS OWN PEOPLE...
AN ENEMY OUT TO **STOP HIM** AT ANY COST...
AND A **PRESIDENT** ABOUT TO BE **ASSASSINATED**...

SLEEPING SOLDIERS

A **TOM MARLOWE** THRILLER

BOOK 1 IN A NEW SERIES OF THRILLERS IN THE STYLE OF
JASON BOURNE, JOHN MILTON OR **BURN NOTICE,** AND
SPINNING OUT OF THE **DECLAN WALSH** SERIES OF BOOKS

AVAILABLE ON AMAZON / KINDLE UNLIMITED

JACK GATLAND

THE LIONHEART CURSE

HUNT THE GREATEST TREASURES
PAY THE GREATEST PRICE

BOOK 1 IN A NEW SERIES OF ADVENTURES
IN THE STYLE OF 'THE DA VINCI CODE'
FROM THE CREATOR OF DECLAN WALSH

AVAILABLE ON AMAZON / KINDLEUNLIMITED

Printed in Great Britain
by Amazon